KATHRYN THOMAS

Off the Beaten Track

My Favourite Faraway Places

KATHRYN THOMAS

Off the Beaten Track

My Favourite Faraway Places

POOLBEG

Published 2008
by Poolbeg Press Ltd
123 Grange Hill, Baldoyle
Dublin 13, Ireland
E-mail: poolbeg@poolbeg.com
www.poolbeg.com

1 3 5 7 9 10 8 6 4 2

A catalogue record for this book is available from the British Library.

ISBN 978-1-84223-330-6

Typeset by Patricia Hope in Sabon 10.75/15

Printed by
CPI Mackays, Chatham ME5 8TD, UK

About the Author

Kathryn Thomas was born in Carlow in 1979. She made her television debut on young people's sports programme *Rapid* in 1998 and has spent the last eight years reporting from around the world for RTÉ's travel programme, *No Frontiers*. As well as continuing her travels, she now also presents RTÉ's *Winning Streak – Dream Ticket* every Saturday night. She was voted Television Personality of the Year at the 2008 Irish Film and Television Awards. *Off the Beaten Track* is her first book.

Acknowledgements

This book would not have happened without the support and belief of everyone in Poolbeg, especially Brian and Paula. When I doubted myself and my abilities, which was most of the time, you always managed to rebuild my confidence again, more often than not with after-hours phone-calls and e-mails!

To everyone I have worked with in Frontier Films down through the years, but especially to Gerald and Susan who have been like a second family to me.

To Stuart in CoCo Television for putting me on this long and crazy road, thank you.

To everybody in RTÉ who has supported me down through the years and entrusted me with the responsibility of communicating with people what a fantastic world we live in. A special thank you to Grainne McAleer, Mary Curtis, Clare Duignan, Noel Curran, Eddie Doyle, Alice O'Sullivan and Cathriona Edwards.

To Joanne and Sinead in Presence Communications, who brilliantly manage to know where I am going and what I am doing before I do.

To all the freelance crew who helped me find my way in the land of television. I would especially like to thank Judy Kelly, Gerry Hoban, Ruth Meehan, Ingrid Gargan, Pat Comer, Daniel O'Hara and Stu Teehan, all of whom accompanied me on journeys documented in this book. To Mark Boland, the cameraman who has been by my side more than anyone else. You are a great friend with a lot of secrets! If you ever plan on writing a tell-all memoir, let me know in time so I can skip the country!

I am privileged to have the most incredible group of friends anyone could wish for. I know I am sometimes unreliable, sometimes far away and sometimes never there when you need me but you have filled my life with great fun. A special thanks to Antonia, Ruth, Shane, Sorcha, Sally, Catriona, Susan, Linda, Yvonne and Mary-Kay for being there forever. To Enda, for hanging in there. You all have me back now.

To my whole family, all the Thomases, Keanes, Lyons, Astons, Wakefields and Taylors, and especially to my Papa and Nana. I love you dearly.

To my Gran, who taught me that being able to see the beauty of the world should not be taken for granted. In her honour I will be donating twenty per cent of the royalties from this book to the National Council for the Blind, whom she worked so tirelessly for.

Finally, to the anchors in my life: Dad, Mum, David, Linda and Stevie. I have learned through travel that there is so much in this world I can do without and, though I don't say it enough, I could not do without you. I love you with all my heart.

For Mum and Dad
You are my world
Thank you for everything

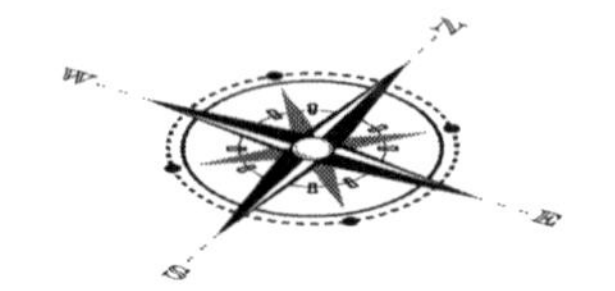

Contents

Introduction

It feels quite strange to be finally writing this introduction as it is the last part of a project which has taken over a year of my life. When I decided to write this book, I knew it would be a challenge but I never really understood quite the extent of the challenge and now, I can't believe it's over! At times, the process has been frustrating, rewarding, time-consuming and fascinating, but most of all, this record has been a great reminder for me of what I have seen, whom I have met and what I have learned.

I do not consider myself a writer and so never thought I could write a book. But, I never in a million years dreamed I would have the privilege of growing up in my twenties travelling the world and would be left with so many stories I wanted to tell.

Ever since I was a child, I had a fascination with travel. Lying on the floor, I would pore over an atlas and, using my finger as a boat, sail across the pages, from ocean to ocean, landing in such exotic places as the Solomon Islands or Outer Mongolia or Zanzibar and try to imagine the beauty and mystery and magic I would find there.

When I joined the already well-established RTÉ holiday programme, *No Frontiers*, back in 2001, I was twenty-two years old, and it really was a dream come true. My role was to bring independent, shoestring travel into Irish living rooms. I took off wide-eyed, ready to report back on any adventure the world could throw at me! In those early years, I was really only finding out about myself, who I was and what I wanted out of my life. They say that travel broadens the mind and I now know that growing up on the road in those formative years changed me in so many ways.

Wandering through the Dogon country in Mali, West Africa, was where I first truly understood how to appreciate beauty in the simplest of surroundings. Trekking in the Himalayas, I felt the enormity of our planet and realised exactly how tiny we are in the bigger scheme of things. My time in Ethiopia made me more aware of how important it is not to judge a book by its cover. The majesty and power of the Antarctic is still with me when I close my eyes. I can feel it. My two-week adventure in Papua New Guinea pushed me to my limit and made me realise that the body I have been given is capable of a hell of a lot more than I ever gave it credit for.

The chapters as they appear in this book are, for the most part, my journeys in chronological order. It made sense to me to compile them in this way as it means the book has become a journey in itself.

Our lives today mean we are constantly juggling our time between work and family, mortgages and bills and our time-out is often overlooked. We work long enough hours to deserve our week or two away in the sun, which frees us temporarily from the stresses of everyday life.

In 2004, when I took over as the lead presenter with *No Frontiers*, I began reporting on a much broader range of holidays and in doing so, I saw a lot more hotel rooms and a lot less tent! But there was never a doubt in my mind that this book should begin where my love of travel does – off the beaten track. There is a different kind of freedom that comes with taking off into the unknown with just a bag on your back and a world full of possibilities in front of you. Backpacking through some of the poorest parts of the world has taught me to appreciate what I have and what I have been given, so much so that coming home after a long trip can sometimes feel like a new beginning. It has instilled in me an endless curiosity with this earth and has become my addiction in life. I hope in some small way that I have been able to capture for you the wonder of the places that I have seen and the generosity of the people I have met, on the journeys that have shaped my life.

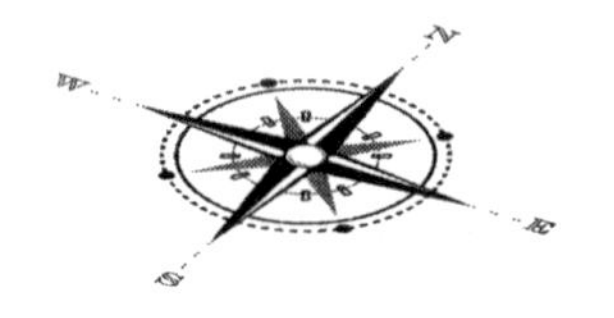

"We shall not cease from exploration, and the end of all our exploring will be to arrive where we started, and know the place for the first time"

T.S. Eliot

Senegal

I watched them on the floor together in the dim light of the club as they moved. His hand at the base of her spine held her close but not close enough that she couldn't shake her hips and move her body up and down against him. Her back was arched, emphasising the curves of her body. Their silhouette moved as one to the mesmerising drumbeats. All around them the dance floor was moving, a sea of bodies writhing to the music and working up a sweat in the heat of the Senegalese night. But I couldn't take my eyes off them and how they danced. Their appreciation for the music was expressed in every move of their hips, their arms, their feet, every shake of their heads. Their connection was so powerful; their dancing told me the story of who they were.

Dance is such a wonderful form of expression. Although I'm not particularly good, I love it and the sense of freedom that it gives you when you become lost in a moment of music that totally consumes you. I feel lucky to have seen so many forms of dance in different parts of the world. The sensual, highly charged tango on the streets of Argentina; the colourful and frenzied flamenco of the Roma people in the caves of Andalucía; the incredible choreographed ballet in the decadent theatres of St Petersburg in Russia. Our own form of Irish dance captivates me, like it did for millions of people all over the world when *Riverdance* exploded onto the international stage, where nothing like it had been seen before.

But nowhere have music and dance blown me away like my times in Africa, where they are such an integral part of people's identities. With so many different countries, cultures and tribal roots, music and dance define Africa's people. To see how they dance, embracing their identity through rhythm, is amazing. And, my God, do they have rhythm! Whether it's the shoulder-dancing Ethiopians, the jumping Masai warriors of Kenya or the spinning women of the Himba tribe in Namibia, they know how to move.

The origins of so much of Africa's music have travelled far and wide and have influenced music as we know it today. I like to believe that music makes the world go round and if you think of a world without music, you think of a world without Africa.

We had come to Senegal, among other reasons, to get a first-hand experience of its world-famous music scene. We had timed our arrival in Dakar to coincide with the return of one of the country's biggest stars, who had just finished his European tour. Youssou N'Dour has been called the most influential African musician of all time. He has collaborated with the likes of Sting, Peter Gabriel, Bruce Springsteen,

Wyclef Jean and Paul Simon, but it was his distinctive voice on the song "Seven Seconds" with Neneh Cherry back in the 1990s that really put him and Senegalese "mbalax" music on the international map. Mbalax is a blend of traditional drumming and praise-singing mixed with the Afro-Cuban style brought back from the Caribbean when black Africans began returning to their homeland in the 1950s and 1960s. This new experimental music with its Muslim chants exploded in Senegal in the 1970s. The young Senegalese who had been listening to Jimi Hendrix and James Brown at the time were now ready to rediscover their culture and Youssou N'Dour was paving the way.

We had pulled up outside Club Thiossane, which looked like an old warehouse at the side of the road. The small dusty car park at the back of the building was full. Cars had literally been abandoned on both sides of the road out the front. Three mangy dogs sniffed around in the dirt as we approached the entrance. The music coming from the building made the hairs on my arms stand on end and I got shivers down the back of my neck. I could feel the electricity of the crowd before we even opened the door. Inside, the place was packed and heaving. The band on stage were fantastic, working the crowd into a frenzied sweat. Four female backing vocalists sang in their native Wolof while the lead singer sang r'n'b style in English. The crowd moved, swayed and ground to the music as if in a trance and were as brilliant to watch as the band were to listen to.

But it was the couple in the middle of the dance floor who stole the show. For the first twenty minutes, I self-consciously shifted from one foot to the other on the edge of the dance floor and, watching them, felt like I had as much rhythm as a one-legged anteater. Two huge women came over, gyrating against me, each other and anybody else they could find. "Come on, girlfriend, shake that booty. Loosen up and move," ordered one of them with a huge smile. With one flick of her hip against mine, I was catapulted to the far side of the room! She roared laughing as I spun around, trying to figure out where I was. I joined her in the fits of giggles and all of a sudden I was pumping and grinding without a care in the world.

After about an hour, with no pre-warning, the place went silent and the familiar, perfectly high-pitched nasal voice rang out through the speakers around the club. The crowd went wild. Suddenly Youssou appeared, wearing a flowing white traditional Muslim boubou and skull cap. He was smaller than I expected but he still had that very recognisable smile. There was an army of people on stage, including six backing singers, six drummers, two saxophone players and three guitarists. I thought to myself, here is a man who has been on the *Time 100* list and has worked with the greatest musicians in the world, yet he is still perfectly at home in a rundown club in the neighbourhood where he grew up. Two hours later, at 4.00 a.m., the "voice of an angel" left the stage and left his club of revellers in a happy sweat.

It was a fantastic introduction to Senegal's music scene. Unfortunately, our introduction to the country on our arrival the day before hadn't been so positive.

It was 4.00 a.m. when we landed in Dakar airport. I stood back from the luggage carousel and watched the crowd of tourists congregate right at the mouth of the baggage belt, pushing and shoving their trolleys, vying for every inch of ground available in a three-metre radius. I have never understood why people do that – crowding in on top of each other, craning their necks as it they expect Jesus Christ himself to come shooting out of the black abyss, holding their sacred bags aloft in the air! Judy sensed my frustration but I didn't notice her raised eyebrow as I ranted on to her.

"Why can't people just move back so everyone can see their bags coming out and collect them in an orderly fashion when they come around on the belt? It's like the people who queue up to get on a plane when their seat has already been allocated to them. That really bothers me."

Another raised brow, except this time I clocked it. "Jesus, Kathryn, you need to get some sleep."

I tried to look offended but then laughed apologetically realising I sounded like one of those world-weary travellers you get stuck beside at an airport bar or waiting on a bus who waffle on about how they have become so disillusioned with the world. She was right. I hadn't slept one wink on the overnight flight from Paris and was shattered. In fact, it was the opposite of how I'd felt all week, when I had been excited and could feel the adrenalin coursing through my veins. We were going to Africa. It was June 2001, I was only twenty-two and, although I had been to Cape Town, I had never been to what I imagined in my head to be "real Africa".

Our twelve-day trip was going to take us through Senegal and over the border by train into Mali. Senegal is the most western point on the African continent, flanked to the north by Mauritania and to the south by Guinea-Bissau. The Gambia eats into its centre. Senegal is a relatively small country compared to its landlocked neighbour Mali, which is five times bigger than the UK. Both promised incredible adventures, and more so, I felt, because we were just a two-woman crew.

Judy and I had travelled and worked together before in Cambodia and Laos and had become firm friends. In some ways we were like chalk and cheese and in others we were so similar. She had worked with *Vogue* in London, had a penchant for designer clothes and, although she could slum it with the best of them, was a self-described high-maintenance kind of girl. I on the other hand had packed bags in Superquinn, never had a manicure before in my life and aspired to be a high-maintenance kind of girl! But we both loved to talk, we both loved to laugh and, most of all, we both had a huge love of travel. We knew how to look out for each other on the road and were aware of the risks that came with travelling. We knew that in both capital cities, Dakar and Bamako, but especially in Dakar, we would need to watch our backs. Theft and muggings were common against tourists, who also had to deal with relentless street hustlers.

We loaded our rucksacks onto a trolley, the camera hidden safely in a bag strapped to Judy's back. The only thing that looked remotely like we had any equipment was the tripod bag I was carrying across my chest. The electronic arrivals doors weren't working and when we did eventually emerge through an emergency exit door, we could hardly get past for the crowd that had gathered. The next five minutes happened in what seemed like seconds. Three guys got between myself and Judy, splitting us up, insisting that they help us with the trolley and carry our bags. I very firmly told them we were fine and that we would be getting a taxi. I looked over and one of them was trying to lift the camera bag off Judy's back. She instinctively took her hands off the trolley to protect it. In that split second, another man snaked in front of her and wheeled the trolley with our rucksacks on it in the direction of the door. We both started shouting for him to come back with the trolley. The two guys walking alongside me were saying, "No problem, he is a taxi man." They tried to remove the tripod bag from my shoulder but I held on to it and ran after our bags, which were being loaded into the boot of a battered car.

"Take them out. We are getting a taxi."

"This is taxi."

"This is not a taxi."

I looked at the taxi rank, which was empty. There was no sign of any airport police around either. Most of the crowd had dispersed at this stage and only five men were remaining.

"What hotel you staying?"

"We are fine, thank you. We will get a taxi to our hotel. Take our bags out of the boot," Judy ordered.

Finally a man in police uniform came over. "Lady, this is taxi. They will take you to hotel. What is the address?" She took the crumpled address that she had scribbled on a piece of paper out of her pocket and handed it to him. Another official came over and we both relaxed a bit. We looked at each other and decided that we had no choice but to go.

With Judy already sitting in the car, I tried negotiating a price before we got in, but the engine had started up and, afraid of being left behind, I jumped in too. Before we knew it, we were both in the back seat, with one guy either side of us and three of them in the front as we drove out of the airport. I shouted at this stage for them to stop, which they did. The driver spoke a little English.

"Do you know where this hotel is?" I asked, pointing again to the crumpled address.

"Yes, yes, I do. Don't worry."

"How much is the charge to the hotel? Tell me or we are getting out."

"Dangerous. Do not get out here."

"I would rather take my chances."

Knowing that I was getting hot-headed, Judy turned around to me, trying to defuse the situation. "Listen, let's just get to the hotel with the gear safely and deal with money later."

I was so annoyed that we had been scammed already, and we hadn't even been in the country five minutes, that I hadn't even begun to worry about our safety, unlike Judy, who was busy plotting in her head what the least painful way to die would be! It was the longest twenty minutes in the world, but we were driving toward the city centre. Eventually, we turned onto the street where our hotel was. The driver pulled in at the side of the road and pointed to a building two blocks up on the opposite side. "There is your hotel. Next street is one-way, so we have to stop here. That will be 12,000 CFA francs." That was four times the fare we should have been paying. Judy took out the money and gave it to him. I wanted to object, but knew at this point that I should stay quiet. I could see the concierge standing at the door in the distance and wanted to yell out to him. They unloaded our bags from the boot, got back in the car and drove off. We looked at each other, said nothing, hoisted up our bags and walked toward the hotel. The concierge came running down the road to meet us. "Why they leave you there? These heavy bags, leave them and let me help you." Two more of the hotel staff came out. We told them what had happened and they all seemed deeply apologetic and embarrassed. "There are a lot of bad people here," muttered the concierge, shaking his head. "There are bad people everywhere," I smiled at him. I tried to tip him for carrying the bags and to pay for the Cokes that he had brought us without asking, but he would not hear of it.

So we had got off to a bad start but that afternoon we met up with Citro and Mara, from Eyeneye Concepts, the company that had helped us organise the trip. Both men came to the hotel dressed in full-length colourful boubous. Like over ninety per cent of Senegal's population, they were practising Muslims. They spoke fantastic English and were eager to go through our itinerary for the next couple of days. While they would meet up with us whenever they could, they had organised a driver and guide, Jawara, who would be with us the entire time, whenever we needed him. The plan was to spend the following day driving around Dakar, soaking up life in the city and its colourful markets. The day after, we would take the early boat to the historic island of Gorée, which was once a vibrant port in West Africa's slave trade. The guys had also arranged to take us to some of the best live club venues in the city. After all of that, we would head south along the Petite Côte to some of Senegal's best beaches and hopefully time it so that we could take in a traditional wrestling match while we were there.

By the time we had finished our meeting it was 6.00 p.m. The guys asked if we wanted to join them for dinner across town, where they were looking after a group of French people who were leaving the following morning, but we said we would just grab something locally and have an early night. They recommended a place down the street and told us not to wander too far. "People here are generally friendly. They will hassle you and walk beside you, asking you to buy whatever they are selling. Although it is annoying, most of them are not dangerous. We do have a problem with pickpockets, though, so just be on the watch."

We wandered down the road to the brightly lit Chawarma Donald restaurant, which was playing funky hip-hop music. It was fairly busy, which was a good sign, but we managed to get a table beside the window and ordered a couple of Cokes.

We were left alone to our dinner of chawarmas – meat wrapped in bread – for less than fifty cent. We got chatting with two Dutch girls at the next table who had been travelling through West Africa for a month. "The nightlife here is insane. Nobody goes out until 2.00 a.m. and they stay partying all night. Most of them don't drink. It's all about the dancing. The clubs and live bands are fantastic. The people are incredible and great fun. Sure, the constant hustling gets frustrating, but you just learn to get used to it."

Citro, Mara and Jawara met us the following morning and we took off to explore the city. Senegal is a former French colony and, driving through the streets of Dakar, I could still see strong French influences intertwined with African ones. From the architecture to the grid-lined streets and tree-lined boulevards to the patisseries and ramshackle corner coffee trolleys selling freshly baked French baguettes under Nestlé umbrellas, I was surprised how European the city felt. We drove right down to Cap Manuel, in the south of Dakar from where, high up on the cliff, we had an incredible view of the sea and Gorée Island in the distance. Not only that but, because Dakar is built on a peninsula, we could see right down the coast of the continent as far south as the Gambia.

Heading back towards the western corniche and the harbour, we passed huge luxury houses on our left and old forts built into the cliff faces on our right, with winding stairs that led down to the sea where fishermen were preparing their dugout canoes for the day ahead. The sun was shining and it felt great to be somewhere totally different. It dawned on me that Irish backpackers had made their mark on the well-worn routes across Southeast Asia and more recently South America, but the African continent for various reasons is not attracting vast numbers of us in the same way. The overriding factor I think is because people are intimidated by travel here.

Senegal itself runs as a fairly peaceful democracy, on a continent where instability and political corruption are rife. The country was granted independence from France in 1960 and its first president, Léopold Sédar Senghor, after fourteen years in power, decided in 1974 to establish a multi-party system to create a fair democracy. There was a change of party power in 2000 after twenty years of the Socialist Party at the helm, when Abdoulaye Wade took over as president, proving that change could happen and could happen peacefully. Senegal's government, which advocates free press, giving every political party a platform, is trusted by the West. The Senegalese are extremely politically conscious and it is not uncommon to see hordes of people poring over newspapers while having their morning coffees on the street or men hurrying along in their flowing robes with radios pressed against their ears, keeping abreast of what's going on.

We drove past the IFAN Museum, stopped to take some shots at the Palais Presidential, protected by poker-straight guards in their bright red uniforms. Then we drove up Avenue Léopold Senghor to the heart of the business district and parked in Dakar's main square, Place de L'Indépendence. This is the main hub of the city, where most of the avenues meet. Yellow and black taxis whizzed past in every direction as bicycles, mopeds and pedestrians all wove in and out of the traffic.

Looking around, I got the impression that the people of Dakar are self-assured, confident and modern in their outlook. Men in suits carrying briefcases and wearing dark glasses walked with a manner of self-importance, talking loudly into mobile phones. Shopkeepers and coffee-shop owners were organising staff and dealing with the morning delivery trucks in a meticulous fashion. The Wolof are the dominant ethnic group, making up thirty-five per cent of Senegal's population. They are followers of the powerful Muslim Brotherhoods, which play an important political and economic role in the country. The women are tall and statuesque, striding self-confidently with their heads held high, dressed immaculately in bright colourful prints.

We got out and set the camera up. Within thirty seconds a crowd had gathered around us, but Citro and Mara kept things under control so we could film. Then we took the lift up to the seventeenth-storey roof terrace of the Hotel Independence, ordered some Cokes and took in the panorama.

What's different about Dakar, unlike so many other African cities I have been to since, is that it is built on the sea. While it is busy with traffic and street sellers and day-to-day life, glimpses of the ocean between skyscrapers and traffic-choked streets make it much more tolerable. From here we could see the busy commercial port, the grand mosque and Isle de Gorée glittering on the ocean in the distance.

The sun was shining as we drove down the Avenue Pompidou, one of the busiest streets in the city, toward the Marché Sandaga. "You can buy everything here and no problem filming. Just be careful," Citro warned. "Pick-pocketing is a big problem. All the people will want to talk to you. Most of them are okay but just be careful."

We pulled up outside the Marché Sandaga, a huge crumbling concrete building, which looked like it had been abandoned twenty years ago. The guys told us that this market was the lifeline for many of the city's residents. The sound of music and voices leaked out to greet us as we approached the building. Inside, we were swallowed up by thousands of people manning stalls, selling everything from bootleg CDs to tailor-made suits, Manchester United shirts, rip-off designer jeans, sunglasses and Islamic prayer books. Everyone was shouting, bargaining, buying and selling as if they were on the floor of a stock exchange. We had entered on the ground floor and followed the guys through a labyrinth of narrow alleyways until we ended up in an area selling mostly meat and vegetables. The women in bright full-length traditional Muslim boubous with their babies on their backs walked between piles of colourful vegetables.

When Judy had got her shots, we followed Mara down a stone stairs into a dark dungeon-like basement where, even underground, the heat of the day could not be kept at bay. This was the fish market and the overpowering smell made me retch so much that I couldn't do a piece to camera. So Judy quickly filmed the images I had to close my eyes to! The fishmongers' bloody hands filleting, their bare feet squelching around in puddles of melted ice and blood, piles of panting fish, fresh out of the ocean, willing somebody to throw them back. Finally, back up on the ground floor, we climbed a rickety stairs, past four little boys wringing the necks of live chickens, up and out onto the roof. It was lined with restaurant stalls, and the smell of pungent spices and sea air was a welcome relief. We sat down and the lads tucked into bowls of gourbane serene, meat served with millet and peanut sauce. After five minutes my appetite returned just in time to share a bowl of yassa with Judy – chicken with rice, lemon and onion sauce. It was fantastic.

After lunch we walked down one of the side streets beside the market, a little off the tourist track. Here and all over Dakar, life is very much lived on the street. We passed a barber at work on the footpath. A line of men queued to sit at his rickety table, in front of an old mirror hanging from a tree. Two men in overalls sorted through old car parts and displayed them on the ground in front of their shop while beside them a tailor worked busily, bent over a sewing machine in the sun.

Like inside the market, as we expected, the hustlers were relentless, trying to peddle anything and everything. At one stage we had a group of about fifteen young guys following us, offering cigarettes, hallucinogenic kola nuts and proposals of marriage. "You not want to marry Senegalese black magic man?" "Ladies, which one of you want me? Who will be the lucky one who is going to marry me and take me home to your Daddy?"

Although it's mostly done in jest, the constant attention does get tiring. Even wandering around with Mara and Citro by our sides, I felt that the cocky self-assuredness and remarks of these young guys are in a lot of cases designed to intimidate Western women. I found the best way to deal with them was to be just as cheeky back and don't let it register with them that you are in any way uncomfortable. So this was my job while Judy was trying to film. "If you want to marry me, I need to know that you can dance. My Daddy won't be happy with a man who cannot dance." All of a sudden drums from a market stall were picked up and an impromptu dance-off began with the group of hustlers, with me in the middle shaking it for all I was worth. By the time we left, we were high-fiving, shaking hands and, most importantly, not being badgered!

The following morning we caught a cab down to the port and jumped on board the 7.00 a.m. ferry to Isle de Gorée. There were only six other people on the boat, the sun was shining and it felt good to be getting out of the city. It was hard to imagine that this tiny island (only 800 metres long) that we could see glittering in the distance had played such a pivotal role in West Africa's slave trade during the eighteenth and nineteenth centuries.

Twenty minutes later, we stepped onto the island and into another world. As we wandered from the jetty up into the small town, brightly painted colonial houses with beautifully ornate wrought-iron balconies lined silent narrow alleyways where clumps of bougainvillea hung in fat clusters here and there, bathed in the soft morning light of the sun. There are no surfaced roads and no cars and it felt like we had been transported back in time to a peaceful Mediterranean hideaway. It was the Portuguese who in 1444 first settled on the island, and it changed hands seventeen times after that between the French, Dutch and English. Because of its sheltered harbour and easy accessibility, it quickly became a strategic port for trading companies, which shipped not just materials like gum, hides and ivory to the Americas, but also the native Africans themselves. The slave trade flourished in the eighteenth and early nineteenth centuries and, although nobody knows for certain, it is estimated that between fifteen and thirty million black Africans were sold into slavery.

In the small museum on the northern end of the island, in the old fort, we learned more about the island's history. The slaves were divided up into ethnic groups, chained together and stamped with company logos using red hot irons on their skin. They were penned in small dungeons not just in the famous House of Slaves but in basements all over the island. We walked down to the famous "Maison des Esclaves", built in 1786, which is the reason most tourists come to the island. We entered a large open-air courtyard, flanked on either side by two sweeping staircases. These led to the first floor, which was where the merchants and their families had lived. Lining the stairs were about 100 children, all about ten years of age, who were on a school tour from Dakar to learn about their history. It was quite a strange but reassuring feeling to see them there in their little school uniforms as I walked through the courtyard and into the dark dungeons below, which had once held their ancestors in captivity. The cells were tiny and windowless. The remains of rusting shackles protruded from the flaking walls and floors.

At the very end of the building was an opening in the back wall called "The Door of No Return" from where, it is said, the slaves were taken from their pens and thrown onto waiting ships, never to see their homeland again. I felt strange and uncomfortable standing in the shade of the thick walls, looking out to sea. I tried to imagine what it must have been like standing tethered in chains, frightened, beaten, branded, alone, separated from your family and friends, with no knowledge of where you were going or what would happen. The feeling of despair must have been overwhelming.

Talking to one of the local guides who lived on the island, I later found out that it wasn't just European merchants who had kept the slave trade alive. When Senegal and the Gambia could no longer satisfy demand, they travelled further inland to find their supplies. Local kings sold their people to the westerners and, on Gorée itself, powerful African women called "signares" also played their part. These women from the Wolof and Jula tribes already had a high standing in these matriarchal societies. French tradesmen and merchants married these women to gain more power and access within indigenous communities, to carry out their trading. Their mixed-race children then had a standing in society with their own servants and in turn had a lifestyle funded by the slaving industry.

At the Congress of Vienna in 1815 the British put pressure on Spain, Portugal and France to abolish the slave trade officially, as they had already done. France eventually did in 1848, pressurised by the threat of constant uprisings within Africa. You wonder how such atrocities and disrespect for human life were allowed to continue for as long as they did over ten centuries. It is easy to write down or type the statistics, "fifteen to thirty million", but when you actually think about fifteen to thirty million human beings being trafficked from all parts of the African continent to different parts of the world, it is almost incomprehensible. There have been many indescribable crimes throughout history but in my mind the tragedy of the African slave trade has to go down as the worst.

We wandered down to the small beach, which by now was dotted with sunbathers and local children playing in the sheltered waters. It had been a heavy morning for the two of us, trying to understand and capture the horrible tragedies that this small island had witnessed. I remember it felt good to be sitting on the beach in the sun with the sand between my toes, the waves lapping against the shore, listening to the local children laughing.

We rose early the next day and drove with Jawara south along Petite Côte to a town called Joal. We passed incredibly beautiful white sandy beaches but didn't stop, as our first priority was getting to a traditional wrestling tournament which the guys had found out about only the day before.

Wrestling is the national sport in Senegal and, like football, draws huge crowds. But people don't just come to watch the fighting. There is mysticism and spirituality connected to Senegalese wrestling. Jawara explained to us that every wrestler carries out a pre-match ceremony to ward off evil spirits or black magic that their opponent could have put on them. This ritual includes a protection dance to the wild beating of drums. They also cover themselves in "gris gris" or charms tied around their arms, waists and legs to bring them luck and enhance their performance. Traditionally, wrestling matches took place to celebrate the end of a village harvest and the strongest man in the competition would receive a cow or a bag of rice. Nowadays, like everywhere else, sport has been modernised and money is the main incentive for young men to become involved.

In 1995, Mohammad Nado, who nicknamed himself "Tyson", shot onto the wrestling scene. He would drape an American flag over his shoulders before every fight, insisting that what he and it represented was power, freedom and money. Before "Tyson", the biggest prize sum for a fight had been $20,000. On New Year's Eve, 1995, in the biggest fight ever staged in Senegal, he was pitted against Yakhya Diop, with prize money of $130,000. He lost the fight but his consolation prize was $120,000 – not bad, considering the average monthly wage in Senegal is 40,000 CFA francs or $80. Kids lapped up the new Americanised role models, as did the advertising agencies and the media, and all of a sudden the ancient sport entered a whole new kind of league.

From outside the stadium we could hear drums beating, whistles being blown and women chanting. We paid the equivalent of twenty cent to enter. Inside, the place was packed as people sat behind wire fences looking out onto a pitch of sand. At one end, ten drummers sat on chairs in a semicircle and to their left six women sat dressed in colourful robes and turbans. These, Jawara told us, were the griots – praise singers who recounted stories of magical powers and ancient warriors to instil courage into the competitors in front of them. Dotted around the pitch, eight different pairs of wrestlers were fighting each other, each match being supervised by a referee. Jawara explained that a festival like this one goes on for four or five days. The men grappled each other in the sand, their dark muscular bodies glistening with sweat. As they were wearing only loincloths, we could see every defined muscle, tense and taut. I had never in my life seen more physically perfect, strong, manly bodies. I looked at Judy, who looked at me, and I knew she was thinking the exact same thing: *Thank you, Lord, we have just died and gone to heaven!*

We settled down on a wooden bench as close to the fence as we could get. There are two forms of wrestling: the newer style, where the fighters can throw bare-knuckle punches; and the more traditional style, which is more acrobatic, where hitting is not allowed. The winner has to make his opponent's knees, shoulder or back hit the sand.

We watched one wrestler prepare for his fight. He danced around in a circle with his eyes closed, chanting quietly. He drank various liquid concoctions, then sat down on his hunkers with his head touching the sand, his bodyguards and supporters covering him with a blanket of feathers. All this was carried out much to the enjoyment of the roaring crowd, who could witness this and the other fights around him, which were happening simultaneously. He then sat up with his head thrown back, his eyes still closed, and chanted in Wolof as those around him joined in. He repeated this over and over and the whole ritual lasted over an hour, which Jawara told us was not unusual. He then squared up to his opponent.

They circled each other for the first few minutes, pawing at each other and slapping each other's arms in a manner that looked almost disinterested. It was as if neither of them could be bothered engaging in the fight. The crowd cheered and, as the anticipation grew, so did their volume and that of the musicians. Then, all of a sudden, their bodies became locked together in battle, sand flying in the air as they grappled for a way to topple each other. Legs flailed in the air, their bodies hunched over. Within minutes, a firm grip under a thigh saw the wrestler we had been watching lift his huge opponent high in the air and land him on his back. Game over! While the preparation ceremony had lasted an hour, the fight lasted less than ten minutes!

In amongst the crowd, there were a few tourists dotted here and there, soaking up the highly charged atmosphere. Jawara disappeared and came back with a small skinny man in his seventies who was the organiser of the festival. He invited us to come down and film out on the pitch. We didn't need to be asked twice to get up close and personal and were down at close quarters in seconds! At pitch level, the wrestling matches became even more of a spectacle. You could see in their eyes how they were playing psychological games with each other. The chanting and drumming travelled right across the hot sand and seemed to enter their bodies and this, along with the roars of the crowd, spurred them on for battle.

When we left that afternoon, the stadium was still as packed and noisy as when we had first arrived. We strolled through Joal, the home town of Senegal's first president, which to me had no redeeming features. It was dirty and squalid and seemed to lack any sort of soul. Those locals who didn't endlessly harass us as we walked sat about in dusty doorways, looking completely disillusioned with the world.

Mountains of rubbish littered every street corner and the smell of rotting vegetables and shellfish was enough to turn my stomach. Even the beach was black with rubbish.

Jawara stayed with the jeep while Judy and I crossed to the island town of Fadiout. It was linked to Joal by a long wooden walkway, which we crossed rather than paying to go by "pirogue" or traditional boat, captained by children no older than ten. The man-made island is completely built of shells and has emerged from the sea through years and years of systematic dumping. We stepped onto the island and crunched our way through the town's shell-paved streets, where the small houses on either side also had walls made of shells. Even though the beach seemed to act as a rubbish dump as well, it was a welcome change from Joal. Kids played together on the quiet streets while one woman sat under the shade of a huge baobab tree, selling souvenirs spread out on a blanket in front of her. She smiled sweetly as we passed. It was the first time since arriving in the country that we weren't hassled to buy anything, so we sat down beside her, bought a few things and asked her about the island. She told us that, like most of the community, she was Catholic, but that they lived happily alongside the small Muslim community.

We crossed another rickety bridge to a separate island, again made completely out of clam shells. This was the Christian graveyard where the small, tightly packed shell-mounds were marked with little white crosses. It was peaceful and the noise of the crunching shells underfoot was strangely satisfying in this little island Catholic community.

Tired after our day's filming, we drove back up north along the coast to Toubab Dialao, where we had arranged to meet Mara and Citro later that evening. We were staying in a traditional home-stay on the beach and, after an hour of searching, we eventually pulled up outside a long thatched hut with a wraparound veranda. The sun was setting, bathing the whole place in a soft orange glow. The woman of the house, Ramla, paused from sweeping sand off the veranda, leaned on her brush and smiled broadly as we enquired if we had found the right place. "I wasn't expecting anyone until tomorrow! My family is home for the holidays. They will leave tomorrow, but don't worry, we will find some room! Come on in."

Inside, there wasn't a sign of anybody. As we stood with our bags on our backs in the big open sitting area, she went from door to door, peering in and closing them over again. "Everybody is sleeping." Eventually, she came back to one of the doors she had opened and screamed, "Up you get, dear! You have to move outside for the night."

A bleary-eyed man, whom we later found out was her husband, emerged rubbing his eyes and his large belly. "It's all yours," he indicated to us.

"Sorry, but we are not going to throw you out of your own bed. We can sleep outside if you have a tent or a mosquito net."

Ramla looked at me. "You are a guest in my house. You are not a guest of my garden."

Her husband chuckled in a knowing way that said there would be no point arguing with her. We followed her into the room, where the bed was still warm after her husband's attempted siesta. She stripped the sheets and within five minutes had fresh linen on the bed. Other than an old wardrobe, a small TV on a rickety table with a coat-hanger sticking out the top of it, and his sandals, there was nothing else in the room.

Outside, the sitting-room began to fill up with people emerging from different rooms until it felt like we were at a busy meeting place in the centre of town. It was only later that we finally worked out that Ramla's "family" consisted of her husband, four sons, three daughters, plus her visiting sister and her five children. Amidst all the chaos there was order as people went about the chores they were given: boiling rice, whisking eggs, kneading bread, lighting mozzie coils on the balcony and playing Senegalese beats on the radio.

Presently, a convoy of headlights appeared in the distance and Mara and Citro jumped out of a battered old jalopy with four others in tow. Word had spread that the possibilities of a beach party were on the horizon and within minutes fires were lit and drums laid out in preparation for the impromptu party to take place after dinner. Feasting on bowls of ceebu jen – fish and rice accompanied by huge mounds of couscous, sweet potatoes and peanuts – we were made to feel like part of the extended family. Ramla insisted the party start as soon as everyone had finished eating. Because nobody at the party drank alcohol, huge bowls of fruit punch were dragged down onto the beach for the party. The cars were arranged so that their headlights lit up a dance floor of sand and the bed that had been especially vacated for Judy and I had no occupants until 5.00 the following morning.

Unfortunately, our time in Senegal ended the same way it had begun – in difficulty. Having said goodbye to Mara, Citro and Jawara at the train station the next day, we waited to board the train for Mali. Judy decided that, as our train was late, she would set up the camera and take a couple of shots of the Victorian exterior. While I stood at her back, trying to keep the crowd at bay, a man walked straight toward the camera and began shouting in Wolof. His tone was aggressive and, as he pointed to the camera, he directed his rant to the gathering crowd, swelling in number by the second. Children ran from street corners, vendors came out from behind their stalls and train commuters stopped to see what all the fuss was about. It seemed that whatever he was telling the crowd was inciting the majority of them to turn on us and join in his anger. We still had no idea what had provoked this anger.

"Let's make a run for the station," Judy said, gathering up the gear. All of a sudden, the man grabbed the camera off the tripod and held it up in the air, threatening to smash it. By now a crowd of about forty people surrounded us and things were getting out of control. Some were trying to defuse the situation and others were clearly enjoying watching the drama unfold. It seemed like an eternity that we stood there, rigid with fear, not knowing what to do.

I was shouting out for anybody who spoke English when, all of a sudden, from somewhere in the crowd a woman pushed her way through to us, slapped the guy in the face, grabbed the camera off him and pushed the two of us towards her peanut stall at the side of the street, where she swung open the little wooden door, hurried us inside, bolted it from the inside and dragged a pallet up against it. The angry crowd followed and gathered outside her stall, taunting us to come out. While we waited in the darkness, she peered out defiantly and a screaming match ensued between her and what seemed like everybody else outside. She explained to us in broken English that the man who had taken the camera believed that we were filming people and that our technology could make them appear naked. We couldn't believe what we were hearing.

The police, who are never far from the train station, arrived within minutes to find out what all the noise was about. By the time the woman had explained what had happened, the instigator of the whole debacle had disappeared. We rewound the shots of the train station for the police and, although interesting, the old Victorian façade was obviously not quite as interesting as what we had been accused of! Finally in the clear, we thanked the lady who had rescued us, once again redeeming our faith in the Senegalese people. The first part of our West African adventure had come to a close, and not exactly as we had imagined it – escorted to the station by two police officers and put on a train bound for Mali.

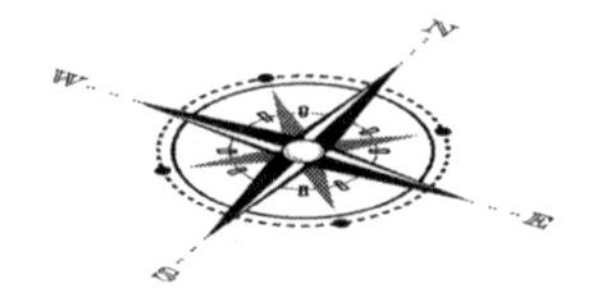

Senegal Fast Facts

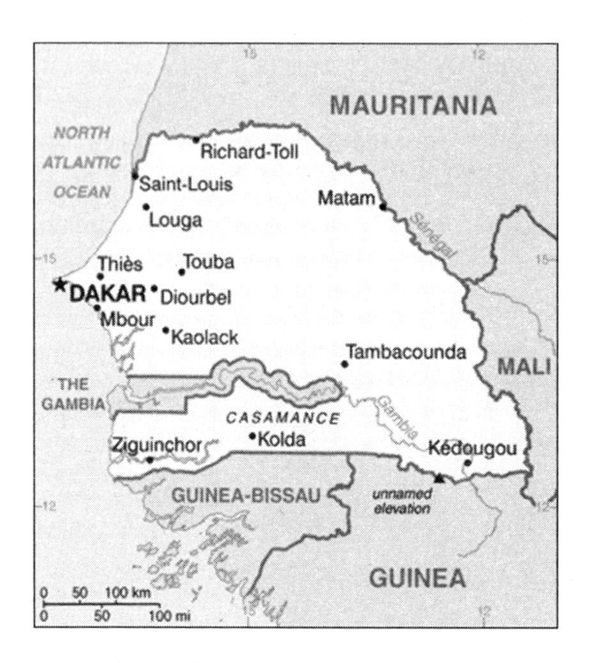

Population: 12.4 million approx.

Official Name: The Republic of Senegal.

Language: Official language is French. National languages include Wolof, Jola, Mandinka, Pulaar and Serer.

Size: Senegal is 196,722 square kilometres and is bordered by Guinea Republic and Guinea-Bissau to the south, Mali to the east and Mauritania to the north, and encloses the confederated state of The Gambia.

Climate: Senegal's wet season lasts from June to September, with a dry season from January to May. Average daily temperatures range from 18°C to 31°C.

Best time to go: The best time to travel is from November to February, before the heat hits in March and after the wet humid season. This is a great time to spot the migratory birds and mammals in Senegal.

Time Difference: + 0 hours from Ireland.

Visa Requirements: Irish citizens holding valid passports are permitted to stay in Senegal for up to three months without a visa. For more information, contact the Senegal embassy in London.

Currency: Local currency in Mali and Senegal is the same, the CFA franc (XOF). The currency is issued by the Central Bank of West African States, an agency of the West African Economic and Monetary Union, consisting of eight countries (Benin, Burkina Faso, Côte d'Ivoire, Guinea-Bissau, Mali, Niger, Senegal and Togo). ATMs are available in major cities and tourist spots in Senegal, as are credit card services. For cash, euros and dollars are the most easily changed currency.

Tipping: It is customary to tip for services provided. As in most West African countries, a ten per cent tip is expected in better-class restaurants; also, bear in mind that wages here are not high so you should avoid tipping too much, as this will set a precedent for others.

Vaccinations: It is highly recommended that you consult your local Tropical Medical Bureau or GP before travelling to Senegal for all relevant vaccines required. The WHO reports malaria transmission in parts of the country.

Safety Information: Medical facilities are poorer outside of the capital city. All regular medications should be taken with you when travelling and a medical kit is highly recommended. It is also recommended you arrange comprehensive medical insurance before travel.

Highlights:

- Take a trip diving around the Cap Vert Peninsula. February to April are the best months.
- Try some deep-sea fishing or fish some of Senegal's creeks and rivers; can be arranged in Dakar.
- Take a trip in the Siné-Saloum Delta, a wild region of mangrove swamps, dunes and lagoons.
- Relax on the Petite Côte (Little Coast) south of Dakar. The main tourist resorts in the area are in Mbour.

Fun Facts

- **The Dakar Rally (or the Paris–Dakar Rally) first took place in 1979 and was organised by Frenchman Thierry Sabine.**
- **The symbols of Senegal are the Lion and the Baobab.**
- **Thie Bou Dien: Senegalese national dish. It is made of manioc, cabbage, eggplants, rice and fish (thiof).**
- **The highest point in Senegal, a peak near Nepen Diakha, is only 581 metres.**

Useful Contacts:

- www.worldtravelguide.net
- Senegal Embassy London: www.senegalembassy.co.uk

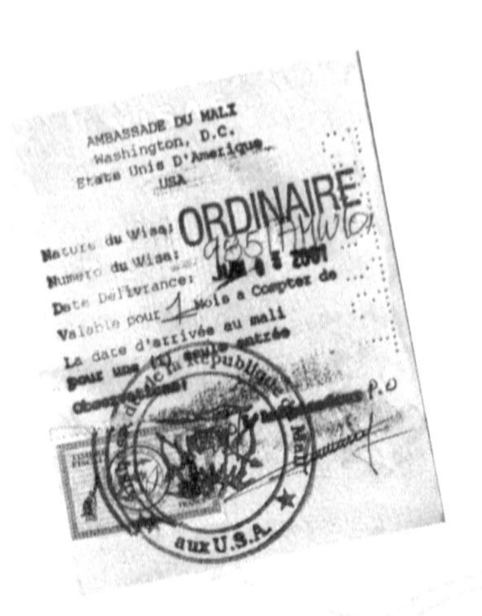

Mali

I have always been a big fan of train travel. No airport queues or check-ins. No stress. It's relatively inexpensive and it's relaxing. I love the sound of a train as it glides over the tracks: *Da-da-da-daaa . . . Da-da-da-daa . . .* How your body sways slightly from the waist with the motion of a train as it carves its way through countries and continents. All you have to do is sit back and watch the world pass your window.

In 1923, when the Dakar to Bamako line opened, it was considered one of the world's greatest train journeys, linking the two main west African cities with the Atlantic. The French had cultivated huge cotton industries in Mali at that time, and the improved trading route meant there were trains running three times a week in both directions.

Unfortunately, we found out that the glory days of the Dakar to Bamako route have long since passed. Forty hours after our police escort from Senegal, our train coughed and spluttered into Mali's capital, Bamako. The journey had been nothing short of excruciating. Although Judy and I had booked a first-class cabin, envisaging some level of comfort for the long trip, we were sorely mistaken. The beds on which we had splashed out fifty dollars were more like park benches under paper-thin mattresses. No bed linen was provided, the lights didn't work, the walls were filthy and there was so much grime on the small window we could barely see out. And if a final nail in the coffin were needed, the toilet down the corridor was clogged before we had even pulled off.

There was no air conditioning at all and as the two days rolled past, the narrow passageway outside our berth became clogged with people. The small windows in the corridors provided them with the only relief from the stuffy carriages on the sweltering train.

The landscape was monotonous and, unlike south or east Africa, there were very few animals left to spot in the National Parks. Because the average speed of the train is only twenty miles an hour, two days of seeing nothing but scrubland and baobab trees nearly drove me around the twist. So, all in all, it was not the most pleasant excursion to psyche us up for the second leg of our West African adventure!

When we arrived in Bamako, Judy and I took a taxi to our hotel. We stood outside for a couple of minutes while we rechecked the address in our guidebook to make sure we had been dropped off at the right place. We were at the dead end of a dead end street, which was deserted apart from the carcass of a dead bird rotting in the sun. The building in front of us (supposedly our hotel), like those either side of it, looked like a run-down garage or service repair centre. The description in our book read: "A good value mid-range hotel with clean rooms and friendly staff. Spotless bathrooms. Interesting part of town." I wondered to myself, as I looked up and down the dusty, empty street, what constitutes an interesting part of town? It was the "spotless" that had clinched it for us, having spent two days on a train whose toilet made the one from *Trainspotting* seem like Raffles Hotel.

A man appeared from a house across the street and we enquired if we were in the right place. "Yes, yes, come in." He slid the bolt across the big steel door. Inside, a wooden table and an old filing cabinet made up the reception. "You rang from Dakar?" he said, as if trying to convince us he was having difficulty remembering the innumerable guests he had checked in that day. He opened up a large notebook, sending a cloud of dust up in the air. There, written in black and white, were our names at the top of an otherwise empty page. For some reason it felt almost reassuring that there was a record of us in this strange, unknown place.

While Judy checked us in, I threw my eyes around the dilapidated building. As if on cue, a huge rat scurried across the hall, stopped, sniffed a bit of dirt on the cement floor, then disappeared into the darkness. Judy, busily counting out some money, hadn't seen it; nor had the manager, who was watching her eagerly. My eyes were out on stalks! The manager looked up at me, smiling patiently. I stood frozen to the spot, smiling inanely back as if nothing had happened.

He gave us the key to our room and, blissfully unaware, Judy followed the giant rat down the corridor into the darkness. We climbed the stairs to our room on the first floor and I breathed a sigh of relief, knowing that, one floor up, our chances of running into that particular rodent again were slim.

Inside the room were two single beds; clean, yes, and perfect – if you were the same width as a knitting needle. Our bathroom was down the corridor but, as there didn't seem to be anybody else staying in the hotel, or indeed anywhere in the vicinity, we decided that wouldn't be an issue. What worried us was the brown pus that was dripping from the corner of the ceiling and running down one of the walls.

We sat on the beds opposite each other, our knees touching in the small cramped space.

Silence.

"Ah, yes, the luxury and glamour of a travel show . . ."

Silence.

"Well, at least it's one step up from the train."

Silence.

We looked at each other, then at the crap dripping down the walls, and we laughed and laughed until we were both in tears. Strangely, I found the whole place quite comforting. It was quiet, it was cool and, apart from Freddie Krueger's intestines running down the walls, it would do us grand.

Before I went on this journey to west Africa in 2002, I knew very little about Mali, except that it was the country with one of the most recognisable town names in the world, Timbuktu. This huge land-locked country, with a population of 13.5 million, is twice the size of France, but it's not easy to find on the United Nations Human Development List. While Ireland ranks as number five top dog in the report, which looks at average lifespan, education and standard of living, it's a long way down the bottom of the list until you come to number 173 out of 177 – Mali, the fifth poorest country in the world.

This is a long fall from grace for the country that used to belong to some of the greatest empires of its time. From the fourteenth to the sixteenth centuries, the Empire of Mali was the crossroads for all the southern African trade with Europe and the Middle East and allowed Trans-Saharan caravans cross to the Atlantic Ocean in the east. Much later, in 1880, France decided they wanted to include Mali into *their* French West African Empire but, unlike Senegal or the Ivory Coast, which have important coastlines, it was never deemed an integral part of the colony and didn't receive the same level of investment.

Through Judy's Lonely Planet contacts in London, we had hired a driver named Moussa for the week, who was to come to our hotel the following morning. Our itinerary meant we would spend just one day in Bamako before heading nearly six hundred kilometres north-east by road, to the ancient town of Djenné to see the largest mud building in the world, the Grand Mosque. After that we would head into Mali's vast semi-desert wilderness to spend three days walking through the Dogon country.

Our driver, Moussa, came to collect us the following morning. He was a shy man but had a little English and, though I had just a few words of French, Judy did well in pidgin conversation. Driving through Bamako felt a million miles away from Dakar. Instantly I could tell it was a much poorer city and the European influence was considerably less obvious. The pace of life was slower and the people did not exude the same confidence and self-assuredness that I had seen in Senegal. Groups sat huddled together along the edge of wide dusty roads, watching the world go by. The vibe in the capital city was much like a big village market rather than a centre of commerce.

The River Niger, which dissects Bamako into north and south, is called "the Lifeline" by the Malians. Originally the city developed on the north side of the river and this is where the busy downtown and market areas exist today. We parked outside the Grand Mosque and followed Moussa down a busy street, where people stepped over and around the sellers and their wares. Although the merchants are not as aggressive as in Senegal, if you stopped for more than a second to look at something, you would immediately find yourself in negotiations.

We turned onto a quiet street and left the throngs behind. Here the men at the stalls and entrances of the low mud buildings we walked past did not jump up to engage us in small talk as we passed. Rather, they sat back and eyed us up suspiciously, whispering to each other behind their hands. This was Bamako's famous fetish market. And I'm not talking whips and chains, leather or lace. Covering every surface of every table were shrivelled monkeys' heads, dried crocodile heads, tortoise shells, ducks' bills, lion paws with matted fur, twisted, gnarled frogs, dried rats and snakes. Jars of ominous cloudy potions and some with clear liquid encasing floating pieces of intestine topped off the delights on offer. The Malians use fetishes as medicines to cure their illnesses, hexes to curse their enemies and different potions to entrap those they desire. Although the majority of the population claim to be Muslim, many of those are what is known as "syncretistic". They combine Islam with their animist beliefs and these fetishes and their magical capabilities, which seem like hocus-pocus to us, are still revered and hugely important all over Mali today. The president is known to dabble openly in a bit of witchcraft and the African Nations soccer tournament is dogged by superstitious teams carrying out sacrifices or using fetishes to influence the outcome of the matches.

Moussa brought us over to an old man with whom he shook hands. "Here, you look, no problem." His friend had the same merchandise as the others and pointed proudly to the biggest pile of shrivelled monkeys' heads we'd seen. "To heal a small child." The old man then picked up a milky-looking liquid, "This will make any man fall in love with you," he said, looking at me and Judy with a straight face. Without hesitating, we bought six bottles between us and left.

By 11.00 a.m. we were on the road to the ancient city of Djenné. The old town was built between the fourteenth and fifteenth centuries and used to be an important part of the old Sahara trading route. Nowadays, except for the busy weekly Monday market, which was taking place the following day, it's a relatively quiet town of 8,000 people. Moussa told us that the 570-kilometre-journey would take us about seven hours. After our rather long train journey, another arduous day cooped up in the car did not sound appealing and I was itching to get out into the African countryside.

The land we drove through, which runs alongside the Niger, was much more fertile and green than what we had seen from the train. Although most of the roads were paved, progress was slow. Traffic was heavy and drivers had to manoeuvre around huge potholes. Moussa was concentrating hard but on one occasion he took his eye off the road to look at an overturned bus on the other side, with what looked like half the population of Mali spilling out of it. Bang! We landed in a pothole hard and our tyre took the brunt. We clambered out of the jeep and did what everybody does for the first few minutes – stood there staring at the burst tyre with our hands on our hips. With us in trouble on one side of the road and the bus crash on the other side, traffic was stopped in both directions. It didn't look like anybody had been seriously injured in the accident, but people were already out of their cars, sitting under the shade of trees and settling down for the long wait before the police arrived. This can take hours. We were lucky, as were those behind us; within an hour, our jeep had been lifted out of the hole, Moussa had put on a new tyre and we were on our way. It was a bumpy ride and almost dark when we pulled into Djenné that evening.

The night air was muggy after the heat of the day but Moussa warned us that the temperature can drop dramatically. Our accommodation was on the roof of a family's mud house. It's common in this part of Mali for backpackers to sleep outside. It is generally cooler and a lot more private than sharing a family's small home. Having spent so long in the interior of cars and trains, it was a welcome relief to be sleeping outdoors. It was exciting. We were given a mat which we rolled out and we lay down for our first night under the African skies. The stars were incredible. From the light of the moon I could see the broken lines of the flat mud roofs of the town stretching into the distance. The noise of the goats and hushed murmurings of passers-by on the street below was soothing. As I drifted off to sleep, I really felt that we were in the heart of Africa.

Peering down from our rooftop the following morning, we awoke to a whole new world. Djenné and its inhabitants were in full flow as traders from all parts of Mali descended on the town for the weekly market. The maze of narrow mud streets flanked on either side by mud houses were thronged with seas of people. We spent so much time looking down, absorbing the scene on one side of the house, that it was a few minutes before we turned around. There, spread out before us, was the huge market square, behind which stood the world-famous "Great Mosque of Djenné". It towers above the town but in a strange way blends in seamlessly as well. Built in 1906, following an earlier thirteenth-century building on the same site, it is the largest free-standing mud building in the world, covering an area of 1,600 square metres. The walls, measuring between sixteen and twenty-four inches thick, are made from sun-baked bricks, held together by mud mortar and plastered over with mud. They keep the intense heat of the sun out during the day and yet still keep the place warm when the temperature drops at night. The butts of palm wood beams, holding the structure together, stick out in symmetrical rows, giving the building a feeling of strength and solidity. These also act as ready-made scaffolding when the mosque needs to be repaired, which it does annually because of the wind and rain. It is a beautiful hand-crafted structure. Staring at it, I could feel the love and devotion that had gone into building it. Non-Muslims have not been allowed inside the mosque since a French fashion-shoot took place there in 1996, in which all the models ran around half-naked.

Makeshift tarpaulin stalls were still being erected on every inch of the market square. Reams of colourful cloth were displayed on the ground alongside baskets of spices and nuts. Women wove around the traders, carrying huge baskets on their heads. What an incredible scene to wake up to!

We rolled up our mats and descended the outside of the building and into the kitchen where the lady of the house had two bowls of steaming millet porridge in wooden bowls ready for us to eat. Although early, it was hot and neither of us felt like eating, but we shovelled a few spoons into us, paid the equivalent of €2 for our stay, and headed out to work.

As the market was so frantic we decided to film away from the main square first and get lost in the narrow warren of mud streets. None is more than two metres wide, not even wide enough to fit an ox and cart; so it's pedestrians, donkeys and goats only! Running down the middle of the streets are open sewer channels. Unfortunately, while Judy was setting up our first shot, her left foot, in an open-toed sandal, went straight into one.

Tangled electricity wires hung overhead, but apart from these, the whole place could have depicted a biblical scene. Old men in brilliant white full-length robes and carrying prayer books looked almost otherworldly compared to some of their poorer neighbours in dusty rags, clutching gnarled walking sticks, who blended in with the brown background.

As we walked, we came across a small square where about thirty women sat on benches under the shade of a huge baobab tree, holding some sort of town meeting. They were like exotic flowers, dressed in electric colours and patterned turbans. Although they didn't exude the swagger of the Senegalese women, they seemed much more flamboyant in their own right.

A small man in a white robe, who had been shyly following us for quite some while, eventually sidled up to us. "They are discussing health problems of the town. Here, a lot of women die having babies, but things are better now. We have trained nurses living here." This was Alijah from the Dogon country, who now lived with his family in Djenné. He went on, "Do you want to come to my house? I have very good view for your camera." As we climbed the stairs of Alijah's adobe house, his two small children ran halfway down the steps to greet him. His wife, who looked no older than sixteen, smiled up at us from the floor where she sat with a baby in her arms. Under instruction in Bambara, he ordered her to make some tea.

Outside, the view was incredible. Alijah was very interested in our work and asked many questions about the programme. We spent an hour with him and his family and he told us all about the Dogon country and the village where he came from. "It is very big place. I hope you have good guide."

"We were going to hire one when we got there."

"Why not hire me? I will do you good price and I know every stone along the Bandiagara escarpment. I know the chiefs of most villages."

Judy and I knew it was not recommended to go walking in the Dogon country alone and that we would have to take a punt on somebody the following day, so why not Alijah? He seemed like a nice guy, easy to be around and someone who would let us work. We said that we would have to check with Moussa but, if he agreed, we couldn't see why not. We agreed a price and, without taking anything with him, Alijah left his house and told his family he would be back in three days.

We strolled back down to the main square and introduced our new recruit to Moussa, who had no problem with an extra passenger in the car. We told them we would be back an hour later, after we filmed in and around the market. It was one of the most colourful spectacles I had ever seen. Because everything was laid out on the ground in the sun, it was open and airy. There was nothing "touristy" for sale. The locals were there to sell to the locals.

I spotted a queue forming in front of an old man, who was stirring a steaming cauldron in the shade of the high walls of the mosque. I watched as he scooped ladles of broth with lumps of meat into plastic bowls. Feeling peckish as well as adventurous, I joined the queue and tried to figure out how much I should pay by looking at the coins in the hand of the man in front of me. On reaching the top of the queue, he handed over his paltry sum. The street chef went fishing in his cauldron, first pulling out what looked like a nice bit of chop. This was returned and instead replaced with a grizzly chicken's foot, claw and all, which was slopped into the bowl of runny liquid. My stomach turned. Then all of a sudden, I figured out the system: the more you were able to pay, the better the piece of meat you got. But by this stage I had lost my appetite and, for want of a better word, chickened out of lunch!

Back in the jeep with our extra passenger, we drove an hour east of Djenné into the Dogon country. This huge 150-kilometre area spreads right through the Sahel along the Bandiagara Escarpment. The Dogon people settled here in 1300 AD after fleeing the banks of the Niger when they refused to convert to Islam. They displaced the Tellem people, who were here before them and whose houses and cave dwellings still remain high up in the cliff faces above the Dogon villages. The Dogons' ancient animist society and belief systems are very intricate but centre on living with one another and their spirit world in harmony. Because the whole area is so remote, the way of life has changed very little in the villages.

Arriving in Bandiagara, on Alijah's advice we stocked up on some essential trekking supplies – sardines, peanuts and toilet paper. Moussa dropped us as far as the jeep would allow, down to a village called Dourou. This was the end of the road for cars of any kind and from here we would walk on dirt tracks across the desert from village to village. There are over seventy of them you can trek to, and most backpackers take in about two or three villages a day. We arranged to meet Moussa three days later, fifty kilometres south, at a village called Kani-Kombole. Until then, we were in the hands of our newfound guide, Alijah.

So, with just a small rucksack each, we set off across the top of the escarpment, in search of a village called Begnimato. Alijah had some family who lived here and he reckoned it was about an eight-kilometre walk away. It was an incredible view from the top of the cliff; the burnt landscape to our west seemed to spread to infinity. The temperature was in the mid-thirties and the heat haze shimmered in the distance, distorting any clear shapes on the horizon.

Alijah had good English and was very knowledgeable about the history of the people. As we walked, he told us that each Dogon community, which can have up to one hundred people, considers itself to be like a big family. Everything is done for the good of the village. The chief is always the eldest living son of an ancestor from within the family branch.

Each village also has a spiritual leader called a Hogon, who is elected amongst the oldest men of the village. His main concern is looking after the purity of the soil. His initiation ritual includes six months without washing or shaving, when nobody is allowed to touch him. After this, one of his wives is allowed to come to his house during the day but he will spend the rest of his nights alone, gathering wisdom from the god Lebe, who visits him every night in the form of a snake and licks him clean. Alijah also told us that it is rare for a man to have more than one wife and, if a woman does want a divorce, it is at the discretion of the whole village.

We didn't meet any other trekkers along our journey as Alijah recounted stories. Considering this was not one of the more remote routes, I began to question whether we should have put our trust in him so unquestioningly. However, just as those seeds of doubt were being planted in my mind, in the distance I could make out pointed thatched roofs sticking out over low stone walls.

On arriving into Begnimato, we were met by the chief who quite obviously recognised Alijah and seemed pleased to see him. If you think the European welcome of three kisses on the cheek is a bit over the top, a Dogon welcome leaves it for dust. With outstretched hands, they greeted each other and then engaged in a long exchange of words with lots of nodding while Judy and I stood there not knowing whether or not we should step in and introduce ourselves. It is customary for the Dogon to greet each other by asking their guests not just about how they are, but how their whole life is – "How are you/your wife/your kids/your father/your village/your harvest/your happiness? . . . etc." to which the usual reply is "Sewa", which means "Everything is fine, thank you", which is used even when all is not well. This is then returned by the visitor and it can sometimes take an hour before the greeting is complete. Luckily for us, after only seven minutes Alijah introduced us to the chief, who invited us to sit down on small wooden stools and have tea. The women of the village sat separately from us in an open-air hut and eyed us up suspiciously as we sat down next to their men.

"What would you like for dinner?"Alijah translated for the chief. After what we had seen in Djenné and rumours that Malians enjoy eating meat of any kind – including dog and cat – we had both decided that we would become vegetarian for the next couple of days.

"Rice would be lovely, thank you."

"No rice with chicken and tomato sauce?"

"Maybe just rice and tomato sauce, thank you. That would be lovely."

This was discussed at length and then the order for later that evening was given to the women so they could begin the preparations. We were shown to our sleeping quarters, which were again on the roof of the chief's house. We had to climb up a tree with steps cut into it and swing our legs up over the adobe ledge onto the roof and dump our bags. We were then free to explore the village.

Dogon villages are either built on the lower plains, high up on the escarpment like Begnimato or against the bottom of the cliffside. The family houses are simple square mud buildings with flat roofs built quite close together. Chickens and goats roam freely in the narrow alleyways. Dotted around them, higher up in the cliff, are the smaller granaries with conical-shaped thatched roofs. The more granaries a village has, the wealthier the community is.

We scrambled up the scree after Alijah and two of the local boys, who were clearly delighted at having been chosen by the chief to show us around. Men and women have their own separate granaries. The men's granaries are square and are used for holding flour, millet, onions and rice. The round granaries of the women are used for storing food, cloth and their jewellery. They are all built on plinths off the ground in an attempt to keep the rats away. They are very basic but, on closer inspection, most of them have exquisitely carved wooden doors depicting different stories and Dogon rites of passage.

Every Dogon village is laid out in a symbolic plan representing different parts of the human body. Alijah and the two boys brought us to the head of the body, which is a hut called a Taguna. Only men are allowed in here to discuss and debate issues and the roof is purposely built too low for standing up. This means that if an argument breaks out, all the men have no choice but to remain sitting, which in turn defuses what could potentially be a rowdy situation!

That evening, the most fabulous sunset washed the desert in a sea of red. We sat around a fire in front of the chief's house in the stillness of the desert until the sun slipped below the horizon and we were left in the dark. Kerosene lamps were lit and homemade millet beer was passed around in a big gourd before dinner. I decided, from the taste of it, that it was probably better that I couldn't see what I was drinking. It had a sour, yeasty taste with bits of grit in it. Certainly didn't match a cold bottle of Coors Light after a long day in the sun! Then dinner was served and it tasted fantastic, as we'd had nothing to eat all day. We chatted a little longer with the chief but the two of us were so tired after the heat of the day, we excused ourselves and headed for bed. Climbing the "tree-stairs" up to the roof in the dark was no easy feat, especially with a dodgy stomach after a few shots of milky millet beer.

This was our second night under the stars and, as we snuggled down into our sleeping bags, I couldn't imagine the most luxurious five-star hotel in the world bettering our accommodation.

"It's a long way from your *Vogue* days," I teased Judy, as she attempted to brush her teeth, spitting into an old plastic bottle.

We lay there in the stillness and looked up at the millions of stars above. The low murmurings of the men sitting beneath us, coupled with the backdrop of goats' bells ringing in the distance, filled me with an overwhelming feeling of peace. The sense of being in the world and being part of the world made me want to burst with happiness. My head wouldn't or couldn't switch off. I felt alive. Lying there confirmed to me once again that it's the simple things in life that give you happiness which, after your health, is the most important tool for survival.

The wind picked up during the night and woke me up. From inside my sleeping bag, I could feel the desert sand storm raining down on top of us. I wasn't cold though and I liked the feeling of being out in the elements with the wind howling around me. I pulled my hat down over my ears and somehow drifted back into a deep sleep.

The following morning, I woke up and peered out to find I was sleeping next to a sand dune in the shape of Judy's sleeping bag. We sat up. There was sand and dust everywhere – in our hair, in our mouths, up our noses.

"How did you sleep?" I asked.

"Great," she said, shaking half of the Sahel out of her hair. "And you?"

"Like a baby."

We gathered up our things and were ready to move on from the village by 6.30 a.m., but I got the feeling that something wasn't right with the villagers. Although people were still smiling, the women in particular were acting quite strangely. We took out handfuls of biros and pencils we had brought with us as gifts and handed them out. This seemed to shift the mood a little and the villagers sang us out as we went on our way.

We finally persuaded Alijah to tell us what was wrong. He explained that the villagers were slightly put out, because the entire village had to go without meat the night before, simply because we had decided not to eat chicken. Although they do eat vegetarian meals, the meat had been especially prepared for our arrival. Because the communal meal is cooked in one big pot, the men were annoyed at what the women served up and the women in turn were annoyed that we had caused them this upset. It had never even crossed our minds that this would have been a problem for the whole village.

"Why didn't they tell us? We would have eaten chicken, no problem. Probably not cat or dog, but we thought tomato sauce would be easier for everyone and that they didn't have to use up their meat on us."

"The chief didn't want me to tell you. You were his guests and he decided you would have what you desired."

Although we had already walked about two kilometres from the village at this stage, I was so embarrassed that I wanted the ground to open up and swallow me.

We were attempting to make our way to a village called Teli, around twenty kilometres south of Begnimato before continuing on to the village of Kani-Kombole, where we would spend our last night. By midday, after walking for five hours, we had covered a lot of ground. The temperature was touching forty degrees, there wasn't a cloud in the sky and there was nowhere to shelter, to escape the incessant heat of the sun. My mouth was constantly dry. I hadn't gone to the toilet since the previous morning, though I had been drinking litres of water – a sure sign of dehydration.

We climbed down the high escarpment and passed small groups of walkers, most being led by guides. We stopped to talk to a French couple who were walking through the Dogon country on their own for two full weeks. They had misread their map the night before and ended up sleeping in the desert, miles from anywhere. We shared our water with them and Alijah marked on their map the best route for them to follow.

Senegal

Let the adventure begin – Judy and I on the road

A street scene in Gorée Island, Senegal

The battlements of the old Maison des Esclaves in Gorée
PHOTO © *Ji-Elle*

The Door of No Return on Gorée Island

The Victorian railway station in Dakar PHOTO © *J.W. H. van der Waal*

Mali

The Grand Mosque at Djenné, the largest free-standing mud building in the world
PHOTO © *Ferdinand Reus,* used with kind permission. All rights reserved.

The Monday morning market at Djenné

PHOTO © *Ferdinand Reus,* used with kind permission.

A typical Dogon village PHOTO © *Dario Menasce*

Above:
The old Tellem dwellings at Teli

The former dwellings of the Tellem people cling precariously to the Bandiagara Escarpment

Outback Australia

Gerry, myself, Grant and Tim, lost in the bush but with no worries

All smiles in the Outback

PHOTO COURTESY OF AND © *RTÉ 2003*

Road to Nowhere

An eye on Uluru

Uluru at sunset

PHOTO COURTESY OF AND © *RTÉ 2003*

Farther along, we rested at the hillside village of Yaba-Talu, where a local basket-weaver stopped his work and offered us a millet beer which, not wanting to earn a reputation in the area of being rude and difficult guests, we politely sipped, trying not to grimace at the horrible taste. He did not live in a mud house but rather in a hole in the cliff.

"You will see many dwellings like this in Teli," said Alijah. "It is cool inside away from the sun and it does not disintegrate in the rain like the mud houses."

We thanked our friend for the use of his cool cave. Just as we set off again, a donkey and cart passed us on the track. After a little negotiation with the driver, we hoisted ourselves up on the edge of the cart and, with grateful smiles, allowed ourselves another break while still inching our way to our final destination.

I have so many magical moments from Mali, but that half hour sitting on the donkey cart is etched into my memory as if it were yesterday. In the still, lethargic heat of the desert, the only sound was the old cart with its rickety wheels crunching along the track. To my right, the dusty figures of Elijah and the driver sat in comfortable silence up the front. Behind me, Judy lay down with her arms over her face, protecting herself from the unforgiving sun, using a mud-caked rucksack as a pillow. Around us, a sea of red emptiness, broken here and there by clumps of small green scrub and twiggy, leafless trees. I felt like I was living and breathing in a different century, an ancient one. The world as I knew it felt so far away.

We parted company with our donkey and cart and continued along the escarpment by foot to Teli, where we scrambled up the cliff to try and reach the abandoned houses built centuries ago by the Tellem people. Before the Dogon, these pygmy people had lived in the cliffs since the eleventh century. They built their little beehive-style houses in the most inaccessible of places, leading the Dogon people to believe that the Tellem could fly.

Looking up, we could see holes in the cliff face which could only be reached by ropes. Alijah explained to us that the entire cliff face was full of bones. It was the tradition of both the Dogon and the Tellem people before them that, when somebody died, they tied vines around their waists. The bodies were then hoisted up by pulley and deposited in little holes in the cliff. Many of these caves have never been explored and those that have show that the Tellem had been a highly developed society, especially in weaving, as far back as the Iron Age.

It was another five kilometres before we finally reached Kani-Kombole. I was never more happy to arrive anywhere in my life! Moussa was waiting for us, holding a plastic bag of cold beers in the air. I nearly cried with happiness. My feet felt like lead and when I took my boots off, the relief made me feel like my brain was melting out of my ears! Judy and I lay sprawled out on the ground in front of the village, like two wounded soldiers. This had everyone in stitches, including the chief who, twenty minutes after our arrival, was still in the process of carrying out his welcome greeting with Alijah.

We climbed up the tree-trunk ladder to inspect our roof for the night. A strong breeze was blowing now. Alijah shouted up to us, "What would you like for dinner?"

We leaned over, gauged his expression and the faces of everyone else in the village.

"Rice and chicken?" we inquisitively chorused.

"That is a good idea," Alijah smiled up at us before translating to the chief. Everyone seemed happy with our decision.

It was our last night in the Dogon country and, when the sun went down, we huddled around the fire picking at the least gristly bits of chicken bone and washed it down with lots of beer. Neither of us had had to touch the Imodium up until then, and we prayed that tonight would not be the night.

Our arrival had prompted the appearance of some local teenagers, who were keen to see what the two women and their big camera was all about. Judy set the camera up on the tripod and rewound some of our footage of the last few days so they could have a look. They were utterly mesmerised and went into fits of giggles every time they recognised somebody from the village on tape.

One of the young boys came over to me with an old battered cassette player cradled in his arms. In one hand he held a dusty cassette. "No wire," he said, pointing to the hole at the back of the recorder and then pointing to a wire that connected the microphone to the camera, hoping that it would be the key to solving his problems. I loved him for his astute train of thought and my heart nearly broke explaining to him that it wouldn't work. I opened up the battery compartment in the back, which was empty except for a thick layer of dust. I rooted in our camera bag and, by some small miracle, pulled out two alkaline batteries. God knows what they were doing there, as we didn't need them for our kit at all. The player needed four and, after a lot of rummaging, Moussa emptied another two from his flashlight. I blew the dust out of the recorder and loaded it up. By this stage, a crowd had gathered around by the light of the fire and suddenly the pressure was on. I looked at the pleading eyes of the little boy as he handed me his battered old cassette. I slipped it into the deck, closed the door and pressed "play".

The noise that came crashing out made everyone around the fire jump out of their skins. Through the crackly, tinny speakers, I could just make the music out to be some kind of old French hip-hop. The tape and recorder had evidently been a present from a previous traveller. The kids screamed for joy in the moonlight.

Overhead, there was a massive roar of thunder, followed by an incredible flash of lightning which lit up the children dancing around the recorder for two or three seconds before they turned into silhouettes again. They were a joy to watch. Not once did they stop dancing, even when the rains came.

That night, because of the howling wind and rain, we couldn't sleep on the roof and instead had to bed down on the floor of an old disused granary. The village still used the mud hut as storage for anything and everything. In all the clutter of sacks and baskets of onions and shovels, it was difficult to find somewhere to lie down flat. We listened to the rain pelting down in sheets outside. Through the open door, every couple of minutes lightning would illuminate the village enclosure. It was spooky but exhilarating, until one flash of lightning put the spotlight on a huge rat that scurried right in front of my face.

We both started screaming and ran out into the rain. Luckily, the noise of the thunder had drowned out our screams, which at least meant we hadn't woken anyone else in the village up. We stood there in the rain, not knowing where to go. I couldn't bring myself to go back in and lie on the floor. So we pulled up two wicker chairs as far under the thatched overhang of the roof as we could and sat in the darkness of the storm. We talked quietly for hours about everything we had seen and all we had experienced in the two weeks since arriving in Senegal.

A cockerel crowed just before sunrise and as the rain had stopped, we walked a short distance away from the village, sat on the wet earth and watched the black plains of Africa wake up. Shades of grey and green, followed by red, orange and yellow leaked across the sky.

I was leaving one of the poorest countries in the world behind, yet the experiences it had given me have enriched my life in ways that I can't explain. My eyes were opened so much and my first time in West Africa, all those years ago, truly made me see how travel can change a person for the better.

Mali Fast Facts

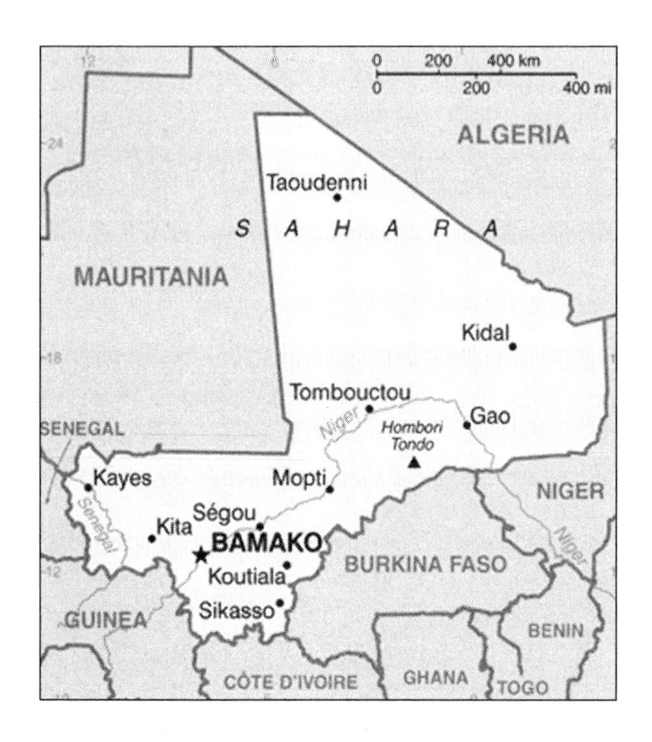

Population: 14 million approx.

Official Name: The Republic of Mali.

Capital City: Bamako.

Languages: The official language is French. The other main languages are Bambara and Fula.

Size: Mali is 1.25 million square kilometres. It is a landlocked republic, sharing borders with Mauritania, Algeria, Burkina Faso, Côte d'Ivoire, Guinea, Niger and Senegal.

Climate: Mali's wet season lasts from June to September, with a dry season from January to May. In the height of the summer months, temperatures in Mali are often reported to reach over 40°C, while reaching a staggering 30°C in the cold season.

Best time to go: The best time to travel is from November to February before the heat hits in March and after the wet humid season. Mali's cultural festivals take place in January.

Where I went: Bamako, Djenné and the Dogon villages of Begnimato, Yaba-Talu, Teli and Kani-Kombole.

Time Difference: +0 hours from Ireland.

Visa Requirements: Irish passport holders need a visa to travel to Mali as a tourist for up to three months. It should be applied for through the Mali embassy in Brussels, Tel:(322) 345 74 32.

Currency: Local currency in Mali is the CFA Franc (XOF). The currency is issued by the Central Bank of West African States, an agency of the West African Economic and Monetary Union, consisting of eight countries (Benin, Burkina Faso, Côte d'Ivoire, Guinea-Bissau, Mali, Niger, Senegal and Togo). It is possible to get ATM's in Bamako. For cash, euros and dollars are the most easily changed currencies.

Tipping: It is customary to tip for services provided. As in most West African countries, a ten per cent tip is expected in better-class restaurants. Also bear in mind that wages here are not high so you should avoid tipping too much, as this will set a precedent for others.

Vaccinations Needed: It is highly recommended that you consult your local Tropical Medical Bureau or GP before travelling for all relevant vaccines required. The WHO reports malaria transmission.

Safety Information: Medical facilities are poorer outside Bamako. All regular medications should be taken with you when travelling and a medical kit is highly recommended. It is also recommended you arrange comprehensive medical insurance before travel.

Other Highlights:

- Visit the ancient city of Gao and visit the mosque of Kankan Moussa and the tombs of the Askia Dynasty. Two excellent markets can also be found here.
- Take a trip to Timbuktu, where the magnificent camel caravans arrive every year from the salt mines to distribute their produce.

Fun Facts

- **A Malian man will only shake hands with a woman if she offers it first.**
- **Salt was once such a valuable commodity that people would trade a pound of gold for a pound of salt. Mali is famous for its salt mines.**
- **The ancient mosque in Timbuktu has a door which has never been opened. It is said that opening the door will signal the end of the world.**
- **Prize-money was offered for the first European to reach Timbuktu. Gordon Laing from Scotland reached Timbuktu in 1826 but never returned home, as he was killed by Tuaregs.**

Useful Contacts:

- General Information on Mali: www.worldtravelguide.net
- Mali embassy in Brussels: Tel: (322) 345 74 32

Outback Australia

I hadn't intended arriving into Sydney without a plan. It *had* all been organised. My friend Shane, who'd been in Australia for seven months, would meet me at the airport and we would take off up the east coast together. Just me and him and the open road. I was so excited. But the day I left Dublin for Oz, he phoned me to say that he had fallen out of an apple tree in Tasmania where he had been working, broken his ankle and, under doctor's orders, couldn't leave the island for six weeks.

So there I was, standing at the lit-up accommodation board in the airport, scouring for a cheap hostel. I was nineteen, had never travelled on my own before and didn't have a clue where I would stay or what I would do. Eventually, I decided on a place in King's Cross and an hour later, I was climbing the stairs to the top of a six-floor grotty building. From outside the room, I could hear loud snoring. The smell of damp socks and BO leaked out from under the door before I even opened it. Inside were six sets of bunk beds squeezed into the room; only one bed against the far wall was empty. Everyone was asleep so I tiptoed across the room, crawled onto the thin, stained mattress, turned my back to the room and cried.

What was I doing in this hellhole on my own and why had the guy at the desk put me in a room full of men? I couldn't believe that mixed dorms were the norm down here. I decided there and then that I would get a flight down to Tasmania the following day. I didn't care how much it cost.

As everybody started to wake up, I realised that I was sharing a room with eleven builders from Glasgow who were all heading off to work on-site. I pretended to be asleep as they all got dressed and left. I then got up and decided to take myself off around Sydney to do the sights before I headed south to the safety of the one person I knew. I went down to Circular Quay where I sat and looked at the Opera House for what must have been about three hours. I do this now religiously every time I return to Sydney because it was while I was sitting there that I talked myself out of running away to Tasmania. I marvelled at such an iconic landmark, thousands of miles from home, in a beautiful city where the sun was shining and I thought, "Jesus Christ, this is fantastic! I am nineteen, I am in Australia, with three months to do whatever and go wherever I want. I am the luckiest girl in the world."

I went into a travel agent and booked myself on an overnight bus to Byron Bay for the following week; I would travel up the east coast from there. This would give me time to enjoy Sydney and get into the swing of independent travel. Although I was nervous, it felt as if a big weight had been lifted off my shoulders. By the time I got back to the hostel, it was late in the afternoon and all the lads were getting ready for a night out. I introduced myself and bit the bullet, asking if I could tag along with them.

From that day until the end of my three-month adventure up the east coast, I was never really on my own. Shane eventually did catch up with me but I learned quickly that Australia is an easy place to meet people who are in the same boat as you. The experience gave me confidence to travel on my own, the ability to drink copious amounts of cheap red wine (or Goon as it is called) out of what resembled foil colostomy bags and the knowledge that I would never again take a job stuffing leaflets into envelopes for eight hours a day, no matter how bad things got.

Although I had a great three months, I felt I didn't get under the skin of Australia. I felt I had done the fun, *Home and Away* Australia but next time I came back I wanted to go into the outback. I remember having a conversation with my instructor when I was diving up in the Great Barrier Reef, during one of the last days of my trip. I told him how, the next time I came back, I wanted to experience the outback or the "real Australia". He looked at me as if I had ten heads. "Real Australia, my arse! Deserts and sand and scrub and nothin' for hundreds of miles, just blackfellas kickin' off with each other and everyone else they can find, off their head. To hell with that, mate! You can have 'real Australia'. This is real enough for me."

Australia is the most urbanised country in the world, with ninety-five per cent of the population living in towns and cities, so the idea of the remote bush and the outback really appealed to me. I wanted to learn more about Aboriginal culture and try and understand the sometimes hostile attitudes of the white Australians I had met along the way toward the indigenous people. In cities and towns that I had passed through, it was so common to see homeless and drunk Aboriginals and in Sydney there is a big problem with drug-related crime coming from within their communities.

From what little I knew about Aboriginal culture, everything about their history, their laws and their beliefs are centred around their creation stories and their knowledge of and respect for the land. In 1985, the Australian government handed back huge amounts of land right across Australia to the traditional owners and although advances have been made in terms of repairing the wrongs inflicted on Aboriginal people, the relationship or vibe I picked up in the three months I was in Australia were mostly tainted and negative.

Five years later, in 2004, I flew into Alice Springs, the capital of the hot "red centre". It is the jumping-off point for tourists who come out to see Uluru or "Ayers Rock" and I had been warned by many people who had been there, that there was nothing else to it. In fact, I had heard it described as a bit of a dump. Either way, with the nearest ocean 1,200 kilometres away and the nearest cities, Darwin and Adelaide, 1,500 kilometres away, it is the key town of Central Australia. Now, I knew it probably wouldn't be the hippest or most happening of towns. But I also refused to believe that the red centre had only an overnight or two in Alice and a daytrip to the rock to offer before people flew out again to the coast. This, after all, was the cradle of Australian civilisation, where 50,000 years ago, the Aboriginal people began their relationship with and understanding of the land. It is engrained in every inch of their being. This is the wild west of the southern hemisphere, where pioneers came in search of gold, miners came to make their fortune and drovers claimed vast tracts of land, the size of small countries, where they could graze their cattle.

We were going to use Alice Springs as a base to explore the outback and to see what else there was to do on holidays in the middle of nowhere. Our crew for this trip were Gerry and myself, who flew from Ireland, and our two Aussie crew, Grant and Tim, fresh-faced from the short flight from Sydney. I had worked with the lads before and it was great to catch up with them again.

We were staying in a motel on the outskirts of town and my first impression of Alice was of a functional rather than a pretty place. It was quite modern and on first impressions had less of a frontier town feel than I had expected. To get our bearings, the lads advised us to take the jeep up to the top of Anzac Hill to get a panoramic view of the town. They imparted this advice while sitting by the pool in their togs drinking beer. Gerry and I, who had left Dublin thirty-eight hours earlier, looked at each other, sat down and joined them. We agreed that it would be just as beneficial to get the low down from the lads, who had been to Alice countless times before. Grant works on the Australian equivalent of *No Frontiers*, which is called *Getaway*, so we whiled away the afternoon swapping travel stories and boring to death everybody else who sat next to us.

Later that evening we headed into town to get a bite to eat. The streets were busy as couples strolled along looking in shop windows and checking out restaurant menus while determined groups of guys and girls hot-footed it to the best watering holes to sink a few beers after the heat of the day. It was May, which is high season in the red centre. May/June and September/October are when people flock out here, as the temperatures are just about bearable in the late twenties or early thirties. Tim recommended the Blue Grass restaurant and we were lucky enough to get a table outside. We discussed our itinerary for the next few days and worked out a schedule which would make the best use of our time.

Halfway through our meal we heard a car come flying down the street. It passed our table and with a massive screech of brakes, turned right at the crossroads in front of us. The door of the car flew open and the body of a young woman hit the cement with a thud, rolling a couple of times before coming to a stop at the side of the road. The car drove on and then screeched to a halt about twenty metres away. We were all so stunned that none of us reacted for about five seconds. It was as if the world had stopped for those few seconds before reality hit with a bang. Finally Grant jumped up from the table and ran towards the girl on the ground. We could see that she was alive because she was attempting to get up but we weren't sure whether she was concussed or drunk like her two friends, who had stumbled out of the car and were staggering toward her. Grant bent down beside her and asked if she was okay. She didn't even register that he was there. The three girls were English, and with the help of her two friends, the injured girl, her legs cut to pieces, was scraped off the road and bundled back into the car. Just as quickly as the whole thing had happened we were left looking at the red taillights disappearing into the distance, laughter still audible in the car over the music on the stereo.

Witnessing this made me feel quite uneasy and reminded me of a crash I had been in during my first time in Australia. After a night out, myself and a Finnish girl called Anna had squeezed into the back of a van with a couple of others to get a lift back to our camp in the bush. The driver was a local guy who had been drinking all day and smoking pot for hours. We knew we shouldn't have got in but it was our only way to get home and we threw caution to the wind. He took a corner too fast, swerved and we found ourselves upside-down in the ditch. Thankfully nobody was killed or seriously injured. There was one twisted ankle and a couple of cuts and bruises but the following morning when I walked back down the road to where the overturned van still lay, I realised how stupid I had been. It's strange, but when you are away on the other side of the world, you do things you would never normally do at home. Even though in some situations you are more guarded, in others the sense of freedom that travel gives you can make you take more risks.

Up early in the morning, we were picked up by Sandi in her "Alice Wanderer" for a tour of the town. Along with her husband Mal, she has been taking tours since 1994 and loves the town she now calls home. "Like anywhere, I guess, it takes time to get used to somewhere but we have lived all over the Northern territory and Alice is home now." We described what we had witnessed the previous night. "I think people go a bit overboard letting their hair down here. Maybe it's the heat and because they are usually here for a short time, I don't know. But all I know is that I have seen some Europeans behave a lot worse than some of the locals in this town."

Eventually taking the lads' advice, our first stop was to the top of Anzac Hill to look down on the town. The relatively small sprawl of shiny white buildings sat gleaming in the sun, surrounded by a sea of green trees which looked like they were protecting the town from the harsh red desert that surrounded it. In the distance, Sandi pointed out Heavitree Gap, an erosion in the rock made by the Todd River, which now provides the only road into Alice Springs. Beyond the gap, the MacDonnell Ranges sat majestically on the horizon. It was a modern-day oasis framed by a piercing bright blue sky.

We drove out along the Stuart Highway to the original site of Alice Springs – the old telegraph station six kilometres outside town. It was here during the construction of the overland telegraph line in 1870 that J.J. Mills discovered water and springs below the dry riverbed. The area is named after Alice Todd, the wife of former Postmaster General, Charles Todd. I was delighted to know, after all these years, who the **** Alice was! The line was established to relay messages between Darwin and Adelaide and it is the best preserved station along the 3,000-kilometre telegraph route. This was obviously known as far afield as Japan because when I went to use the toilet there was a queue of about sixty Japanese tourists ahead of me. Probably being a bit over-cautious about getting dehydrated, I had already drunk three litres of water in the three hours I had been awake and certainly was not in a position to stand in a long queue. I wandered off down a dirt track until I felt I was out of the way enough to go about my business, which I did cautiously on account of the long grass, where snakes were known to lurk.

I then stumbled upon an old graveyard for the station's employees. The grave of the second stationmaster, Ernest Flint, who died on 17 July 1887, simply reads "RIP The Surveyor". I wondered what it must have been like living here in utter remoteness back in the 1870s, where, if you were sick and didn't get better of your own accord, you died. The small community of stationmaster, four linesmen, teacher, cook and blacksmith, had to be completely self-sufficient with their cattle, sheep and vegetables. Provisions only came once a year from the south. I imagined how exciting that one day of the year would have been, how torturous the wait until the supplies arrived. I wondered how, over a hundred years ago, these first European settlers would have conducted themselves with the local Arrernte people and how they were received. It seemed so long ago until I read a notice on the station wall which put things somewhat into perspective: "It is worth remembering that the probable occupation of this site spans 330 generations of Aborigines as well as five generations of Europeans."

Back in town, we stopped for a coffee just outside Todd's Mall. Small groups of Aborigines sat in the shade of trees on the grass, some selling paintings, others chatting amongst themselves. Two or three men lay sprawled out on the grass. Sandi explained that because a lot of the indigenous communities are now dry areas where no alcohol is permitted, a lot of men with drink problems have drifted here where they can get drunk without letting down their clan. "With all these people coming and going, the tourists, the locals, people are always passing through and you're always seeing new faces. It's a town in motion and for exactly that reason, don't ask me how, I feel at home here."

I wasn't overly excited about visiting the Flying Doctors Museum in Stuart's Terrace. Being more of an avid *Neighbours* fan, I never watched the fictional drama series which was broadcast in Ireland and across the world in the 1980s. The show was based on the real Royal Flying Doctors Service, which was set up here in Alice in 1939 by Rev John Flynn. It was the first air ambulance service in the world, bringing medical aid to the outback for the first time. It's a completely non-profit organisation and although they now receive substantial government funding, the organisation still relies on a lot of national charitable donations. As well as emergency evacuations and treatments, they also provide routine health checks, medical treatments and advice, 365 days of the year. Nowadays, the usual crew attending a call would only be the pilot and a nurse, with a doctor available to diagnose over the phone. What I thought was really inspiring were the simple but ingenious ideas of medical chests, of which 3,500 have been distributed to different parts of the bush. Inside are compartments of pills which have all been numbered. Also inside is an anatomical body chart with each different part of the body numbered. The doctor can ask the patient over the phone to tell him or her what number hurts and they can then prescribe the correct pill number to treat the ailment. On average, the Royal Flying Doctors attend 665 patients a day. The tour itself is tiny and took us about an hour to do, which is quite concise considering that the service travels twenty-one million kilometres every year.

By this stage I was beginning to understand a bit more about the realities of living in the bush and next on the agenda we had been given special permission to take part in a live class at the School of the Air. There are 120 students between the ages of four and thirteen who live on farms, in national parks and Aboriginal communities who have their classes with a teacher via radio and satellite link-up. They do their homework by email and have home tutors, like parents or older siblings, to help them as well.

I sat beside the teacher, John, in a dark room with a projector, four computers and a webcam. He introduced me and the crew to the class, even though there was nobody else in the room. He told them that we were from Ireland and that we were out making a TV show. He asked a girl called Natasha to tell us a little bit about herself. I was looking at a superimposed photograph of Natasha on the map as her voice rang into the room through the speakers.

"Hi Kathryn. That sounds like a cool job, travelling all over the world."

"It's a great job, Natasha, I love it. Now am I right in saying your farm is one of the biggest farms in the Northern Territory? Do you know that it takes me about four hours to drive across my whole country from east to west?"

She giggled. "That's what it takes to drive across this station!"

Kirsten then came online as her photograph flashed up. "I'm eleven and my farm is 400 kilometres away. My best friend out here is Jenny. She's a tame kangaroo and my other best friend is Nicky, who lives down south. I see her once a year at our annual class get-together."

I had great fun listening to the stories from different parts of the red centre and was absolutely mesmerised at how technology like this had changed the lives of so many children, who would otherwise have had to travel anything up to eight hours to get to school! John told me that the fee for the year is $300 and that covers the cost of the equipment needed as well.

After a lunch at the Red Ochre Grill, we said goodbye to Sandi and headed for the Ooraminna cattle station, about fifty kilometres south of Alice. It is the smallest farm in the region, covering a mere 160,000 hectares! Bill Hayes, who runs the farm along with his family, had offered to drive into Alice so we could follow him out to his place in case we got lost. We assured him that there was no need for that and, with our map, we were sure we could find it ourselves. Slightly reluctantly, he responded, "Alrighty, but when you feel you have gone too far, keep drivin', make sure you have plenty of fuel and water and hopefully I'll see you when I see you." By our calculations, it would take us less than an hour to get there. We left Alice and just a few miles outside of town, turned off the main road onto a red dirt track which stretched without a bend to the horizon.

The land cruiser bounced along the dusty track as we drove across the red scrubland, pierced with clumps of prickly spinifex, to a soundtrack of Tom Petty. In a way, it reminded me of parts of Arizona or New Mexico but felt entirely different. The light in this part of Australia is incredible and the contrast of the vast expanse of flat red earth against the clear blue sky is intoxicating and alluring. Your whole body absorbs it and you feel such an incredible sense of peace that you forget this is one of the most hostile environments on the planet. We stopped every couple of miles so Tim, the cameraman, could get another shot of the long red road to nowhere. "Aw mate, this is better than the last four!"

Taking a photograph, I noticed something that looked like a small lizard dart across the road. We all stood around and looked at it. Then Grant piped up in an authoritative English accent, "I do believe that – where I jest not, my friends – is a thorny devil." I refused to believe him. "I'm telling you, that's what they are called."

"That's not their proper name, that's Aussie speak!" I laughed – until we got to Ooraminna, where his sighting was confirmed and I was $100 poorer.

Two hours later we drove through what looked like a deserted town. In fact, we found out later, it was a film set for a movie called *The Drover's Boy*, which had never been made. There was a reproduction police station and jail and a couple of outbuildings. The film was to be based on true accounts of Aboriginal women who had worked as drovers or cattle herders and got together with white farmers. Women were not allowed to be hired so they used to camouflage themselves as men by tying scarves around themselves to flatten out their breasts.

The Ooramina homestead itself is built on a hill overlooking a vast expanse of land which take in views of the MacDonnell Ranges and the Simpson Desert. Bill and Jan were waiting on the bleached wooden terrace to greet us when we arrived. Bill and Jan are the sixth generation of the Hayes family, who originally arrived out here with bullocks and drays in 1884 to replace the wooden overhead telegraph poles with steel ones. They are the stereotypical outback family – laidback and hardy, with tough skin that has adapted to horrifically high temperatures. Without asking us, Jan handed us all an ice-cold beer while Bill told us a bit about his property. About fifteen years ago, like on every other farm, his cattle were affected badly by drought and so the family had to diversify their industry. By turning to tourism and giving people an insight into the running of an outback station, it allowed them to sustain their traditional way of life.

Sal, Bill's son-in-law, pulled up in his battered Ford F-250 to take us on a tour of the station. Like Bill, Sal personified the image of the Australian bushman – a big powerful-looking man wearing a blue plaid shirt, shorts, R.M. Williams boots and the traditional Aussie wide-brimmed hat. He certainly did not look like your average tour guide. His Ford was covered in dust, just like himself. He grabbed a beer out of the eskey, drank it back in about ten seconds, slapped his impressive belly and smiled. "G'day! You lot ready?" We drove out across the expanse of land hoping to spot some of the 5,000 herd of cattle. I felt like I was on safari and I thought how odd it would be to feel this excited hoping to spot a cow on a farm in Ireland! The heat haze shimmered low on the craggy ground and distorted definite lines and shapes, making everything feel fluid and surreal.

Sal told us, "There is no natural water on the property so we have to make sure the thirty-two watering holes are functioning at all times. In some areas there are forty or fifty kilometres between watering holes so I reckon you're more likely to die of thirst out here than a snake bite. We do a round trip of 230 kilometres every three days to make sure everything is right." As we drove along I asked Sal about the station's relationship with the local Aborigines. "Yeah, we get on all right. We have respect for each other. Nobody knows how difficult it can be out here and that you have to work so hard or the place will kill ya. Those boys know the land better than anyone and they know we have a respect for the land as well."

That evening we sat with Bill on his veranda watching the sun go down, listening to the silence of the vast emptiness. Between the silences, we played a game where Grant came up with the names of other Australian animals, such as the bridled nail tail wallaby or the long-nosed bandicoot, and we had to guess whether they were true or false. This led us onto unusual Australian place names like Mooflake, Grong-Grong and Hat Head. By the time we giggled our way through Gympie, Tittybong and Come-by-Chance, it was time to go to bed.

The following morning we got ourselves back on the old south road, heading for Titjikala, an Aboriginal community 150 miles away. Gunya Titjikala is Australia's first exclusive indigenous resort and we were all intrigued to find out what exclusive camping at $900 a night in the bush entailed. The venture was set up by Mark Provost who, having travelled right across Australia with his wife and kids, had experienced little or no interaction with the indigenous people of his own country. Even though my first trip in Australia had only included the east coast, in the three months I was there, I had no proper encounters with any Aboriginals. I would chat to them busking in Circular Quay or selling souvenir didgeridoos in tourist shops, but that was the extent of it. I knew there were tours led by Aboriginal people where you could learn about their "Dreamtime stories", but you were bussed in and bussed out. So I could see how this venture would work, albeit that it would not be easy to set up. Living within an Aboriginal community is difficult to organise because, since their land was returned to them, a lot of their communities are still off-limits to outsiders and you need permission from the elders to enter. For a remote community that has had its land returned, I imagined that tourism could be seen as a threat or a dirty word. Although at first the Titjikala community had expressed reservations, it had finally been agreed that the community could not but benefit from the project. Mark's tour company invested all of the money and owns a fifty per cent share in the resort. The other half is directly owned by the Titjikala community, who are also the sole employees running the whole place.

The sun was bright in the sky and everyone was too tired to slag Gerry about his music selection. It felt good to be on the road again, into the endless outback plains, even if it was to the soundtrack of Nick Cave. Every now and then we passed an upside-down rusty wreck of a car or the remains of one that had been burnt out. They looked forlorn but not out of place in this wild west backdrop. I sat up and screamed like a child every time I saw the huge kangaroos that appeared out of the long grass, bounding across the plains at speeds that would rival Michael Schumacher. I was surprised at how big and powerful they were, with hind legs strong enough to lift their weight high into the air.

A cemetery sign greeted us as we drove into the Titjikala community, followed by six barking dogs and then by a group of children, wild with excitement on seeing our jeep. They ran straight for us in the middle of the red dust road, and Gerry had to stop before he ran them over. They climbed up onto the bonnet and clung to the bars at the back, smiling and shrieking with laughter. Gerry drove forward slowly, afraid that one of them would fall off. We figured they might throw themselves under the car if they had to listen to much more of Mary Hopkin's "Those Were the Days" blaring out the window. A group of six women sitting under a gum tree looked up from their card game briefly, waved with the enthusiasm one would expect in forty-degree heat and turned their attention back to the game.

There are about 300 people living in Titjikala and they are made up of the Arrernte, Luritja and Pitjantjatjara tribal groups. Driving past, we could see the collection of about thirty small houses with tin roofs and wire fences where the community lived, with an average of ten people and several dogs per house. It was about half a mile away from the "luxury resort". What appeared in the distance were three safari-style tents on stilts. We parked and were greeted by a group of about fifteen women and children, who stood up from around the fire. We all shook hands and although they were very friendly, they were very shy, with only some of them comfortable enough to look us in the eye. We sat down on the red earth and an eskey full of water and Cokes was opened, followed by a lunch of kangaroo tail and fried potatoes. I normally wouldn't eat red meat, especially something's tail, in the middle of the afternoon – a tuna salad would have been preferable – but I was here for the experience and certainly wasn't going to turn it down, especially when I heard it would be witchety grubs for dinner. Any initial pangs of guilt I felt about the Skippies I'd seen bounding across the landscape, which had got me so excited on my drive here, were soon replaced by the wonderful taste sensations of the gamey meat. Loretta, one of the local women, also made me feel better by telling me that kangaroo meat is much lower in saturated fat than most other meats.

While the lads went off to get some shots, I dragged my backpack up the ladder to check out my tent. It had a shaded veranda and from twenty feet up in the air, I had a fantastic view over the Simpson Desert. Inside, a massive double bed with crisp white linen sat on a highly polished timber floor. The bathroom to the rear had an eco-friendly flushing toilet and free-standing bath open to the sky. It was cool under the thick canvas, even in the shade of the afternoon sun. I began to understand what we were paying for, but I also felt I would prefer to pay less and sleep in a swag under the stars. It was not that I wanted to experience the Aboriginal way, as most of them now lived in basic houses with electricity, but because I was dirty and dusty and unwashed and felt that that's the way camping in the bush ought to be.

Outside, I sat down around the fire with the women and they told me about their life in the community. They spoke very candidly. "Life is hard sometimes but, y'know, many people who left are back now because they can work. We take turns with different groups so everybody has an opportunity to be involved. My brother went away for fifteen years because there was nothin' here for him. But he is glad to be back now." I asked them about the fact that Titjikala is a dry community where no alcohol was permitted; did they mind that tourists were allowed to bring alcohol into the resort? "Nah, there are still some fellas here who go to the next town to buy drink and come back here to cause trouble, sniff petrol, y'know. The police were here last week. But it's only some fellas and the tourists don't drink that way." Another woman continued, "The kids are now doin' what our grandparents were doin', learnin' about bush tucker and where to get it. They wouldn't be out bush, I don't think, if it wasn't for the tourists that come out here."

When the guys returned, I climbed into the 4x4 with Loretta and her mates and the guys followed us as we went in search of tucker for that night's dinner. I was told that Lila, the driver, was the champion at finding and collecting witchety grubs. She looked to be in her fifties and when she turned around and gave me a proud smile, she didn't have a tooth in her head.

As we wandered through the sand, Loretta pointed to the tracks of a dingo while the group spread out to different trees and plants in search of grubs, goannas and honey-coloured ants, which are a treat in these parts. Sure enough, it didn't take Lila long. Sitting cross-legged on the ground, she split open a large root she had cut away from the witchety bush. There, squeezed into the root, was what looked like a fat, puffy white caterpillar. She pulled him out, held him up proudly and plonked him into an empty jam jar. The jar wasn't empty for long. Two hours into the hunting expedition, we had three full jars of grubs and one with the lid on that was crawling with edible ants.

The kids reminded me of myself when we were sent to pick strawberries for my Gran. We would eat the ripe, juicy fruit all day until we were nearly sick. Here, the kids sucked the honey ants into their mouths as they crawled up their arms or chomped into half a witchety grub, throwing the remaining part, still wriggling, back into the jar. I could not bring myself to eat one there and then, especially when Loretta told me they tasted better when they were cooked. So we brought our catch back to the campfire, where the grubs were thrown straight in to cook in the ash.

I was feeling much more confident about eating something that was cooked until I heard what sounded like tiny high-pitched screams. It was the grubs expanding and bursting in the heat. I thought I was going to be sick. One of the kids reached into the ashes, plucked a big fat grub out and handed it to me as casually as someone would offer you a bag of crisps. As I bit down into the white flesh, it popped in my mouth. I chewed and smiled while trying not to retch. It had the consistency of scrambled egg.

The "tourist dinner" was a little more palatable; Nile perch followed by a gorgeous dessert of wattle-seed cheesecake. After dinner, with tea served in billycans, the girls hung around and seemed comfortable enough in our company to spend nearly two hours asking us questions about the TV programme, where we had been and what our country was like. It was so relaxed and quiet, with our voices only competing with the crackling of the fire and the gentle breeze, which eventually cooled the desert down so much that we all turned in for the night.

We took our time driving back to Alice the next day and were all knackered when we got back into town, but after a thirty-minute power nap and a feed, I was ready to hit the town. Gerry, who had done all the driving, called it a night and despite endless pleading I couldn't get the guys out either, so I decided I would head out for a few on my own and see who I might meet.

It was warm and I was quite light-headed after two glasses of wine and decided an ice-cold beer was the way forward. Meatloaf's "Bat Out of Hell" was blaring from inside a place called Bo Jangles, which, believe it or not, was enough of an incentive for me to walk through the saloon-style double doors. The place was packed and had the feel of a real wild west tavern. I eventually managed to get to the bar just as a couple were leaving their seats – or rather, saddles. Leather saddles lined the bar where people could sit and munch on bowls of proper peanuts in shells. I mounted my saddle and asked the barman for a beer. "How 'bout a Pure Blonde?" he smirked. "Why not?" I said, "Mine is out of a bottle as well!" He was from Darwin and was down to work the season before heading back to college. I also met a group of four Irish girls who had just arrived into town, having spent two months pearling up in Broome.

An Aussie waiter walked past me carrying a tray of glasses. "Are ye not goin' to dance?" he asked, pointing up towards the roof. Afraid I was the blonde the staff had decided to pick on, I refused to look up until he disappeared into the crowd. Then I peeked. Nailed to the ceiling, as if someone had fallen out of them, were dozens of pairs of boots and shoes! I began to understand that the whole place was Aussie humour poking fun at tourists. Although I didn't end up dancing on the ceiling, I did end up dancing on the bar with a lasso, three Swedish backpackers and a dwarf from New Zealand wearing a motorcycle helmet. I figured it was time to leave when I went to the bathroom and couldn't open the door of the cubicle. The hinges are painted on the side of the door that is supposed to open, so you end up standing there like a lemon pushing and pushing the wrong side until a local takes pity on you and pushes the other side of the door which opens and you realise you have been had again! Great fun!

The final leg of our journey landed us into Ayers Rock Airport, on a forty-five-minute Qantas flight from Alice. There we hired a jeep and drove to the Ayers Rock Resort, known as Yulara. It's not so much a resort as a town; in fact it has become the fifth-largest town in the Northern Territory! It is made up of five different standard hotels owned by the one company. Wandering around it felt a bit strange; it seemed huge, with over 1,000 staff catering for up to 4,500 people, and it made you forget that you were in the middle of nowhere. The rock itself is twenty kilometres away and we were not due to see it until 4.00 the following morning for sunrise. We checked into the three-star Lost Camel resort and within about five minutes we were all in the pool trying to cool off. The temperature gauge on the wall read thirty-eight degrees. Every time I got out of the water to lie down to read I felt I needed to get back in again to cool off.

Later that evening we headed across to the Outback Pioneer Hotel to cook our own dinner on Australia's biggest barbeque. A huge square griddle sat under a corrugated iron roof surrounded by long communal tables. You bought whatever meat you wanted at the counter – emu sausages, kangaroo steak or burgers – and tried to find space in the charcoals among the crowd to cook your own grub. The atmosphere was fantastic and the place was packed with people who had either seen the rock or were venturing out the following morning. Music blared over speakers, the beer flowed and it felt like a proper outback barbie.

We were trying to do our last piece to camera when two guys, who had obviously had a few beers, came and sat down beside me.

"Hey gorgeous, what ya filmin'? Need any help? My mate Nigel here wants to be on television."

"Thanks for the offer, but we are just trying to get this last piece in the can so we can wrap and eat dinner."

"You can eat me." He and his friend roared laughing at their hilarity. "So have you been to the rock yet?"

"No, we are planning to go tomorrow if we ever get finished up here tonight." The sarcasm went over their heads. Generally I have no problem with Aussie men and in fact I like that sometimes they can be a bit brash and gobby, but these two Neanderthals were a stereotype too far.

"If you're climbing the rock, don't try and take a piece home with you. It's bad luck. One of our mates put some bits in his rucksack and when he got back to Sydney, he got a dose of the claps!"

"Maybe he packed his own bits in the wrong rucksack to begin with," I said. They stared at me blankly and walked off.

Gerry knocked at my door at 4.00 the following morning. "We're leaving in fifteen minutes." It nearly killed me to get out of the bed which I had only been in for four hours. It was freezing. I layered up with two jumpers, a fleece and a woolly hat and we headed off into the darkness of the desert to find a good spot to watch the sun rise over Uluru. We had flasks of hot coffee and didn't have long to wait before the dawn broke, shedding light on the world's biggest monolith.

It emerged out of the ground in shades of grey and black, as did other groups of early risers, keen not to miss this particular daybreak. I don't know what I thought I would feel, but when I saw Uluru for the first time in the distance, as the sun rose higher in the sky giving it its distinctive red hue, I was quite nonplussed; it looked exactly as it does in photographs and on postcards and in a funny way seemed dwarfed by the flat landscape.

I eavesdropped on an American man, which wasn't difficult, who was reading loudly to his wife from his guidebook. He was wearing a torch on his head. "Uluru (which he pronounced Ullar-oo) is 3.5 kilometres long and 380 metres high. It is made of feldspar-rich sandstone which is mainly grey and white. The distinct rust colour is caused by a thin coating of iron oxide on the outer skin. The changing colours of red are caused by light refraction as the sun moves around and sinks in the sky." She didn't seem interested. "Can we go back for breakfast?" She took the words right out of my mouth. I felt I needed to be in closer proximity to the rock to get a better sense of its scale.

After breakfast, we met our guide, Jack, one of the traditional Anangu owners, who was going to take us around for the day and give us some local knowledge. The government handed back the land to his people in 1985 and, in 1993, Ayers Rock was given its official Aboriginal title "Uluru".

The road out was busy and we passed minibuses, coaches and jeeps, to-ing and fro-ing from the most visited landmark in Australia. As we sped toward it, the closer proximity gave everything a much better sense of scale. It loomed and soared over the ground and when we reached the base, the grandeur was undeniable. It is thought that Uluru is only the "tip of the iceberg" as it were and that in fact there are perhaps another five kilometres of the rock under the ground.

We had decided not to do the entire seven-kilometre walk around the base and Jack had picked out some key spots where we were allowed to film and where he could explain some of his creation stories. He explained that the term "Dreamtime" can be quite misleading and that his people prefer to use the Aboriginal word "Tjukurpa" to describe their laws and beliefs. Aboriginals believe the world was created but that it was featureless. Ancient heroes in the guise of plants and animals rose up from where they had been sleeping and roamed the land. Wherever these ancestors were active and their work was done, they transformed into natural features like hills and stars and plants that still exist today and always will into the future. Every Aboriginal clan has a distinct collection of sacred sites that are part of their creation stories and Uluru is one of Jack's. Unlike the Bible or the Koran, none of these creation stories was ever written down and they have been passed on by word of mouth. Not everybody knows the full collection of stories because some may only be heard by men, some only by women and some only by the elders of a clan. That is why Uluru is so important, because different parts of the rock are connected to different stories.

As signs around the rock clearly say, out of respect for their sacred site, the landowners prefer that visitors would not climb the rock – not to mention the fact that tourists die every year attempting the precarious 380-metre climb. At the time we were there, the number of deaths had reached thirty-five. After spending a couple of hours with Jack, only shooting very specific angles and locations which he gave us authority to do, I felt that climbing it would be the equivalent of holding a rave in a graveyard. Nevertheless, I could see people scaling up the side like a trail of ants, obviously feeling it wasn't enough to travel all that way just to look at it.

Up close, it was incredible, much more puckered and marked and less smooth than the picture postcard image.

Every time I looked at it, it appeared different and I thought that may have something to do with my growing understanding of Uluru and its importance to the Anangu owners spanning 30,000 years. There is something magical about it. As the afternoon sun began to sink lower into the sky, the rock darkened from a glowing orange to a light red to a deep moody bold red.

This was the end of our trip and it seemed like the perfect setting to say goodbye to the outback. We drove to a quiet spot, put the cameras away and climbed up on the roof of the jeep to witness the majesty of Uluru at sunset. I thought of my first time in Australia, where with trepidation and fear I sat in front of another iconic Australian landmark in Sydney until I found the confidence to travel on my own. When I did, it opened up so many doors for me, not least the urge to return to Oz, which had allowed me experience all of this. There is not much to do in the outback for those just interested in ticking off lists, but that's not what this place is about. For me, it is about coming out and understanding that this great emptiness commands and deserves your respect. This was the end of another Australian adventure and I knew I would be back for more.

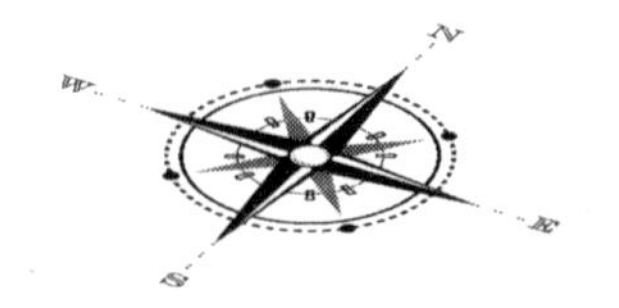

Outback Australia – Northern Territory Fast Facts

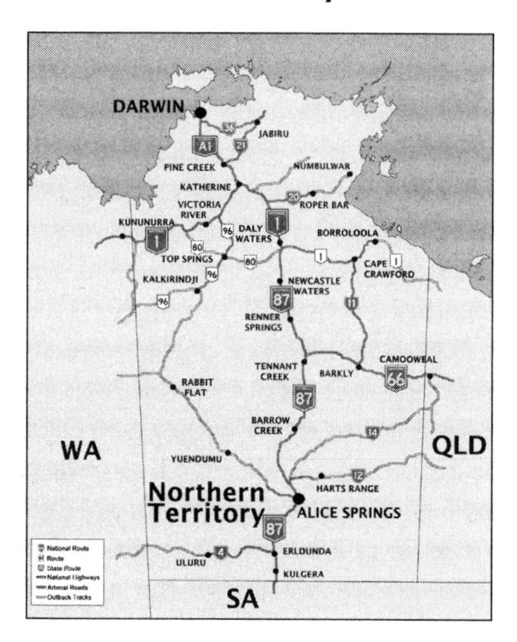

Population:

- 20 million approx in Australia
- 217,000 approx in Northern Territory
- Alice Springs has a population of 26,000 approx
- Uluru has a population of 500 approx
- Titjikala has a population of 330 approx

Size: Australia is 7,617,930 square kilometres and is the planet's sixth-largest country, consisting of six states and two territories. The Northern Territory is the most barren of all areas in the whole of Australia. It encapsulates a total area of 1.35 million square kilometres, twenty per cent of the whole country. However, just one per cent of Australia's population lives there.

Climate: The Northern Territory has two distinctive climate zones. The northern end, including Darwin, has a tropical climate with high humidity and two seasons, the wet (November to April) and dry season (May to October), and Central Australia has a desert climate.

Best time to go: The best time to visit Central Northern Territory is from March to May when you will miss out on the summer's extreme heat but still be far enough away from the cold season. Temperatures can get as high as 48°C (118°F) in summer and can drop as low as -7°C (19°F) in winter.

Where I went: Alice Springs, Ooraminna Cattle Station, Titjikala Aboriginal reserve, and Uluru.

Who to go with: There are numerous companies that offer tours to Australia and therefore you should shop around for the best option. Another option is a "Do it yourself" holiday, which is quite easy to organise for Australia. Some of the larger tour operators to Australia from Ireland include: Trailfinders, Aus Travel and The Australia Travel Centre.

Time Difference: +9.5 hours from Ireland.

Currency: Local Currency is the Australian Dollar. ATMs and credit card services accepted countrywide.

Tipping: It is customary to tip in Australia for services provided. Naturally, tips depend upon quality of service.

Visa: Irish passport holders require a valid passport and visa (Electronic Travel Authority - ETA) for travel to Australia. An ETA (Visitor) Visa allows a person to stay in Australia for up to three months. This Visa can be applied for online (www.eta.immi.gov.au) at a cost of about AUS$20.

Electricity: 220-240V 50Hz

Vaccinations needed: There are no vaccinations required for Australia.

Other highlights:

- Climb the Sydney Harbour Bridge.
- Have a day out at the races at the Melbourne Cup.
- Visit the Great Ocean Road.
- Swim the Great Barrier Reef and visit the Whitsundays.
- Enjoy a glass of wine on one of Australia's numerous wineries.

Fun Facts

- **Apparently the first European settlers in Australia drank more alcohol per person than any other community in the history of mankind.**
- **The Tasmanian Devil does exist, and it has the jaw strength of a crocodile.**
- **Australia has the world's largest cattle station (ranch). At 30,028 square kilometres, it is almost the same size as Belgium.**
- **Tasmania has the cleanest air in the world.**
- **The Sydney Opera House roof weighs more than 161,000 tons.**
- **The Great Barrier Reef is the largest organic construction on earth.**
- **Termite mounds are the tallest non-human constructions on earth.**

Useful Contacts:

- Australian High Commission Dublin: www.ireland.embassy.gov.au
- Australian Tourist Board: www.australia.com

Books to Read:

Guide Books: *The Lonely Planet*, *The Frommers Guide*, *The Rough Guide*.

Down Under by Bill Bryson.

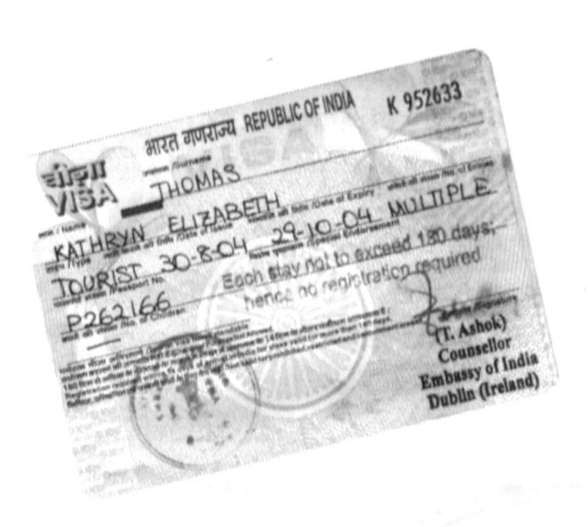

Himalayas

There is something about climbing a mountain that surpasses any other physical challenge. The struggle to the top is forgotten in an instant when you reach the summit and that warm, glorious sense of achievement trickles through your veins.

The first time I climbed Croagh Patrick, I set off in foul humour, having had a fight with my boyfriend. The weather reflected my mood; it was windy and lashing rain. He turned back and went to the pub and I turned to the mountain with fury and climbed like my life depended on it. Climbing is such a solitary exercise and gives you plenty of time to think. But the higher I got and the more difficult the climb became, I had to focus my attention on the mountain as opposed to what was bothering me. Anyone who has climbed Patrick knows that, in strong wind and rain, the last 100 metres to the top isn't easy and you are literally on your hands and knees in parts, dragging yourself to the summit. But standing at the top, inhaling deep breaths of air, looking down on the submerged drumlins of Clew Bay seemed to put everything into perspective. Used as a euphemism for overcoming any adversaries, no mountain is insurmountable. As Edmund Hillary famously said: *It is not the mountain we climb but ourselves.*

In 2004, I had the incredible opportunity to climb the greatest mountain range in the world, the mighty Himalaya. When I first heard about the trip, I had visions of us climbing in balaclavas, snow shoes and protective thermals, battling against snow and blinding blizzards, crippled with the onset of frostbite. I certainly didn't think we would be climbing in balmy temperatures in the high twenties. I had the privilege of completing this once-in-a-lifetime experience with two great friends: Mark, whom I love to bits and who knows me better than most; and Pat, a big man with an even bigger heart, a kinder and more gentler soul you couldn't meet. We were all novice trekkers but expert risk-takers and there was something thrilling in knowing that we were going to throw caution to the wind on the roof of the world.

Our trek would take us through the northern Indian state of Ladakh. We only had one day in Delhi before we had to catch our flight to Ladakh the following morning. After checking into a basic hotel in Connaught Place, we decided we would do a quick taxi tour of New Delhi, taking in the India Gate before heading into Old Delhi to see the Red Fort and the Jama Masjid, the country's largest mosque, and immersing ourselves in the labyrinth of narrow lanes and alleyways to complete the sensory overload. I had been in the Indian capital before and the one thing I tried to explain to the lads is that you need to give the city time. I had been appalled and abhorred by the place at first – the poverty and the filth, the noise and the traffic, the begging and the sheer volume of people and cars. Nothing about Delhi is discreet, but in time you do find yourself adapting to its pace and slowly you can see its immense beauty through the squalor.

Even though it was 7.00 a.m., the streets around Connaught Place were packed. At our first set of traffic lights, the car was surrounded by four street urchins, three of them without arms and one with a mangled leg, pleading in the window for money. Our taxi driver tried to shoo them away. "These children, more and more of them here every day. Very, very sad. Never give them money. Sometimes the parents, they break the arms or the feet so more peoples will give them the money." It is horrible and gut-wrenching having to look anywhere but into their eyes. You breathe a sigh of relief as the lights turn green and the children are left behind. But you cannot escape the poverty here. It is everywhere.

We did a brief tour of the Jama Masjid mosque, which has the capacity for 25,000 worshippers. Unfortunately, tourists are not allowed in during prayer time, so you have to use your imagination wandering around the vast expanse of emptiness. From there we walked to the Red Fort, which in my opinion is as impressive as the Taj Mahal. The impressive thick sandstone walls, some measuring thirty-three metres, provide a place to escape the frantic world outside. The turrets and wide courtyards transport you back in time and remind you of India's former glory.

But to really experience Delhi, I wanted the lads to spend an hour or two in the old town. We waved down two bicycle rickshaws, with me in one and Mark and Pat in the other.

The lads were hoping to get a few shots of me weaving in and out of the crowds but before we could translate our wishes to the drivers, the lads took off, with my driver in hot pursuit. They tried filming looking back at me but quickly we realised it was a futile exercise. As we went deeper into the bazaar, the streets got narrower and narrower until we were moving at a snail's pace. On both sides vendors were selling their wares and beggars sat hunkered on the street outside eating-houses, their hands outstretched waiting for leftovers to be tossed out into the street. The air was heavy with the smell of over-ripe bananas being pushed past us in giant wheeled carts, mixed with the pungent smells of spices and dog shit. Pigs caked in mud sniffed piles of vegetable skins rotting against a wall. And all the time people, throngs of people coming and going in both directions. This meant that our rickshaw was in fact going slower than the pedestrian traffic, so we paid up, jumped out and followed the crowd. At a narrow junction, I looked up and glimpsed the outline of the mosque's minaret, flitting in and out of view, as overhead laundry blew in the dank air. Nothing can prepare you for your first time in Delhi and it is a city that I love spending time in now.

Lying in bed that night, I couldn't sleep. I felt excited. A mixture of jetlag and the intensity of the environment we had been in all day wouldn't allow my brain to slow down and switch off. Images of the day flashed before me and I thought of the girl I had seen in the muddy alleyway, stepping out of a rickshaw, beautiful and magnificent in an emerald green sari. She held her head high and seemed oblivious to the squalor around her. God, it is far away from the world we know. I turned my attention to the journey ahead of us, to a totally different Indian experience, the vast emptiness of the roof of the world, and the possibilities and contrasts reminded me again why India is such a traveller's dream.

The following morning we left Delhi at 4.40 for the hour-and-a-half flight to the northern region of Ladakh. Once an autonomous Himalayan Kingdom, it is now part of the Jammu and Kashmir state of northern India. Now, my knowledge of Indian politics wouldn't be great but I did know that Pakistan and India have never been the best of buddies and Ladakh shares its borders with Tibet and China in the East. Throughout history, it has always been a strategic location and a very important trading point on the Old Silk Route. So this predominantly Buddhist state, sandwiched between two mountain ranges, the great Himalaya and the Karakoram, has seen a lot of war and still has a strong military presence.

The view from the plane was incredible. Rising from a blanket of bare brown hills, snow-capped peaks reached into the heavens as if trying to pierce the sky. As the sun rose, the highest snowy peaks were hit first, glowing a vivid pinky-orange which then spread to the lower peaks until the whole skyline was lit up like a Christmas tree. In the valley floors below, fertile strips of green grass sat either side of milky blue glacial rivers which snaked past tiny villages and disappeared again behind mammoth mountain faces. It was beautiful, a rugged Utopia. I thought about the monks in isolated mountain monasteries and their Buddhist philosophies and how, even up here in this remoteness on the top of the world, surrounded by peace and tranquillity, they still could not escape the clutches of war.

When China closed its borders with India, the government decided in the 1970s to open it up to tourism. I didn't know anyone or hadn't spoken to anyone from Ireland who had climbed here before I left. We were doing what was classed as a "moderate" and not too difficult trek through the Indus valley for four days. My training had consisted of one hill walk around Howth Head, treating myself to a pint in The Summit afterwards, and that was about the height of it. I wasn't so much worried from a fitness point of view; it was the altitude I was worried about. Leh, the capital of Ladakh, at 3,600 metres is one of the highest capitals in the world along with Lhasa in Tibet, Addis Ababa in Ethiopia and La Paz in Bolivia.

You would think that up here, a nice flat plateau would have provided the perfect runway to land a plane. Not so. On our approach, the plane didn't descend so much as drop out of the sky in a matter of seconds. Every part of my body felt like it was in my mouth. We hit the runway with a bounce and immediately the brakes began to screech, working hard in order to stop on time at the other end. The runway was shorter than usual on account of a large mountain that we were hurtling towards. We whiplashed to a stop. As I peeled my head off the back of the seat, I could feel my internal organs sliding back into their original positions. I turned to Mark and Pat and couldn't work out which one looked sicker.

I was glad to have my two feet on the ground as I walked down the steps of the plane onto the tarmac and into a little bus, even though we were only about twenty metres from the airport building. I could feel my lungs working that little bit harder trying to take in the thin but pristine air and I wasn't sure whether it was the altitude or the fact that I was close to hyperventilating after the landing! Pat, who had taken a seat up the front of the bus, went to stand up as we got to the terminal and collapsed back onto his seat. The altitude had already started to affect all of us and a wave of uncertainty about the next few days washed over me.

Our smiling guide Angdu was there with a sign to greet us. "Jooley, jooley," he beamed as we all shook hands. There were maybe twenty men, women and children standing behind him. Their features were definitely more Tibetan than Indian. They were mountain people with mountain faces, deeply creased with flushed ruddy cheeks. And their smiles. If ever a smile personified a face, it is the smiles of the Ladakhi people – honest, open and sincere, beaming like the sun that reflects light all over their valley kingdom. They instantly reminded me of the Bolivian people I had met in La Paz. Like a lot of mountain people at this altitude, they are small in stature and Pat, Mark and even I seemed like giants towering over them.

A lady came forward and draped a white piece of material like a bandage around our necks, which we found out later is a sacred welcome gift. Similar can be seen adorning statues and flagpoles all across the countryside. The entire crowd gathered behind Angdu seemed to be smiling and waving hello to us – "Jooley, jooley". For a brief moment I thought they were all part of our trekking group. Two of the men, wearing traditional triangular hats with the edges turned up like two ski slopes over their ears, insisted on helping us with our bags to the jeep. As far as airport etiquette goes, this is usually my one pet hate. People kidnap your trolley or bags in a flurry of activity to a waiting car or taxi and then expect a tip. It drives me insane and I have been known to lash out at poor young fellas who are just looking to make a quick few cent. But these people were so good-natured and mannerly, and I wasn't quite sure if they were with us or not, that I couldn't refuse and so I just let them take my bags. They placed our luggage aboard then smiled, waved and walked off. Angdu explained that they had just turned up to welcome us and everybody else to their land and to welcome their own people back.

We piled into the jeep and headed for town. "I understand you must be tired, so I will not talk to you like a tour guide today. We have plenty of time after you have slept and you are breathing properly. Then you might want to listen to me!" I felt like kissing him! I loved him already. I had experienced too many tour guides who, when you get off a flight after thirty hours and it's the middle of the night in your head, start waffling on about dates and history and kings and populations until you think your head is going to explode. You don't even know your own name and you are expected to remember the name of an ancient ruler from the fifth century. Angdu knew that our plan was to take it very easy in Leh, for at least two days, so we could acclimatise before we ventured even higher on our trek and knew there would be plenty of time for talking and learning and listening tomorrow.

We drove in blissful silence for half an hour across landscape that looked like the surface of the moon – barren and empty, with craters and strange rock formations. From every angle in the far distance snow-peaked mountain tops glistened against the blue sky. I couldn't believe that only an hour and a half ago, I had left one of the most densely populated cities in India and was now in the least populated and most inaccessible part of the country, with only one person for every two square kilometres. It not only felt like we had flown to a different country but that we had flown back in time. Yaks and hairy goats wandered through the streets of Leh while the local villagers in their long goncha robes and top hats went about their day-to-day chores buying and selling vegetables, metal and wool.

We pulled up outside our guest house in Changspa, about a fifteen-minute walk to the centre of the village. The owner, quite a dashing man dressed in a beige suit, and his young son came out to meet us. I could tell immediately that he very much enjoyed the role of host, and that he was probably gushing a little bit more than usual because we were a camera crew. "I had the BBC out here, they stayed for three weeks. They interviewed me. I was very good." I imagined that the three of us looked somewhat less impressive than a six-man Beeb crew arriving with a truckload of equipment and a not-so-tight budget. Our host was definitely what you would call a fan of Western policies. That night as we sat around an open fire in his front garden, having a few beers, he told us that he used to be in the military. "I do believe my country was a better one under English rule. If I could turn back the hands of time and change history I would." We did put forward our view that, as an island nation, which had also once been under British rule, we were a better country without them, but he wasn't really interested. Anyway, I looked up to the sky above his house and complimented him on having the most beautiful set of stars I had ever seen. We at least agreed on that.

The next morning I woke up with what felt like the worst hangover, although I only had two beers the night before. I had slept for a good seven hours but my head felt heavy and I had no energy. After I had showered and got dressed, I felt like I could have gone back to sleep for another seven hours! At breakfast Angdu said this was totally normal and that our bodies were just getting used to the change in air pressure. "We will have an easy day today. We can drive through town. People are celebrating because it is our annual festival and I read on the internet that the Irish people like to celebrate." He gave a shy but knowing smile.

"What else did you find out about us?" I asked.

"Well, that you have a good computer industry like India and that you can sing."

"I'd say the three of us could put at least one of those rumours to rest."

I also didn't want to bring up the fact that the little internet café across the road from the hotel was still using the old dial-up and it had taken so long the previous night to open and send emails that I had given up. I felt frustrated at first and then actually quite liberated at the prospect of being at the top of the world with no phones, no fax, no internet, just straightforward one-to-one communication.

We drove into town and the atmosphere was buzzing. We had arrived in time for the Ladakh Festival, which is held every year on the first two weeks of September, to honour and preserve the age-old traditions and customs that were the lifeblood of this "crossroads of Asia". The seventeenth-century Royal Palace, which dominates the town, towered above the villagers dressed in traditional costumes and masks. Drums were beating and the haunting sound of traditional flutes echoed around and down the valley. We took our shots as they sang and danced in the market square before they headed off in a snake-like procession which wound its way to the polo ground high above the town.

I couldn't believe that the sport that people go crazy for up here is polo. The "Ladakhi Festival Cup" is the highlight of the fortnight. As our van zig-zagged up the hill to the top of the town, we passed the festival procession and hundreds of spectators making their way up to the polo field. Men, women and children, some carrying bunting and dressed in bright colours, reflected the mood of excitement and festivity. We paid at the entrance and already, on the long brown dusty field, the two teams and their small but hardy horses had gathered at either end. A modest platform of tiered seating had been erected for special guests and dignitaries at the far side of the field, opposite to which the hundreds of spectators would line the ground four and five deep. This plateau on the roof of the world was encased by an old crumbled white-washed wall, beyond which snow-capped peaks jutted into the sky. A man in a long gown and turned-up pointy slippers read out the names of the players through a megaphone. He was almost drowned out by the piped music coming over the crackly speakers at the entrance to welcome the fans.

By now the sun was high in the sky and it was hot. A small battered truck was driving slowly up and down the burnt pitch, spraying water in an attempt to keep the dust at bay. When the crowd had gathered and the excitement had reached a crescendo, the whistle was blown and the ball was thrown in. The horses charged in both directions, kicking up clouds of dust, much to the delight of the crowd. This was polo like I had never seen it before. There didn't seem to be any rules. Riders were ruthless and fierce, colliding into each other, yet time and time again, their sticks connected with the ball with unbelievable accuracy. The game moved up and down the pitch in a frenzy and as the crowd along the sideline got excited, straining not too miss a second, they ended up on the pitch, sometimes escaping a trampling by seconds. At one stage, like a bullet from a gun, a small dog, almost camouflaged against the brown pitch, came charging out from the crowd and was racing two horses for the ball. The crowd went wild and the referee blew to stop the game. Twice more the dog appeared on the pitch, causing three of the horses to tumble, sending their riders flying.

I was standing beside an Australian couple who seemed to be the only other tourists at the game. They had just finished a ten-day trek and were on their way home. All of a sudden an intercepted ball shot over the heads of the locals and whacked the Aussie guy right on the temple, two feet away from me. He doubled over in pain and shock. Given the speed at which the ball was travelling, it was unbelievable that he wasn't knocked out, let alone killed stone dead. The concerned locals whispered among themselves. Eventually he convinced them he was fine and two official-looking men approached us and handed me, the Australian and his girlfriend motorcycle helmets to wear for the duration of the game for protection. I never thought I would find myself in such a situation – watching a polo game in the Himalayas wearing a motorbike helmet. Certainly not polo as we know it, chaps!

The following morning, with our bags packed we left town and drove an hour to Thikse Monastery. Along the drive Angdu explained that eighty per cent of the 25,000 Ladakhis are Buddhist and fifteen per cent are Muslim. Before China took control of Tibet, Ladakhi monks used to go to there for the highest religious teachings. Ladakhi and Tibetan are quite similar languages and with such spiritual connections and similar landscapes, Ladakh is often referred to as "Little Tibet".

As we approached, the monastery complex looked like an ordinary whitewashed village built into the side of a mountain. It was only when it was framed against the sky that the terracotta, yellow and blue building at the top distinguished it as somewhere special. The 500-year-old monastery is home to about 100 yellow-capped monks who live in the small houses on the hill. As we climbed up the steps to reach the big open courtyard at the top, the red-robed monks clutching scrolls smiled a friendly welcome and went about their business.

Some of the younger monks in their early twenties were eager to chat and practise their English. One of them showed us to his one-room house. It was empty except for a mat on the floor, a writing desk and a chair against the wall.

By contrast, inside the courtyard itself was a blaze of colour. Murals and ancient script decorated the walls. To the right of a big open courtyard were another set of steps which led to a building that housed a fifteen-metre-high gold figure of Maitreya, the Buddha of the future. The overall atmosphere in the monastery was one of peace, happiness and openness. It was not austere like I thought it would be and I was reminded of my friend Jason, whom I had met when I was travelling in Australia. A bigger stoner you could not meet, yet he ended up spending nine months in a silent monastery in Tibet. Silent – as in, nobody speaks, at all! He was intrigued by the concept of the place and wanted to see how long he could last. He was welcomed with open arms and spent nine months smiling but without uttering a word.

It was so tranquil and the view from the rooftop across the valley was breathtaking. I thought about what day-to-day life must be like here for the monks, where everything centred around their religion. My knowledge of Buddhism was limited but I knew that central to the philosophy is striving to end or alleviate the suffering of any being. I just felt content sitting there in the sun, watching life go by. I couldn't help but feel wonder and a sense of awe for these men.

From Thikse we drove to Ridzong. This was the starting point of our trek and when we jumped out of the jeep our team were there, lined up and waiting to greet us. These men would all be instrumental in getting us over the mountains for the next four days. Tondu, who was only about five feet tall, was our chef; Jolden, who looked like he was in his late twenties and was well built, was in charge of packing and setting up our camp; Donda and Reezing were a father and son herding team and they were in charge of our eight donkeys (whose names I never got).

Our tents were already set up in a sweet-smelling apricot orchard. There was a pot of water boiling over the fire and dinner was being prepared. When I say dinner, I mean a fabulous three-course meal of homemade vegetable soup, barbeque chicken with chilli rice and beans, followed by a homemade coconut cream sponge. We didn't waste any time putting it away. It was absolutely delicious and I was shocked that Tondu could achieve such exotic tastes and flavours cooking over a little burner with provisions which had been strapped to a donkey! We asked the team to join us, but Angdu explained that it was customary for the guests to eat first. Only when they had their fill and were satisfied would the rest of the team eat. We joked that, in that case, they would starve for the next few days. Angdu, the only one who could speak English, told us that indeed they had been worried when they had first seen us that there might not be enough food for the trip. To make the point, Pat stood up beside Reezing, who only came up to his elbow. Everyone fell about in stitches.

We were still in high spirits when the sun dropped from the sky and gave us our first taste of how cold the desert was going to be at night. Angdu made me laugh, talking about a typical day's weather in these parts. The way he told the story was reminiscent of the banter of an auld fella in a pub in Dublin. "Ladakh is a land of wind and sunshine where a man can, with his face in the sun and his feet in the shade, get sunburn and frostbite at the same time." Temperatures rarely go above the high twenties in summer but can reach minus twenty in the winter. The people here do not pray for rain but sunshine to melt the snow on the higher slopes to irrigate their crops. On average, they get 300 days of sunshine a year and less rain than the Sahara desert!

It was difficult to think of sunshine when it was this cold going to bed. I snuggled into my sleeping bag and pulled my woolly hat down over my eyes and ears. It smelt of hair and for some reason that was really soothing. As I lay there I thought of my family and friends trying to visualise where on the planet I might be. I do this a lot when I'm trying to put it into context myself. I smiled as I spoke out loud to them, like I would if I was on the phone. "I am 13,000 feet somewhere up in the Himalayas, in a tent pitched in an apricot orchard with lots of men and eight donkeys." I listened to the wind whistling around the tent and I drifted off.

I slept like a baby and woke up feeling a hell of a lot better than I had for the previous couple of days. I hoped this was a sign that I had acclimatised. It was 6.00 a.m. and a cup of sweet milky tea and a basin of hot water were delivered to the door of my tent. I washed as best I could, dressed lying down in the tent and emerged to a breakfast of omelette and potato cakes set up on a small table with fold-out chairs. I was surprised to see a tablecloth covering the table and marvelled at how comfortable everything had been so far.

Mark's head was sticking out of his tent. Still lying in his sleeping bag, cup of tea in hand, he was enjoying his first fag of the day. Pat, an avid photographer, was snapping away like a man possessed. The sky was a clear blue but the sun had not had a chance to heat up the mountain air, so we all stayed layered-up for breakfast. None of the rest of the team slept in tents, preferring to bed down on the ground with the donkeys. While we ate, the lads struck the tents and repacked everything with high-speed precision, dividing the load between our donkeys.

With our hiking boots tied tightly and our knapsacks on our backs, we set off on the first day of our trek, leaving the rest of the team to catch up with us after their breakfast. We climbed a gradual ascent for about an hour, Angdu and I walking in tandem while Mark and Pat walked in front of or behind us to get the shots. After an hour of stopping and starting, Angdu was aware of our shooting needs and was totally comfortable in front of the camera.

Unsurprisingly, our team caught up and overtook us quite quickly, singing as they went by. Seventy-five-year-old Donda made me giggle. Though he was wrapped up in sheepskin layers and a crusty hat and clutched a gnarled walking stick, a pair of mirrored aviator sunglasses looked completely at odds with the rest of him. The culture here involves gifts rather than tips; the glasses had obviously been a token of appreciation from a previous trekker.

We eventually reached the ninth-century Ridzong Gompa, which is still used today as a meditation centre by monks. Like Thikse, there was a calmness and serenity here as the monks went about their daily lives. Angdu explained that, traditionally, a family donated one son to the monastery, usually the eldest, but this custom was changing. I asked about the girls of Ladakh, how they were educated and if they studied Buddhism in the same way?

"Yes, we have nunneries," he told me, "but for years their job really was to look after the monks in the monasteries, give them food and clothes. They did not get the same respect as the monks and they were not educated in the ways and teachings of Buddhism. That is changing now. The monks realise they need to keep Buddhism alive and strong for everyone."

We continued downhill through some woods and then followed the Wulhu river upstream, where the verdant green grass stood out in sharp contrast to the barren landscape that surrounded us. We passed a lot of families, some of them Tibetan refugees living as nomads up in these highlands, raising yaks, sheep and goats. Prayer flags attached to the roofs of their small temporary shelters danced in the wind. I was beginning to understand that religion is not just an important part of life in Ladakhi monasteries; the spiritual philosophy of Buddhism and its influences are engrained in every person up here. It is their whole identity. Angdu explained that there are no churches or places of worship as such because everyone has a space inside their home, however small, where they pray.

Dotted across the landscape as we climbed higher again were what looked like giant white pawn chess pieces. These "chortens" made out of clay and painted with white lime wash, are mostly burial mounds. Some are filled with sacred manuscripts and devotional objects and you must always pass them in a clockwise direction to ward off evil spirits. We walked close to one where colourful streams of prayer flags fluttered and spun in the wind. Some were worn to shreds but each rectangular flag of colour attached to the long string had different prayers or mantras, mainly written in Tibetan characters. These are continually added to by pilgrims and travellers who pass them on their journey. I attached the yellow wipe for my sunglasses and wished everyone who passed a safe journey home. I then secretly prayed for a foot rub and a long soak in a bath!

We walked mile after mile of dusty uphill track. It wasn't easy. I struggled with my breathing at times and Pat and Mark were both suffering with really bad headaches. We had to take things extremely slowly as we all knew the dangers of altitude sickness. We were all taking in a lot of water. Eventually after four hours we climbed up the last 320 metres to the brow of a hill from where we could see the village of Yang Thang nestled in the valley below. It was a stunning view and for a moment we all forgot about our tired bodies. This was where we would camp for the night and the sight of it in the distance made us all breathe a collective sigh of relief.

Yang Thang is a small village of about twenty houses. Angdu explained that the population of these mountain villages is kept low by various factors. Many boys go to the monasteries and therefore do not need any land to farm, nor do they have family to support. Also, because so little of the land is suitable for cultivation, these remote villages have lived by a social law that keeps numbers under control. When a son marries and inherits his father's land, his younger brothers must then share his land – and also his wife. The elder brother is always seen as the husband and the father and once the first grandchild is born the grandparents move out of the main family house to a smaller one on the land. The children refer to their uncles as "little fathers". This system of polyandry was made illegal forty years ago but, out of necessity, Angdu explained, it is still prevalent all over Ladakh. The village is completely self-sustained. Women worked the small irrigation channels in the fields to ensure the melted-ice water from the mountains was evenly distributed. Barefoot, rosy-cheeked children smiled and waved as we passed them by.

That night, by the light of two kerosene lamps, on our insistence we all ate together. Angdu was the only one of our team who spoke English, so he translated our questions to the rest of the group. We found out a lot about each other. Much to our amusement, they could not conceal their shock when they found out that, at the age of twenty-five, I was not married and had no intention of it either. In Ladakh, an unmarried woman of twenty-five is fit for the scrap-heap. I was, to all intents and purposes, over the hill!

Since the lads had never heard of bingo, I suggested a card game of gin rummy. On every round, the loser had to make the tea or boil more water or stoke the fire. After that night, it already felt like we were more of a team, which was fantastic. These men wanted us to experience their environment in the best possible way and were keen to do anything to help.

The following day we had a seven-hour walk in front of us to the village of Ule-Phu at 13,500 feet, so we set off early. The landscape had really opened out and every bend revealed even more breathtaking views. To help us focus on our climbing, we sang songs and played I-spy – "I spy with my little eye, something beginning with R", to which there was a unanimous roar, "Rocks!" "I spy with my little eye, something beginning with C." "Clay?" "No." "Clothes?" "No." "Clouds?" . . . and so on and so on until we had covered everything between us and the horizon. The game lasted about five minutes in all!

We passed through Ule-Phu and continued uphill for 40 minutes to a lone house on top of the hill. This was the home of the Luxar family, who had agreed to let us pitch our tents in their garden. It was the most extraordinary isolated home with the most beautiful view I had ever seen in my life.

The sun was shining still and I sat in front of my tent for what must have been two hours. I thought of my friend Enda, who had worked with me on *No Frontiers* and had passed away earlier in the year. He loved climbing and hill walking and I knew this would be his idea of heaven. I tore out a page of my diary and I wrote to him:

How are you, my dear,

Just a quick note to say that I have made it to the top of the world and I am thinking of you. It was a difficult climb today but now that I am here, I can honestly say, I have never been anywhere more breathtakingly beautiful in my life. It is almost too much to take in. A husband and wife and their two children live in a stone house perched at the top of a green hill surrounded by miles and miles of nothingness. The whole scene is how I imagine a child would draw a picture of a house on a hill in the middle of nowhere! There are no roads and everything the family have in their house, including a massive oven, had to be brought up in pieces, bit by bit, hour after hour, and assembled at the top. They smile like they have not a care in the world, they are happy in utter isolation and they want for nothing. I hope that you are happy and free wherever you are and that your adventurous spirit is still flying high. I have taken a stone for you, one that I hope the Himalayas will not miss, and I will bring it back to you in Navan. I will leave this letter for you here, under a rock, as close to heaven as I can get.

I miss you
Lots of Love
Blondie

That night the wind blew up into a howling gale and we all ate dinner by candlelight on the floor of the family home. We knew our tents would stand less of a chance blowing away if we were in them so, as soon as we'd eaten, we ran out and bedded down for the night. The noise of the wind whipping against the tent was almost deafening. I felt scared but exhilarated at the same time. My body was crying out it was so tired, but I couldn't sleep. I thought of the boys lying curled around the open fire inside the stone house a couple of feet away. It was about time there was a role reversal and that we were the ones left outside to the elements of the mighty Himalaya. I lay there and the thought that I would probably never get back here again, never meet these people again, made me sad. All of this would become another memory that would eventually fade. And it was up there on the edge of the mountain that cold night that I decided I would write this book.

We were all still there the following morning, but only just. Mark's tent had collapsed on top of him and the protective outside layer of mine had blown away, which explained why it was so noisy. After breakfast, Richsing, the youngest son, sat on his hunkers at the edge of the hill, cupped his hands and started shouting across the valley in the direction of a house on the other side. "This is how they communicate with their neighbours," Angdu informed us, smiling. I could just about make out a lone figure who lifted her hands and called back a response. There was about a three-second delay before her voice reached our side of the valley. "She is going to buy supplies in Yang Thang and will get some wool for this family. She will return in two days."

We said goodbye to our hosts, thanked them for their hospitality and turned toward Hemis Shuckpan, six hours away. We had to re-trace our steps for about an hour down the mountain. I had two massive blisters on my ankles and was generally feeling quite weak from lack of sleep as well as physical exhaustion. We struggled and again the donkey train passed us out, the men leading them on, not even breaking a sweat.

Every now and then we passed big mounds of rocks. Kneeling down close to one of the piles, I could see that each stone had been inscribed with a mantra or carved with an outline of Buddha. In amongst the rocks were old and new crinkled rupee notes, more offerings of people who had passed long before us. These added up to quite an amount, especially if you were a poor family living in these parts but they were left untouched, in thanks to Buddha.

Things were really beginning to take their toll on us. Pat was having real trouble catching his breath today and I felt so bad for him. Trying to shoot and think creatively while your body just wants to shut down is excruciating. We had no choice but to keep going, knowing that we were due to meet the van the following day, not too far from our camping ground. What we didn't know was that the most difficult part of our trek lay just ahead of us. We had to climb up an almost vertical 260 metres of loose gravel to meet the track which would eventually lead us down into the village. It was like walking in sand; with each step we took, our feet were swallowed up in the soft ground and it felt like we were getting nowhere.

The sun was burning the top of my head, my thighs were killing me and it felt like I was carrying a tonne of bricks in my knapsack. The jokes and words of encouragement and general good feeling over the last few days vanished as we all felt the frustration and difficulty of the last challenge.

And then we got to the top. Adrenalin seeped into every vein in my body as I took in the vista. In what looked like a green lake below, surrounded on all sides by craggy mountains, the shiny roofs of Hemis Shuckpan's houses glistened in the sun. In Ladakhi, shukp means cedar and the cedar trees lining the lower mountain slopes danced in the breeze. Another oasis in this barren but beautiful desert. Even though we still had one day left it felt like we had been, seen and conquered the mountains.

We were all in much better form on the descent into Hemis Shuckpan. Old stone walls lined the path into the village and divided the green plots into fields. Either side, women harvesting on their hands and knees in the fields peeped through the wheat ears and smiled in welcome. The whole place reminded me of the west of Ireland and for the first time in a week, I felt a pang of homesickness.

The guys had set up camp in a small field on the outskirts of the village. By this stage it was three in the afternoon and Mark and I walked along the edge of a river until it disappeared around a bend. Changing into our swimming gear, we jumped in, not to swim but to have a wash. It was the most wonderful feeling, the cold water invigorating against our tired, dusty limbs.

Walking back up the road, we met Angdu who told us that, by chance, there was an audience with a local oracle the following morning and that we were welcome to come along. Over dinner that night, he explained that an oracle is like a female shaman or a witchdoctor, who is able to cure diseases and foretell the future by allowing spirits to possess her body.

We turned up at a decrepit and derelict-looking house the next day. Taking our shoes off at the door, we walked down a dark corridor and into a room packed with people sitting on the floor. In the middle of the room was a low table on which sat a pitcher of water and what looked like a dagger wrapped in a cloth. The smell of incense filled my nostrils.

Pat, Mark, Angdu and I squeezed into the back of the room and sat down.

Then the oracle entered wearing a cloak and lots of different scarves tied across her head and face. She looked haggard. She knelt down in front of the table and began chanting, swaying back and forth, getting louder and louder until she was shrieking and making wild gurgling sounds. A young girl stood behind her and mopped her brow, which was visibly dripping with sweat. From another container she threw salt over her left shoulder and water over her right. Angdu whispered that the spirits she had evoked were entering her body at this point and it was only when she was "possessed" that she would be able to heal the people who had come to see her.

The oracle's whole body went into spasm. When she next spoke, the voice that came out of her was not that of a woman but of a man. She looked straight ahead and all I could see were the whites of her eyes. The room seemed to grow smaller and I felt faint.

A young woman lay in the arms of her mother. The older woman pushed back her daughter's hair to reveal a large tumour on the side of her neck. The oracle bent down and placed a small tube against the diseased skin. She began sucking. All the while she kept chanting, her eyes rolled back in her head. Even though we had been given permission to shoot, I felt afraid because we had the camera rolling. Pat and Mark both looked freaked-out, but for everybody else in the room, what was happening seemed to be a normal occurrence. The sick woman was screaming in pain and then passed out. The oracle kept sucking at her neck. Then she began to spit out black and green mucus into a bucket on the floor. I couldn't believe what I was seeing with my own eyes. She hadn't even broken the skin, yet tar-like lumps of mucus were somehow being sucked out of the young woman's body through this pipe.

For forty-five minutes, men, women and children offered themselves up to her in the hope of finding cures. Then an old man in rags knelt down in front of her. After a whispered conversation, the oracle stood up and ran out to the dark corridor. Angdu told me to follow, so I did. A cow was tethered to the wall. The shaman knelt down in front of the cow and ran her hand over the belly. She then shrieked again and began sucking through the tube that was placed against the cow's skin. The farmer looked on nervously. Green bile ran down the oracle's face as she spat the thick mucus onto the floor. Then she put her lips directly onto the cow's hide and, without so much as a drop of blood, spat out a two-inch nail that apparently had been lodged in the cow's stomach. The farmer looked relieved, kissed her hand and led the cow out of the house.

I felt at this point that I was the one in an altered state of consciousness and had to go outside to get some air.

As we trekked down into Konka La, "no name pass", and climbed to the summit of Meptak La, I couldn't take my mind off what I had seen that morning. The whole experience was another insight into the spirituality of the Himalaya. A mile away, I could see our white jeep in the distance waiting to pick us up and drive us back to Leh. It was parked beside a giant prayer wheel whose contrasting shades of deep burnished red and gold stood protected under a wooden pagoda. When we eventually reached the wheel, Angdu spun it in a clockwise direction and I joined him, chanting the mantra, "Om Mani Padme Hum" – "May all living beings be free from suffering".

I thought about the people I had met along the way and, apart from the oracle, I couldn't remember a single face without a smile. I know it might sound conceited coming from a western tourist, but the people of Ladakh seem genuinely happy and I have no doubt that this is because of the hugely strong influence of Buddhism all across these desert mountains, not just in the monasteries but in all the villages. Religion is not just a part of life here, it is who these people are. On the drive back I reflected that, although far from converted, my time in the mighty Himalaya had left me spiritually awakened.

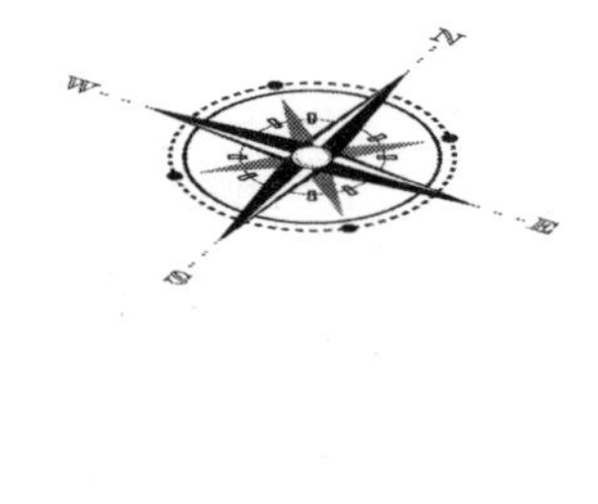

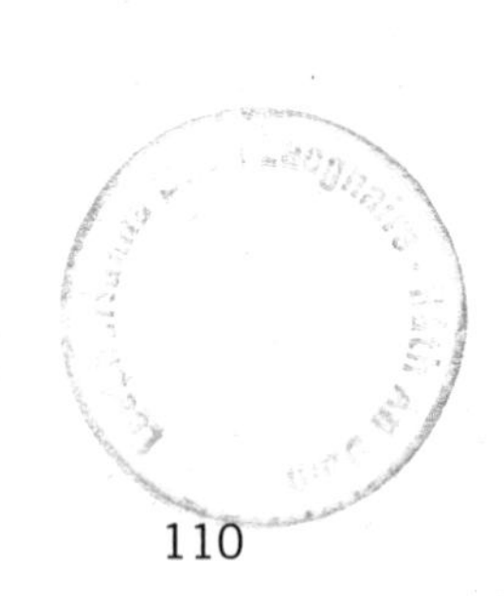

Women wearing traditional costume at the Ladakh Festival

Action on the polo field at the top of the world

Himalayas

Local Ladakhi lady – a face that tells a thousand stories

Below:
The hardy donkeys of the Himalayas

Taking a break to read the spiritual mantras of the prayer flags

Mark and Pat, my Himalayan henchmen

Below: Five-star dining in the Himalayas

Antarctica

The stillness and majesty of the Antarctic landscape

Spectacular iceberg off the coast of Antarctica

Stretching the legs after three days on board

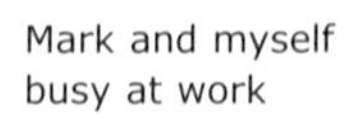

Mark and myself busy at work

Antarctica

All wrapped up, ready for our first night camping on the ice

The snoring seal that disturbed our sleep

Up close and personal with one of the locals

Mr Penguin pointing us in the right direction

View from the top of Spigot Hill

Himalayas

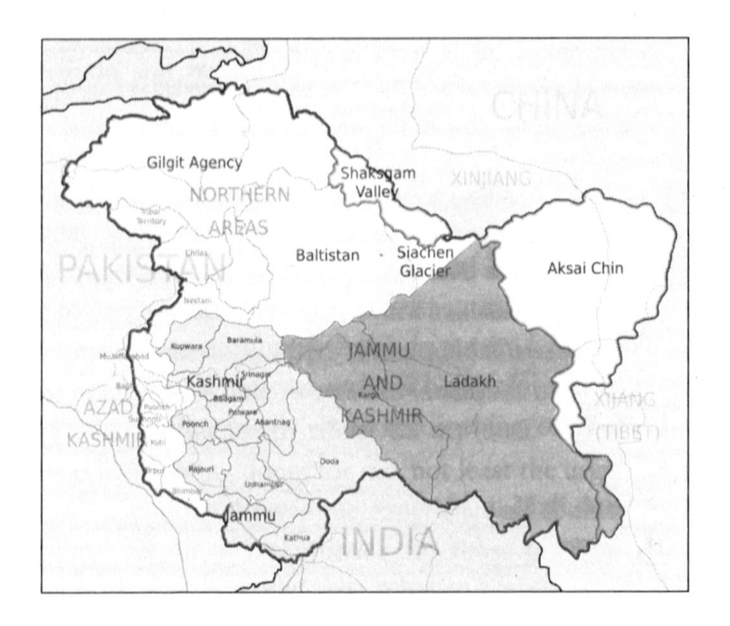

Population: Nearly forty million people inhabit the Himalayan region which consists of three parallel zones: the Great Himalayas, the Middle Himalayas and the Sub-Himalayas.

Official Name: Himalaya is a Sanskrit word meaning "abode of snow".

Size: The Himalaya extend over 2500 km east to west and 250 to 425 km north to south. The Himalaya stretch across five nations. Pakistan, China, India, Nepal, and Bhutan. The Himalayas is the world's highest mountain range and includes nine of the world's top ten highest peaks.

Climate: Within the Himalayas, climate varies depending on elevation and location. The Sub-Himalayan foothills average a summer temperature of 30°C and average winter temperature of 18°C. The Middle Himalayas average a summer temp of 15° to 18°C and winters are below freezing. At elevations above 4,880 metres (16,000 feet), the climate is very cold with temperatures below freezing and the area is permanently covered with snow and ice. The eastern part of the Himalayas receives heavy rainfall; the western part is drier.

Best time to go: Trekking is available throughout the year depending on your preference of areas to visit. Ladakh in India is favourable from mid-June to September, Bhutan region from March to August, Nepal is favourable throughout the year and Tibet from April to November.

Who to go with: I recommend you shop around the numerous tour operators that now offer trekking in the Himalayas and find a company or tour operator that suits your needs, your experiences and your level of fitness. I travelled with Himalayan Kingdoms, based in the UK.

Where I went: Delhi, Leh, Indus Valley, Ladakh Himalayan Range.

Time Difference: New Delhi is +5.30 hours from Ireland.

Currency: This will depend on the region of the Himalayas you visit.

Visa: Since the Himalayas occupy five countries, you will need a visa for the country where you begin your trek. If you cross a border on your trek you will also need a visa. You should consult with your tour operator prior to departure regarding the appropriate visas that are required.

Vaccinations Needed: Depending on the country where you begin your trek, vaccinations may be required. You should consult your local Tropical Medical Bureau or GP for advice.

Trekking Tips:

- Develop basic fitness prior to departure. Consider carrying a backpack and camping for a few days; this will help you to select the trek best suited to you.

- The way to prevent altitude sickness is to give the body enough time to get used to the rarefied air. A slow and steady ascent is vital. Adequate hydration is also helpful.

- Take a well-packed medical kit, including a good blister pack.

- Bring some reading material for your nights camping.

Trekking Essentials: A good quality rucksack, which has broad straps to hold a foam mattress, a knife, sleeping bag, good quality and comfortable walking shoes, rain gear because rains are really unpredictable in the mountains, matchboxes, umbrella, camera film/disks according to the duration of the trip, water bottle, disposable bags to collect and carry garbage, and torch.

Fun Facts

- **The Himalayas cover about 0.4 per cent of the Earth's surface.**
- **The Himalayas continue to rise one centimetre every year.**
- **The first woman to climb Mount Everest was Junko Tabei.**
- **At 6,300 metres (20,700 feet), Siachen in the Himalayas is the world's highest battlefield, where the bigger enemy is the bitter cold. Temperatures hover at –30°C and often touch –60°C.**

Useful Contacts:

General information on trekking in the Himalayas:

- www.visit-himalaya.com
- www.myhimalayas.com
- Contact the Tourist Authority of the country where you begin your trek for more general information and visa requirements.

Books to Read:

Himalaya by Michael Palin.

Trekking and Climbing in the Indian Himalaya by Harish Kapadia.

Inside Himalaya: The Journey by Basil Pao.

Antarctica

I remember the first time I visited the Shackleton Museum in Athy with my Dad. My brother David had a rugby match and my six-year-old sister Linda had been injured earlier that morning attempting to capture a wild cat with an overturned shopping trolley; so it was just the two of us. With no siblings to engage in devilment, he had my full attention as he told me the story about the great Irish explorer Ernest Shackleton.

It was 1914 and while Europe was preparing itself for the Great War, Shackleton was preparing himself and his twenty-eight-strong crew to cross the "unknown continent" by foot. He had been part of many voyages to the Antarctic but this was *his* time to shine. He set sail from the Pacific island of South Georgia in his boat *Endurance* on what would become one of history's greatest adventures. Dad described to me how the boat became stuck in thick sea ice and drifted for nine months before it was crushed, leaving the men stranded on the ice. They drifted for five months on an iceberg, eventually reaching Elephant Island. Shackleton had no choice but to cross 800 miles of treacherous seas in a small rowing boat with five others. He returned four months later to rescue every one of his men, alive.

I remember being confused; the land Dad was describing sounded so harsh, as I had imagined Antarctica to be a Christmas world with nothing but snow and snowmen and Santa Claus and reindeers. Looking at the black-and-white photographs in the museum that day, I obviously had very little comprehension of the enormity of this feat. In the years that followed and as my love for travel and exploration grew, to me, what Ernest Shackleton achieved, what he navigated and survived, makes his the greatest story of all time.

It was a Thursday afternoon in November 2005 when confirmation of our Antarctic trip finally came through to the office. I had just put the phone down to Peregrine Adventures, the company based in the UK who were working with us to co-ordinate the trip. The months of production planning, research and logistics were all in place. I rang Ruth, the director, and Mark, the cameraman, to confirm that we were booked on board a Russian ship, the *Vavalov*, departing from Ushuaia in South Argentina on 8 December for an adventure to the seventh continent.

Walking home from the office that evening, it was cold and wet, exactly like the night before, but this time I was smiling in the rain, pushing against the head-on wind that was driving against me as I walked along Stephen's Green. The conditions seemed to heighten my sense of adventure and I thought of how Ernest Shackleton must have felt back in

1914 when he eventually got the green light to embark on his voyage to the Antarctic. Little did he know what lay ahead of him and his crew. I didn't know what lay ahead of me and mine, but I did know how lucky I was to have the privilege of visiting one of the most hostile yet beautiful environments on earth.

It's a long trip from Dublin to Ushuaia in Argentina, which is hardly surprising considering that it claims to be the most southerly town on the planet. It is actually in Patagonia, which is sometimes mistakenly assumed to be its own country rather than a region covering the southernmost parts of Argentina and Chile. It took us two days to get there, flying from Paris via Buenos Aires.

Ushuaia is the jumping-off point for most people who come to hike the glaciers but was also the point where we were to board our ship to begin our ten-day adventure. There's not much to the place but I liked the town; it felt hard and wild and bleak. It is surrounded by water on three sides, where old fishing trawlers and naval vessels bob in a grey sea against a grey sky. Along the harbour front, clapboard buildings with shuttered fronts give the impression that this place has seen its glory days, but farther into town you get a much better impression of where it is today. It caters well for its two main industries, fishing and tourism. There are loads of restaurants, bars, nightclubs and even a strip joint for the wayward sailors, weary fishermen and wishful tourists.

I always think a town like this attracts all sorts of weird and wonderful people, like Alice Springs in Australia; the tourists come for one thing and everyone else who is there seems to have drifted to escape the world for one reason or another. The people that live here have become their environment and I liked it and them for that reason.

That first day we did have the choice to take a daytrip to the Tierra Del Fuego National Park about nine kilometres outside town, but rather than squeeze in an excursion after our mammoth flight, we chose instead to wander around this last outpost, gathering up the last essentials, including extra socks, chocolate and a large supply of wine and vodka.

The next morning, weighed down with rucksacks, camera gear and shopping bags, Mark, Ruth and I boarded the *Vavalov*. When we were handed a glass of champagne and shown to our first-class cabins, we smiled at the fact that, although we were retracing Shackleton's footsteps, we would be doing it with a little more comfort! We tipped our glasses and toasted Shackleton's men and luck to our journey.

With everything stowed away I decided to go for a nose around. The ship is primarily used as a research vessel during the winter months and takes tourists in the summer season from November to March, when the ice floes have melted enough to navigate the waters. So although it is perfectly comfortable, it doesn't ooze luxury or opulence like some of the cruise ships you'd associate with sailing the Caribbean or the Med. It puts basic functionality ahead of anything else. On the top deck there were the first-class cabins, each of which had one wide single bed under the porthole window and a set of bunk beds at its foot, the top part of which could be folded away for extra space. There was a writing desk and a small en-suite bathroom. Small but perfectly formed.

At the other end of the top-floor corridor was the ship's library, full of books about polar environments, expeditions and wildlife. Downstairs on the second floor were most of the guest cabins, which had four berths. This was also where the bar was located – the main meeting point of the ship. Below deck were the staff quarters, dining room, a projector room, a pokey gym with a few machines and a sauna. For those on board who chose to use the sauna the way it was originally intended, outside on the deck there was an icy plunge pool. I wondered which facility was more underused, the gym or the outdoor plunge pool?

Having settled into their cabins, most people came up on deck to wave goodbye to civilisation as we pulled out of the Argentinean port and travelled down the Beagle Channel. Watching as the twinkling lights of the town and isolated houses on the hillside faded into the distance, I was reminded of how uncontactable we would be for the next ten days. We had been told there was a satellite phone on board only for emergencies and usually the idea of this would thrill me. Being cut off from everything but your experience allows you to feel a real sense of escape when you're travelling and today there are surprisingly few places left on the planet where you cannot send a text or receive a call. We have laughed numerous times over the years when somebody's phone would ring in the most out-of-the-way places, "Hey Kaks, are you heading into town tonight?" "No, don't think I'll make it, I'm standing on the Great Wall of China"; "Mark, you around tomorrow night for dinner?" "Sorry, I'll have to ring you back, I'm just doing a piece to camera with some of the jungle tribes of Papua New Guinea, good luck"; or "Now is not a good time, Mum, I'm hanging out of a helicopter harness trying to take some shots. I'll buzz you when I land."

Today was different, though. With no means of contact, I would not be aware of my Gran's condition. She had had a horrible year, having been diagnosed with pancreatic cancer. When the doctors felt they could do no more for her, she insisted on being discharged from hospital to be at home. The night before my trip, I had driven to Carlow to see her. For those few hours, I sat on the side of the bed. Although she was weak, she told stories in the way that she always did to her grandchildren, with humour and intelligence. Even as a child, I could have sat and listened to her all day. She asked two requests of me before I left; firstly, to toast her with a glass of Martini extra dry on the deck of the boat once we had reached the White Continent. She handed me the bottle and we laughed at the thought of my padded gloves trying to hold a Martini glass gracefully and agreed that I could use a plastic cup if necessary. Secondly, she told me to always be true to myself at home and when I'm away. We both knew that, once I had boarded the ship, it would be nearly impossible for me to get home if anything happened and she made it very clear that she didn't even want me to entertain the idea. I looked at her, not wanting to say goodbye, willing her to at least see Christmas, a couple of weeks away, but at the same time not wanting to leave anything unsaid. We hugged each other and cried, I told her I loved her and we said goodbye.

Now, as the land vanished from the stern of the boat, I felt she was with me and I tried to visualise us sitting down to the upcoming Christmas dinner, me boring her and everyone else with my photographs of the trip.

Mark, Ruth and I spent two hours shooting in and around the boat and scoping out the passengers who we would be living with over the next ten days. To be honest, the night before we had wondered if we would be the youngest people on board. But far from being indoctrinated into a blue-rinse cruising club, at the introduction meeting in the bar, it became apparent very quickly that there was a real mix of people onboard – different ages and nationalities, couples on honeymoon, people celebrating anniversaries, a gay couple, one family with their children, friends and a lot of people travelling on their own, fulfilling a life-long dream. With our name badges pinned on, we clumsily shuffled around the room introducing ourselves. One thing that seemed common to everyone on board was that we all possessed a real sense of adventure.

Another thing common to most people was feeling lousy. There was quite a roll at sea at this stage and groups that had been standing around now took to the chairs and booths around the room, reaching into pockets and bags for sea-sickness tablets. The bar, which was the communal area of the ship, was where we first met our entire crew, who briefed us on our trip and told us that it generally took people a day or so to find their sea legs. This was because we had to spend two days crossing the open waters of the Drake Passage, renowned for being one of the roughest seas in the world, before finally reaching the Antarctic continent.

Dinner on our first evening was an experience. Walking around the buffet counter in the middle of the dining room was difficult enough but, once you sat down, holding onto your own dinner plate also proved tricky. Three times I had somebody else's plate in front of me as mine slid down the other end of the table. We all reconvened in the bar and I nearly died when somebody told me it was 10.00 p.m. I looked outside and it might as well have been 3.00 in the afternoon. At that time of year, in that part of the world, the days are long and the nights short. Outside the white sky made the sea look an ominous grey but the ship was warm and I felt safe as we coasted over the waves.

I got talking to Peter, who was seventy-nine and part of a contingent of fifteen passengers on board from Australia who had been re-routed due to pilot strikes. Instead of flying from

Melbourne to Buenos Aires and down to Ushuaia, they had to fly via Tokyo, LA, Houston, Buenos Aires and finally Ushuaia. Talk about a mammoth journey before then boarding a ship to spend two days crossing one of the most treacherous seas in the world! Their luggage hadn't made it so they all had to buy new thermals and specialised clothes for the trip in Ushuaia. Peter was quite badly shaken up, feeling sea-sick and terribly weak only hours into the journey. I didn't know whether I felt more sorry for his condition or at seeing him having to wear a luminous pink long-sleeved T-shirt with yellow padded pants, obviously the height of fashion in Ushuaia.

Slowly, people began to drift off, realising they would have to turn in while daylight still blazed outside. By 11.00 p.m., Mark, Ruth and I had grown to become a merry little band of ten holding court at the bar. With us were Lindy, a gregarious Aussie woman in her fifties with a very impressive bosom, which she introduced us to by names; her friend Jane; Biggles and his wife Kate, who own their own winery just outside Brisbane; and Duncan, a travel agent, also from Brisbane. He had sold this trip to numerous clients and on hearing two years of positive feedback, had decided he had to do it for himself. Then there was David McGonagle, the well-respected Captain of our ship, and Martin Grey from the Orkney Islands in Scotland, who was one of the expedition leaders. Not only did he look like your stereotypical highland Scot, rugged and strong, but he also enjoyed a story and song. Tanya was the barmaid on the ship and figured out immediately that it would probably be in her best interests to look after us for the next ten days.

So the session started and by midnight (it might as well have been midday) we were the only ones left in the bar.

Everyone was in great spirits and any wobbly walking on the way back to cabins was blamed on the rolling waves. I was in fits of laughter as I heard Duncan chime up from the bottom of the boat, "Goodnight to the Irish, up there in your first-class cabins while the rest of us have to slum it in steerage. I hope the spins get the better of you and that you cannot figure out how to open your bloody portholes." There was a loud crack and more hilarious laughter. "God, Lindy, those girls are impressive. Can I kiss them goodnight?"

A loud ascending alarm ricocheted through my brain. "Good morning, shipmates. This is your Captain. It is 7.00 a.m. and breakfast is being served in the dining room, after which Martin will be giving us a whale identification lecture." *Jesus, Mary and Joseph, what was that?* I hadn't noticed the intercom built into the ceiling of my room. Is this how we were to be woken every day? I crawled out of bed, frantically scanning the walls and the ceiling for an "off" button, or at least something that would turn the volume down, but there was none. Unsteady on my feet and forgetting I was at sea, I stumbled forward with the motion of the boat and hit my head off the edge of the cupboard. Vowing never to drink again, I crawled back into bed and decided I would stay there for the next ten days. Ruth came in and told me to get up, that the crew were waiting for me to come down before they started the "whale identification lecture". When I tell you I would rather have gouged my eyeballs out with a blunt spoon, I am not over-exaggerating. The only thing I felt like identifying was two Alka-Seltzer in a large glass of cold water.

I eventually made it down to the bar to a loud cheer from the rest of the room. I apologised sheepishly and slunk myself into a corner beside Mark, who also looked like he should be in a dark room under the covers. The rest of our merry little band of revellers didn't look so merry this morning either. Duncan looked like he might vomit at any minute; Lindy was green and, even more disturbing, quiet; and Biggles looked like he had drunk his entire winery! Martin, on the other hand, was sprightly as he spoke to us about spotting minke and humpback whales, migrating birds and Adélie penguins.

Outside on the deck, the air was noticeably colder than the day before. It was bracing and certainly good for sore heads. I spent most of the morning spotting whales with Duncan, the two of us trying to put some of Martin's information into use. Were they minkes or humpbacks? We saw giant albatross and other birds flying overhead before torpedoing into the water for fish or gliding down to land their rear ends in the icy waters. I also photographed the boat and her passengers and pored over books on the Antarctic in the library with endless cups of hot chocolate. That evening we went below deck to the projector room to watch Morgan Freeman's *March of the Penguins*. After the first night's festivities, let's just say an early night was had by all.

The following morning, I opened the porthole of my cabin and was hit with a blast of cold air to the face. I was also hit with one of the most breathtaking scenes imaginable. Rising out of the ocean, as far as the eye could see, were incredible icebergs of all different shapes and sizes. Some were as big as office blocks and some small enough to bob and roll in the current. Those on the horizon were bright white, illuminated by the sun, those closer to the boat cobalt blue, lighting up the surface of the water with their underbellies. The jagged edges above the surface were only the tips of the icebergs, some extending fifty, sixty or seventy metres into the deep. The whole scene was made picture-perfect by a light snowfall, creating a magical wonderland. I ran next door and was greeted by the picture-perfect image of Ruth's rear-end framed by the porthole. She was hanging out the window, taking in the view and snapping away on her camera.

We all gathered on the lower deck, prepared for our first trip in the Zodiacs. These inflatable boats would be our secondary means of transport over the next few days, manoeuvring us through the waters and landing us onto the icy continent. Togged out like Michelin men with the necessary warm gear and lifejackets, we exited the *Vavelov* for the first time in two days. We motored gently through the water, navigating our way between the icebergs. Our first encounter was with a huge male seal, which lunged out of the water to take some time out on the ice and warm up a little in the sun. He raised his head lazily as we passed by and, realising we were a safe distance away, went back to the business of getting some shut-eye. He looked so peaceful. We also spotted a pair of Adélie penguins shuffling along in the snow, their feathers wet and gleaming in the sun, having just come out of the water.

Everything was so still and beautiful. At water level, the icebergs were put into a whole different perspective again. I felt like Alice in Wonderland travelling through a magical ice sculpture park. Martin explained to us that an iceberg is freshwater ice that has broken away from a glacier and that typically only about one-ninth of it is visible above the water. Because the density of pure water is less than that of salt water, most is submerged by the extra weight. I tried to visualise motoring along beside the B-15, which he told us was the largest recorded iceberg in history, measuring an area of 11,000 square kilometres when it broke from the Ross Ice

Shelf in 2000. It broke apart again in November 2002 and the largest piece still had an area of 3,000 square kilometres, still the biggest recorded on earth. Imagine, a bloody 3,000-square-kilometre iceberg!

After the *Titanic* sank in 1912, killing 1,517 of its passengers, and because of increased numbers of expeditions threatened by icebergs, there is now a worldwide study that monitors them by satellite year round. There are tabular and non-tabular icebergs, tabulars having steep sides and a flat top like a plateau and non-tabulars coming in all different shapes. Then you have bergy bits, and the smallest of all icebergs, measuring less than one-metre high, are called growlers. Martin piped up loudly that we were surrounded by growlers and of course this had all the immature people in the boat sniggering away until it was explained to everyone else amongst us that this was a fondly used expression, namely by the Irish, for a woman's vagina, which led nicely into an hour of smutty jokes. Ah yes, in one of the most unpolluted, pristine places on the planet, we in our Zodiac, the good people of America, Canada, Australia, England and Ireland vied to be the winners of the filthiest joke contest. Unsurprisingly, Australia won.

After we returned to the *Vavelov*, a good feed of lunch was accompanied by loud chatter all around the dining room about who saw what as people eagerly pored over their digital photographs.

In the afternoon, Ruth and I got togged out again for our first kayaking trip. This was an optional extra, and an expensive one at that, so there were just twelve in our small group. The plan was to circumnavigate Pléneau Island, which lies at the southern entrance of the Lemaire Channel. Beth-Anne, our kayak leader, gave us our safety talk. We hung onto every word, nobody wanting to overturn. "Okay guys, you really must concentrate on what you are doing and keep one eye on your fellow paddlers. If you do go overboard, you will not survive in the water longer than a few minutes. Hypothermia sets in when the water draws heat away from your body and if your body drops below ninety-two degrees, everything begins to shut down, you lose consciousness, your breathing slows and lastly your heart stops beating." I looked at Ruth and then at the plastic kayaks bobbing in the water, which all of a sudden did not look as sturdy as they had done in vertical lines fastened to the back wall of the equipment room below deck. Feeling slightly nervous, I slid into the water and pulled the spray deck tightly across the cockpit of my kayak. I bobbed away, afraid to move a muscle as I waited for the rest of the group to enter. Then, slowly, we paddled away from the *Vavelov*, spreading out slightly as we pushed forward into the ice.

After three days surrounded by people on the ship and in the Zodiac boats, the sense of solitude in the kayak was a wonderful feeling and my nerves quickly subsided. We were soon surrounded by a flotilla of gentoo penguins and blue-eyed shags, which quickly overcame their shyness to satisfy their curiosity with a closer glimpse of our bobbing plastic boats. No noise from engines, just the cracking of ice off the tip of the paddle and the slight scraping sound as the bottom of the kayak pushed forward through the brash ice.

But then I stopped and really listened to how loud the "frozen continent" actually is. The glacier we were paddling beside was creaking and grinding over the rocks; I could hear ice crackling and popping as the glacier melted and the trapped gases were released. It's difficult to describe how this whole environment enters your body, it consumes you and you are reminded of how small and insignificant you are in the bigger scheme of things. As if to emphasise what I was feeling, two humpback whales swam past us at a distance of about twenty metres. My fear had turned to awe. Unfortunately, we couldn't penetrate the ice in the shallow waters closer to the island and had to change course, paddling instead to the gentoo penguin rookery. We sat and watched these quirky, curious little creatures until we were all numb with the cold and were lured back to the warmth of the ship.

The following day we took our first steps onto the Antarctic continent, the first piece of solid ground in three days. Clambering out of the Zodiac into deep crunchy snow at Spigot Hill felt like a real achievement. "It is only an achievement, Kathryn, if you climb the 300 metres to the top and back down again, so start hiking," ordered Captain McGonagle. It took us thirty-five minutes to climb to the top, following the guides in a winding trail, sometimes knee-deep in snow. Every so often a misjudged step or photo opportunity had people up to their waists in snow, much to the amusement of the rest of the group. The view from the top was incredible. The *Vavelov* was moored in the bay below us, the Zodiacs shining like little red jewels against the snow. The sky was grey and everything else was different shades of blue and white. Desolate, empty and awesome. As I looked around, it struck me that it wasn't a matter of what was here – the beauty and appeal of the place was all about what was *not* here.

On a daily basis, we were informed of our route depending on the weather conditions and we were lucky enough to be able to enter one of the most perfect crater islands in the world, Deception Island. It got its name from the fact that it is difficult to find the one small entrance at which to enter the crater itself. Although a strong head wind blew down on top of us, our captain navigated the ship through the small opening. We could see where the cold Antarctic waters mixed with the thermal waters of the bay. Steam rose in places from the black sand beaches but, standing on the deck, I wasn't so sure about utilising this once-in-a-lifetime opportunity to swim in the "warm waters" of the Antarctic.

We anchored in the middle of the crater and transferred to Whalers' Bay in our trusty Zodiacs. Our expedition leader Gregg told us how sailors and explorers had used Deception Island as a refuge from storms and icebergs since the nineteenth century. But it was the whalers of the early twentieth century who had left their mark on the place. Huge rusting boilers and tanks lay broken and lonely along the shore. Whale carcasses had been boiled down here to extract whale oil, which had been a lucrative commodity until the Great Depression saw oil prices drop. Whaling then became uneconomic and the island was abandoned in 1931. We were told how forty-five whalers had been buried in the station's cemetery, before it was itself buried in volcanic eruptions in the 1960s.

It was an eerie sort of place that reminded me of pictures I'd seen of Pompeii. The last traces of man were rusty piles of metal preserved in a ruined state by an environment that had got the better of them in the end. I thought of the men who had died here, thousands of miles from anywhere, and was again reminded of the courage and bravery of Shackleton's men, not just for being part of a dangerous expedition but for not letting the windiest, driest, coldest place on earth beat them down.

This psyched me up enough to strip down to my swimming togs and run across the snow-covered beach into the sea. We were warned to keep moving once we had got in and so I swam parallel to the shore for about 100 metres, hitting pockets of hot and cold water as I went. It never felt too cold in the water but certainly re-dressing on the beach was done with speed and reckless abandon, piling layer upon layer until the majority of swimmers looked like colourful yetis returning to their lairs, where the ship's small sauna almost reached bursting point. Funnily, nobody opted for the added extra of the icy plunge pool.

Our next landing was at the Vernadsky Research Station on Galindez Island. It is the oldest station on the Antarctic peninsula, now owned by the Ukraine who bought it and took it over from the British in 1996 for the grand sum of one pound. The small island has a couple of out-buildings beside the jetty, where we moored our Zodiacs, and one main wooden structure which was the research station itself. The scientists who live here study upper atmosphere and climate change, mainly concerned with the hole in the ozone layer. In fact, this was the first place in the world where scientists noticed the widening hole.

Two of the scientists, Roman and Vasily, took some time out to give us a tour of the station. They were in their early thirties, very friendly and eager to explain their work. The programmes they study contribute to present-day weather forecasting and to studies of past climate. With so many environmental concerns today, research like this is invaluable and I really admired them. It was great to see them so enthusiastic about their work. Talking to Vasily, it was clear that they also viewed their time here as a unique opportunity before returning to continue their careers in research stations in their own country. When the Ukrainians first bought the station in 1996, twelve people spent that first winter on the island – two geophysicists, two meteorologists, a glaciologist, a diesel mechanic, a carpenter, a cook, an electrician, a communications manager, a doctor and a traveller. With major renovations and an extension built in 1980, the island now has accommodation for twenty-four. There was a general policy that people did not stay longer than thirteen months to ensure that nobody went round the bend.

It snows on average 250 days of the year, with temperatures in the winter reaching minus twenty degrees Celsius and, in summer, only rising to plus two degrees. I tried to imagine what life was like here in the depths of winter, when night lasted for twenty hours. I had read how Shackleton and his men had played games and music and put on shows to keep themselves sane.

"Are there any females amongst you?" asked James, a retired English army officer (with a straight face, I might add). It sounded like he was talking about a very rare species of mountain gorilla and, by the tortured look on the Ukrainian scientists' faces, it became apparent that women were not a common sight in these parts. The majority of day-trippers who did appear from vessels like ours did not really fulfil the required role. I have to tell you, I didn't feel particularly attractive in my padded boiler suit and inflatable lifejacket, but I thought what a nightmare it must be for these men, living on an island in the Antarctic, to see us shuffling around their sleeping quarters, knowing the promise of what lay beneath all our layers. . . .

We all retired for a drink at the bar, where Roman told us the story of how in the 1970s the British scientists received a shipment of wood, which was to be used to construct a new jetty. Instead, they constructed the Antarctic peninsula's only bar. For this, "they were temporarily reprimanded, but they will be eternally toasted!"

It had become customary for the more daring female day-trippers to donate their bras and knickers, which were strewn up over the bar in exchange for a shot of home-made vodka and a thankful smile from the barman. I must say I was tempted to leave a little part of me behind, but my 34A bra was a little too petite in comparison to the women who had gone before me. We all agreed, including Lindy herself, that she would take one for the team and left a rather impressive two cups behind.

Before we left, we all got our passports stamped with an official Antarctic stamp. Although it is a stateless continent that does not belong to any country, we all agreed it was probably our best stamp yet!

Before we returned to the ship, we motored across Stella Creek to Winter Island. This was the original site of the research station before it moved to Galindez Island in 1954. Meteorology was the most important research carried out at the time. Outside the original wooden hut, a timber sign dating from 1947 tells you that this is "British Crown Land". The original hut, "Wordie House" still stands intact. It is named after James Wordie, who was a member of Shackleton's Imperial Trans-Antarctic Expedition between 1914 and 1916. The little hut looked tiny and so dated compared to the modern set-up of Vernadsky Station where we had just come from. I walked in and it was like being transported back in time. The hut, which only ever housed five people at a time, comprised a kitchen and one bunk-room which still had the two sets of beds. Original records and log books remained on the table, old tins of Bird's custard on the shelf. Behind the door an old pair of wooden skis hung from the wall and there were still bags of coal in the storehouse. I came out of the hut having felt that I had intruded on somebody. The place gives you a very real understanding of what life must have been like here in the 1940s. Stepping into the sunshine, blinded by the reflection of the white snow, I thought to myself, *what a surreal and wonderful world!*

Back on the boat, we recapped our day at the research station. The women felt sorry for the lost souls alone on the ice and pondered on what life would be like without women for months on end. The men called it paradise. It was only later that night, through observations by Mark and Duncan, qualified by one of the crew, that I found out that while we, the tourists, were being shown around the laboratories at Vernadsky, a Zodiac of Russian and Ukrainian girls who worked on our ship were dropped off to the quieter sleeping quarters of the research station to "catch up" with some of their old friends and acquaintances! The news made me happy for these men, whom I was sure were sleeping a little more soundly that night.

With renewed male–female appreciation all round, it was the perfect night for a party. Huge plastic bags were emptied onto the floor of the bar and colourful costumes spilled out, waiting to be chosen. It was a "tropical island" theme party so we donned Hawaiian shirts, sombreros and an array of silly foam hats over our thermal gear and headed out onto the deck, where the BBQs were already cooking up a storm. Geoff, the chief birdwatcher, pumped out the Caribbean music while the others served up fruit punch and set up the limbo-dancing competition. The whole scene was absurd: it was minus one degree Celsius, 10.00 p.m. (yet it could have been 10.00 a.m.) and as massive icebergs floated past our ship, we recreated a tropical island in the Caribbean. When news of my Bob Marley CD reached the captain of the ship (who, I might add, was wearing a chicken on his head), I was ordered to go and retrieve it and we danced until the sun went down – which it didn't!

To forego the comfort of my cabin for a night camping on the ice was something I had been looking forward to all week. Although the entire Antarctic trip had felt like an adventure, I wanted the experience of one night in the elements, in a tent with the wind whistling around me. The initial raise of hands volunteering for the camping trip had been twenty-five but common sense prevailed and only twelve of us boarded the Zodiac, waving goodbye to our ship, which we wouldn't return to for ten hours. We bounced across the waves in the cold and moored on an ice floe kilometres from the *Vavelov*.

Ruth, Mark and I decided we would squeeze into a two-man tent for warmth and began setting up camp by stamping around in circles, compacting the snow so our tent pegs would hold firm. Thin foam mattresses and thermal sleeping bags were then unrolled and extra thermal layers were put on. We were under strict instructions not to leave a trace of ourselves behind – no food, no rubbish, not even yellow snow would be tolerated. Our toilet facilities consisted of a large bucket hidden behind an even larger block of ice. We had been warned to try to do everything that needed to be done before exiting the ship and not to drink too much water after that. But the cold and nervous excitement and thoughts of having to get up out of one's sleeping bag in the middle of the night meant that there was a queue of nervous pee-ers waiting to use the facilities almost immediately after we had finished pitching the tents.

Proud photographs of our camp accomplishments were being taken in front of our tents before we turned in for the night, when suddenly there was a loud groan, a huge crack and a deafening rumble that enveloped the stillness around us. It was as close to what I imagine an earthquake would sound like. About one kilometre from our camp, a massive piece of ice, the size of a large detached house, broke away from the cliff face and crashed into the sea, creating huge waves, the tsunami after-effect spreading and rippling in every direction. For a split second, it frightened the life out of everyone, including our two guides who had never seen anything like it at such close proximity before. It was as incredible to hear as it was to watch. We all stood there open-mouthed. Yet, as soon as it happened, it was over, and five minutes later stillness reigned again. The only sound breaking the silence was the lapping of the small waves that eventually made it to the shore where we were camped. Tired but restless, Ruth, Mark and I cuddled up in our tent for warmth. We thought about home and laughed at the thought of our friends and families trying to visualise us lying on the bottom of the world in the snow.

I woke up after what I knew could only have been a few hours' sleep, desperately needing to pee. I lay there willing the urge to go away, trying to guess which one of my fellow campers was snoring so loudly, half-afraid they would cause another avalanche. Annoyed at having to get up, but knowing I could not put mother nature off any more, I scrambled out of my sleeping bag, threw on my boots, windcheater and ski jacket over my already many layers and unzipped myself out of the tent. It was snowing lightly and in the dull light I figured it had to be about 4.00 a.m. I trudged past the other tents to the toilet. I looked across the bay and could see the *Vavelov* in the distance, proud and sturdy, holding her passengers safe and warm. The thought of them made me will myself to be as quick as I could, but it is tricky trying to co-ordinate operation free-flow when every one of the muscles in your body wants to contract against the cold. Not entirely sure if I had finished but not willing to risk frostbite, I quickly buttoned up and made my way back across the snow.

It was then I found the source of the snoring and it stopped me dead in my tracks. Not more than five metres behind our tent were two gigantic Weddell seals and their young pup. I stood rooted to the ground and just watched them. One of the adults was asleep and the other two members of the family eyed me up with lazy curiosity. I had never heard of seals attacking humans but these guys were big and didn't look one bit afraid to be so close to our camp. I looked around at our little makeshift canvas dwellings, covered with a thin layer of snow. They looked so out-of-place and I couldn't help but feel we were intruding. I was wide awake now and I woke Ruth and Mark to tell them what I had seen. But neither of them shared my enthusiasm at that particular time.

It felt good to return to the warmth of the boat for breakfast. Ruth, Mark and I were really excited as we had all our footage in the can and this was a day to relax and take it all in. On our final kayaking trip that morning, we paddled along the coast of the bay where we came across the remains of a minke whale that, according to Beth-Anne, looked like he had met a violent death at the hands of a group of orcas. We watched Wilson's storm petrels dancing gracefully across the water, scoping out the territory, and soon others were hovering in position getting ready to feed on the greyish section of whale carcass. It was incredible to watch this scene in the grand, white, silence. There were cumulus and cirrus clouds overhead and the sun was shining, highlighting the beautiful, dark mountain peaks. It was the perfect setting to say goodbye to this white land.

Back on board a few hours later, we were re-crossing the Drake Passage on our journey home. We rounded the famous Cape Horn in fine weather and calm seas. As we drew back into the pier at Ushuaia, where we had set off on our voyage ten days earlier, I felt like both the happiest and saddest person in the world. Everything felt different and I wanted to reverse out and sail back to the beautiful, empty nothingness, where all is quiet and still. Now, even as I sit here writing this, memories of my time in the Antarctic are of grandeur, awe, inspiration and fun. I smile thinking of all the stories I recounted for my Gran that Christmas. The magic of Antarctica will always remind me what an incredible world we live in.

Antarctica Fast Facts

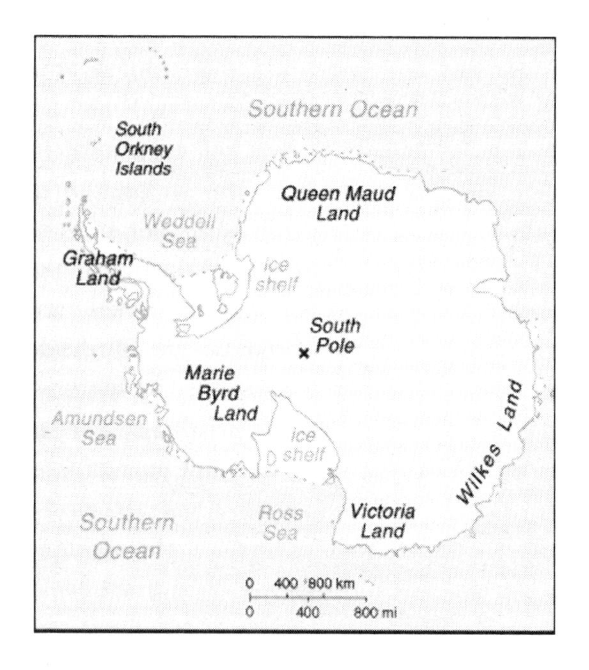

Population: During the summer months there are about 4,000 people on scientific bases with around 25,000 tourists visiting at this time of the year. During the winter months only about 1,000 people remain on scientific bases.

Size: Antarctica is 5,339,543 square miles or 1.4 times the size of the USA.

Climate: Antarctica is known as the driest, coldest and the harshest of all the continents. At the South Pole, the temperature varies from −20°C at the height of summer to −70 in mid-winter. Temperatures during the summer tourist season are higher due to the location that most tourists visit, averaging 0°C to 5°C. There are two seasons in Antarctica: a short four to five-month summer season from November to March and a long eight-month winter season from April to November.

Best time to go: There are no tours to Antarctica during its long winter months from March to October but tours are available from November to March with December and January being the height of summer and with up to 20 hours of daylight and milder weather in the tourist regions.

Who to go with: There are numerous companies that offer tours to Antarctica and these can be found on the International Association of Antarctic Tour Operators website (www.iaato.org). These operators promote and practise safe and environmentally responsible tourism.

Time Difference: +11 hours from Ireland. Time is largely irrelevant as the tourist season has about 20+ hours' daylight each day.

Currency: Most of your spending will take place onboard your vessel in the applicable currency.

Visa Requirements: Since no-one owns Antarctica no-one needs a visa to visit it. However, you will need visas for any countries that your ship visits en route to Antarctica.

Electricity: This will depend on the vessels that you will be travelling on to Antarctica.

Vaccinations Needed: There are no vaccinations required for Antarctica but depending on where you are boarding your vessel to Antarctica, some vaccinations may be required. You should consult your local Tropical Medical Bureau or GP.

Other Highlights:

- Run "The Last Marathon" on King George Island.
- Climb Observation Hill near McMurdo Station and see Mount Erebus and the Ross Ice Shelf.
- Try star-gazing on an exceptionally clear night.
- Send a postcard home to family and friends from Port Lockroy post office.

Fun Facts

- **Antarctica's telephone dialling code is +672**
- **"Great God! This is an awful place" – The words of the explorer Captain Scott when he reached the South Pole on 17 January 1912.**
- **90% of the world's ice (29 million cubic kilometres) and approximately 80% of its fresh water is locked up in the Antarctic icecap.**

Useful Contacts:

- International Association of Antarctic Tour Operators: www.iaato.org
- Antarctica Online – Source of information and photos on Antarctica: www.antarcticaonline.com

Venezuela

Bridges and waterfalls are two of my favourite things in the world. Random, I know, but true. I am Aquarius, the water sign, so maybe that's it? I could sit for hours in front of Sydney Harbour Bridge or the Millau Bridge in France or the Golden Gate in San Francisco Bay or even our own Ha'penny Bridge in Dublin and feel absolutely enthralled just looking at them. As well as being structurally beautiful, I think it's the seamless nature of how they function that I find fascinating. I have to blame this totally nerdy obsession on my Dad, as that's what he does for a living – he builds bridges.

With waterfalls, it's the opposite. I love the way they just exist with reckless abandon, unharnessed, eroding through rock, tumbling and plunging and stopping for nothing, doing as they please. Both are majestic and powerful in different ways.

Angel Falls is the highest free-falling waterfall in the world. It is three times the height of the Eiffel Tower and a full fifteen times higher than Niagara Falls. I had always wanted to know what it would feel like standing at the base of her 3,230-feet drop and looking up. Hidden away in Venezuela's Gran Sabana valley, it is not easy to get to. There are no roads to the falls or anywhere near them and the only way to access them is to fly in to a remote airstrip on a small plane, navigate the rivers of the three-million-hectare Canaima National Park in a motorised canoe, overnight in a hammock in the jungle and shanks' mare it from there. That, to me, made it all the more appealing!

Venezuela is not yet a must-visit country on the well-worn gringo trail through South America. Tucked away in the north-eastern corner of the continent, it seems to be a little bit out of people's way. Researching Venezuela before Gerry, Mark and I left on our quest to Angel Falls, I was amazed at how little I knew about the country. It sounded like a traveller's paradise: 3,000 kilometres of Caribbean coast, deserted islands surrounded by coral reef, steamy Amazonian jungles, the snow-capped peaks of the Andes mountains, the swampy untouched Orinoco delta. Everything I read about the country seemed to have an "*-est in the world*" attached to it: the long*est* river, the tall*est* waterfall, the pretti*est* women. (Venezuela holds more Miss World and Miss Universe titles than anywhere else on earth.) It is also home to the bigg*est* snake in the world, the anaconda. Not only that, it is the fourth-larg*est* producer of oil in the world. This is one of the main reasons the US keeps a watchful eye on Venezuela and why their left-wing democratically elected president Hugo Chavez has come out with a tirade of public abuse and

Going with the Orinoco flow

Downpour in the Delta: rains wash over a Warao stilted village

The Warao children of the Orinoco Delta

Who needs clothes when you've got a good pair of wellies?

You could get lost in the beautiful pools of their eyes . . .

Base camp with Angel Falls dominating the background

In awe of the majesty of Angel Falls

PHOTO COURTESY OF AND © *RTÉ 2006*

My first shower in two days — in the spray of the Angel Falls

The grandeur of the Orinoco Delta at sunset

Above:
There's always work to be done in Vietnam's highland villages

The welcoming committee in Poom Cong village

PHOTO COURTESY OF AND

Above:
Talking to local kids on top of a hill

Three hours carrying her heavy load and this Vietnamese girl is still smiling

Working the paddy fields at the start of the day

Trying to get a breath of fresh air in our salubrious "first-class" train carriage!

scathing remarks about George W. Bush, calling him "an asshole" and "the devil".

The arrivals hall in Caracas airport was packed to bursting point. Every time the double doors opened, spitting out weary travellers, the crowds who jostled for space at the facing railings triggered a Mexican-wave-like effect with their makeshift signs. We were to meet a guy called José, our guide for the next two days. We scanned the scribbled signs to see if any one of them made reference to us. Nothing. Looking lost and slightly confused at an arrivals hall in South America where everybody is touting for business sends out an immediate signal that you are gullible, naïve and a potential meal ticket. People were falling over themselves trying to sell us coach tickets, discount hotel rooms, hire cars, internal flights. One sign read: "No plans? Come with me and I'll show you good time." I couldn't see who was offering this service, but there was no need because, just then, I spotted our man.

Bent down low against the railings, his eyes closed, seemingly unaware of the mayhem all round him, was a man who held a sign at a skewed angle. It simply read: "NO FUN TEARS". I doubled up laughing so much when I saw it that Gerry and Mark thought I was having some sort of episode. This eventually woke José, who tried to pretend he hadn't been sleeping at all. "No fun, just tears. That's us!" said Mark under his breath.

"Ola, Ola!"

Slipping out from under the railing, we were greeted with enthusiastic slaps on the back and bear hugs by our guide, which we failed to return adequately, having just stepped off a seventeen-hour flight from Paris. He was a small round man in his late thirties, with a thick mane of black hair, a toothy smile and a pair of grubby sunglasses perched on the end of his broad nose.

We climbed aboard our small battered mini-van and hadn't even driven out of the loading bay in the airport when José grabbed a microphone from somewhere between his legs, cleared his throat and turned around to face us. Gerry and I were practically sitting on his knee and Mark was in the back seat, already falling asleep.

"Okay, ladies and gentlemen, we have a loooonnnnng journey ahead of us," he boomed into the microphone, then paused and smiled, clearly enjoying the sound of his own voice as it ricocheted around the van through the crackly speakers over our heads. The tired and dishevelled-looking driver gripped the steering wheel more tightly in an effort to conceal the fact that he wanted to kill him and I knew it wouldn't be long before Gerry or Mark wanted to do the same. "Let me say that again – a looooonnnnnnggg journey. Traffic is bad; they have slowed down the speed limit along the highway because the big bridge, the only one into the city, is falling down. Can you believe it?" He scratched his balls and chuckled to himself. Then, singing in a low voice with his lips pressed against the wire head of the microphone, he repeated, "The bridge is falling down, down, down." He looked back at us for a reaction. I forced a smile. Gerry and Mark sat there stony-faced, looking like they were going to pummel him into next week.

I tried to break the tension. "What do you mean the bridge is falling down, José? Is it not dangerous?"

"Maybe, but don't worry, it has been falling for a long time. They have been trying to fix it but nothing is working.

There is one old road through the mountains, but this is very bad so nobody uses it."

I wondered how bad the old road could be if 50,000 motorists were willing to risk their lives every day travelling over a 220-foot-high bridge that was falling down? And this was not just any bridge. My bridge fetish meant that I had read about the Viaduct 1, which opened in 1953 as part of the La Guaria highway, linking Caracas to the coast. It is a beautiful bridge, with one huge single arch, flanked on both sides by its supporting columns. Designed by French engineer Eugène Freyssinet and built of ninety-seven per cent concrete and three per cent steel, the 820-foot span was then the longest pre-stressed concrete bridge in the world. At the time it was regarded as the biggest engineering feat in Latin America since the Panama Canal. But obviously something had changed since 1953.

Traffic was slow as we approached the bridge. José was still prattling on, this time telling us that three years earlier he had worked with a BBC crew. "Yes, they were great days. They liked me a lot. I am going to visit them but I am so busy that maybe they will have to come over here if they want to see me!" I wasn't sure whether I was more nervous for my own safety crossing over a 220-foot-high bridge that was falling down or that José might meet an untimely demise at the hands of Gerry, who just couldn't take anymore.

"José, my crew and I have just flown seventeen hours from Europe," he growled. "I'm very sorry, but we do not need to be guided today. We just want to get to our hotel and sleep and we can all talk tomorrow when we are rested. We certainly do not need to listen to you on a microphone, especially in a fucking minibus. We are not on a forty-seater coach."

I thought I could detect a snigger from the driver in the front but other than that, utter silence. Like the cars in front and behind us, we snaked slowly across the bridge, sneaking looks down to the valley floor beneath us. Nobody uttered a word until we reached the other side. Looking back, it was quite easy to see where the road was raised considerably and buckling in the middle under pressure.

Exactly seven months after that day we crossed, the bridge was officially closed. Two months after that, on 19 March 2006, the whole structure came crashing down, leaving the city isolated from its port and airport, and leaving thousands of people without access to their jobs in Caracas. It has since been rebuilt and reopened. I remember at the time having a horrible dream one night, in which the bridge buckled and our little white van went plummeting into the canyon below, with José singing "It's a Long, Long Way to Tipperary" into his microphone.

It wasn't just the bridge or José and Gerry's tiff that made the drive into Caracas so memorable. The city is built in a low valley, 1,000 metres above sea level, surrounded by the Avila mountains. As we approached I could see huge barrios or shanty towns clinging precariously to all sides of the mountains, left and right of us, enveloping the lower slopes like ragged blankets. Houses were built on top of each other out of what looked like bits of scrap metal, salvaged bricks and concrete. The higgledy-piggledy do-it-yourself mountain settlements looked like they could topple over with the slightest gust of wind. In the past fifty years, the population of Caracas has grown from 200,000 to over 11 million people and it was clear to see that the poorest of those had literally been pushed to the edge of society.

Towards the flatter city centre, the disparity between rich and poor became even clearer. A confusion of highways, ugly skyscrapers, gleaming tower blocks and shopping centres built in the 1970s are the result of rash urbanisation, when the discovery of oil made Venezuela an extremely wealthy country. As far as I could see, back then there was no such thing as a need for town planning, just a need to modernise. Leaning against these glass structures and piled up under concrete flyovers, smaller barrios had sprung up. I thought to myself how, in other countries, including Ireland, poverty is hidden behind doors and windows and restricted to certain areas. If it was exposed like this, all around us as we went to get our skinny lattes in the morning on our way to work, would we resolve to do something about it? Here, you can't ignore it; it's everywhere, it cannot be brushed under the carpet, because there is no carpet to brush it under.

When we eventually reached the Hilton Hotel, the lobby was thronged with young people carrying banners with messages like "No Imperialism" and "Don't Bow to America". To the side of the reception desk, a huge stand informed us that we had arrived just in time for the Sixteenth World Youth Festival. As it turned out, so had 20,000 other young foreigners from more than 100 countries across the globe. While they were there for "peace and solidarity", all I wanted was peace and quiet and to try to get some sleep. The entire hotel was booked out and the only rooms they had left were at the back of the building on the first floor, looking directly out to where the bands and street processions were warming up for the week-long festival. From my window I looked out at the activists and thought about why I didn't have stronger political leanings. These people were obviously advocates of Hugo Chavez, the democratically elected leftist leader of the country since 1998. Chavez calls himself an anti-globalist, whereas some people, namely the Americans, call him anti-

American. He is both loved as a hero of his own people and despised by those who feel the country's oil wealth has not been distributed to those who need it.

I drifted off to sleep to the sound of whistles, firecrackers, beating drums and blaring megaphones.

José came to collect us in the lobby the following morning and Gerry apologised for his humour the day before. "No worries, I had another crew out here two weeks ago and they were much more grumpy than you lot. Let's go and I show you my Venezuela."

With a few hours' sleep under our belts and with no microphone ringing in our ears, José was much more tolerable. Back in the van, we exited the hotel, straight onto a highway and into a tunnel where we sat in traffic for half an hour, nearly poisoned by the gas fumes. "Because petrol is so cheap here, nobody uses public transport," José explained.

We finally made it to the Mount Avila Cable Car and the view from the top was incredible, confounding everything I had felt about this city. It seemed to be one big mess.

The sun had burned the morning clouds and from up here, the scale of the city's barrios really became apparent. I had been to Rochina in Rio de Janeiro, Brazil's largest favela, but the difference here is that the sprawl across the low valley seemed endless. José Felix Ribas is one of the largest barrios in Latin America, with a population of 120,000 living on 237 acres. José told us that his uncle lived there in a one-bedroom house with his wife and six children. The previous day, he and his neighbours had been laying new footpaths and sewers in the alleyways between their houses with grant money from the government. "He loves living there and would not like to move out. It is where he grew up and where he wants his children to grow up. They have good doctors in the barrios, free of charge, mostly from Cuba. Castro sends them over and, to say thanks, Chavez sends back cheap oil."

Later that afternoon we headed downtown and began our sightseeing tour at Plaza Bolívar. Tourists are warned to be mindful of their cameras when wandering around the city, so Mark, with €50,000 worth of filming gear, was an obvious target. To be honest, he would rather have myself and Gerry held hostage than part with it, so we thought the best plan was to be accompanied by an armed guard. Though I can't remember his name, he was the smiliest man with a machine gun I had ever met. Disconcertingly, he looked remarkably like José and it was obvious by their easy manner and sharing of cigarettes that this was not the first time they had met! Either way, he had a gun and was quite happy to pose for our crew photos, so he was a welcome addition to our group.

I had travelled quite extensively in South America and so I knew a little about the revolutionary figure of Simón Bolívar. Born in Caracas, he was responsible for giving not just Venezuela her freedom but also Panama, Colombia, Ecuador, Peru and Bolivia. I had no idea how much he was revered in Venezuela, but it soon sinks in when you realise that he is on every bank note and that most streets seem to have been named after him. In fact, Hugo Chavez's 1999 constitution changed the name of the country to the Bolivarian Republic of Venezuela. Bolívar sits right in the middle of the square on top of his rearing horse, looking every bit as heroic as a revolutionary leader should. What a way for your greatness to be remembered, cast in bronze to last more than 100 lifetimes! I thought of Oscar Wilde reclining in St Stephens Green, a bronzed Patrick Kavanagh sitting in the sun along the banks of the canal and

Phil Lynott standing proud near Grafton Street. Over coffee in the main square, Mark decided he would like to be cast and placed outside Lonnegan's pub in Stillorgan, smoking an eternal fag; Gerry, in his own garden with his entire guitar collection (so it would look like he could play) and me overlooking the beach in Wexford, with an open umbrella so the seagulls couldn't crap on my head.

The city's historical centre covers about ten blocks. Strolling through old Caracas is safe enough and, although I had prepared myself to be harangued and harassed, we had quite a pleasant afternoon. Maybe it was because we didn't spend long enough getting under the skin of the city but, to be honest, there was very little about Caracas that I liked. It certainly wouldn't be high on my list of return visits.

The following day, we said goodbye to José (whose Christmas card list we would probably not be on) and flew east to Puerto Ordaz, where we were picked up and transferred to Tucupita. This is one of the main access points to Venezuela's famous Orinoco Delta. There on the banks of the mighty Orinoco River a motorised canoe was waiting for us. Our driver, Antonio, a local Warao Indian, helped us to load up our bags and as soon as we had everything on board we shot off downriver in search of the Orinoco Delta Lodge. And believe me, if you are not a local, it would be nearly impossible to find.

The Orinoco Delta itself is a labyrinth of waterways, canals and channels which spread out from the main river to cover a 41,000-square-kilometre area of jungle before converging again into thirty-seven different channels, which then flow out into the Atlantic Ocean. The first Europeans had sailed up these channels when they arrived in Venezuela.

Seeing the traditional stilt houses of the native Warao Indians along the banks, they had been reminded of a "Little Venice", the Spanish being Venezuela, which is how Venezuela got its name.

We bounced up the wide stretch of river, holding on tightly to the wooden benches in an effort to stop our rear ends slamming against the hard seats. About twenty minutes later, we turned off into a smaller channel. Here we couldn't travel so fast as we had to navigate our way around huge floating clumps of green water hyacinth. The wind had begun to pick up and, although it was still warm, the air felt heavy with rain. Antonio manoeuvred the boat so that the nose was pointing directly at a collection of stooped bamboo fronds on the far bank. "This is a good shortcut. Cover your faces." Before we knew what was happening, Antonio revved the engine and headed directly toward the bank. *Jesus wept,* I thought to myself, *he's trying to kill us.* I gripped the side of the boat, put my head between my legs like they tell you to do on a plane and waited for us to crash into the muddy bank. Long branches and leaves scratched off my back. I gritted my teeth. Then, all of a sudden, silence.

I opened my eyes, looked up and realised that we had entered a dark hidden lagoon. The jumble of gnarled trees on both sides met in the middle, blocking out the natural light of the sun. The water all around us was black and the whole place felt eerie. This was the stuff of real adventure and felt a million miles away from Caracas, the Hilton and José's microphone. We were heading into unknown territory, miles from anywhere and with no real clue what we were going to find.

Antonio raised the engine out of the water and we poled deeper into the lagoon. "Look around, everywhere we are being watched." I kept scanning the trees, expecting to see a Predator-like creature waiting to pounce. At first I could see nothing as my eyes darted around. Then, guided by Antonio's finger, I saw six sets of eyes and three snouts floating on the water about five metres away from the boat. "Cayman," he whispered. "Like alligator, but smaller head." The eyes were motionless, like floating glass marbles, and it was only the gentle flaring of the nostrils, which created small rings in the water, that gave them away.

Suddenly there was a splashing sound in the water right below the boat. I jumped out of my skin.

"Fish?" I enquired hopefully.

"Yes. Piranha," he replied as if that was okay. "We will fish them tomorrow."

Gerry and Mark were in their element and started shuffling around, trying to unpack the gear to get the camera out. "Will you stop rocking the boat?" I whispered angrily. "Did you not hear the man?"

I have a wonderful ability when I'm afraid to visualise the worst possible scenario that could happen – in this case, a huge scaly creature swinging Tarzan-like across the trees, pouncing on our boat and ripping out our oesophagi one by one before feeding our still-beating hearts to the frenzy of piranhas.

The lads started giggling and turned the camera on me. In a whispered David Attenborough impression, Mark began, "And here we have an unusual rare species with a big scared head . . ."

The sounds of the jungle at such close quarters were intensified. The constant underlay of buzzing, croaking and clicking was pierced every now and then by the shrill cry of a howler monkey crossing a branch over our heads or the squawk of a macaw hidden in the trees. We saw turtles in pairs sitting motionless on fallen soggy trunks, iguanas scurrying through the rotting leaves along the bank. Then Antonio himself frightened the life out of me. "Look, look, look! See, on the ground over there!" I grabbed Gerry's arm and dug my nails into it, while all the time scanning for what I knew would frighten the life out of me. Then I saw it: huge and writhing, wrapped around a long branch, was the biggest snake I had ever seen in my life. Hardly surprising, really, considering it was an anaconda, the largest snake in the world. "They can eat humans," went on Antonio. "Many Warao children have been killed. That is why they sleep on stilts." Its head was bigger than my two hands put together.

We eventually came to a little clearing where Antonio lowered the engine and we were back out into daylight again. It was raining heavily now, monsoon rain where the heavy drops pounded off our heads. Finally, we arrived at the lodge just as the sun was about to set. Built in the same style as the Warao houses we'd seen on our journey, the lodge with its vaulted thatched roof opened out onto the river. It was certainly the most remote tourist lodge I had ever stayed in. We unloaded our bags and stepped up off the jetty into the huge open bar and lounge. Big wicker tables and chairs were scattered around among the dining area and cases of books, posters, maps and photographs lined the bamboo walls. Small colourful birds flew in and out, sometimes pausing to rest on the furniture. A small business centre had been set up in a cage in the corner of the room where you could send and receive your emails in the middle of nowhere. It still never ceases to amaze me how technology has spread and functions in some of the most way-out places on the planet. We checked in and got the keys for our huts. "Get dry and long clothes on, before the mosquitoes come," Antonio warned us.

Still soaked to the skin, we wandered down a springy boardwalk to our cabins, each one accessed by its own separate gangplank. The huts were open on all sides but had mesh screens to keep the mozzies and everything else out. Generally I'm not too bad with critters except toads and frogs but after today, my skin was crawling and I felt jittery. I jumped under a cold shower, screened by a bamboo wall, and tried to wash the creepy-crawly feeling off my skin. I got dressed and now that I was dry I was feeling better. I doused myself in 100 per cent DEET and, wearing long sleeves, I walked back up the boardwalk to meet the lads at the bar.

The sun was just disappearing for the day, colouring everything with a tinge of red as it went. By now, the walkway was lit up with oil torches and through the foliage, as I walked along, I caught glimpses of the glowing, silent river in the sunset. The air was heavy with humidity and a sense of satisfaction from the day and at that moment, the whole environment became very romantic. That feeling didn't last long. When I got to the bar, Gerry and Mark had their camera out, taking a picture of a giant tarantula crawling up the barman's arm. "C'mon, Kaks, come and have your photo taken. He's grand." They assured me that he had become a pet after living for years in the eaves over the bar – I kid you not.

Sitting up on a stool with a cold beer, at the other end of the bar from the poisonous resident and his new friends, I took in the peaceful surroundings. I thought I could feel myself getting bitten through my clothes but just put it down to paranoia at the few mozzies who were circling me. Every inch of me was clothed except my face, neck and hands. But then I looked toward the guys, where I could make out clouds of mosquitoes who were attaching themselves to the backs of their shirts. I began to itch, just at around the same time that Gerry and Mark did. Neither the strongest repellent on the market nor layers of fabric were stopping these guys. The barman told us to go back to our rooms and wait until it was dark before we came back out to have dinner, which is exactly what we did. We all emerged an hour later like lambs to the slaughter. But while the mozzies had subsided, we realised we had left it too late. I had never been anywhere that, even with the repellent on, I had been bitten through my clothes. I couldn't believe it.

After a lovely meal, albeit itchy, we decided to have an early night. We walked back to our huts by torchlight and, as I scrambled around in the dark, shining my torch into my rucksack, a loud croak behind me made me scream at a decibel level to rival a banshee. Swinging around, in the light of my torch I saw a massive, slimy, warty toad sitting on the floor of my hut. I mentioned elsewhere that I have a fear of two things – toads and fish. Actually, I'm not that keen on birds either. I dropped everything, jumped over the toad and ran out, still screaming. Not only Gerry and Mark had come running out with the disturbance; the entire population of Venezuela seemed to have gathered outside my room to witness the atrocities that could warrant my terrified reaction. "It's a giant toad," I gasped, almost hyperventilating. One of the local girls who worked in the kitchen and couldn't have been more than fifteen, grabbed one of the oil lamps and sauntered into my hut. She emerged two minutes later, triumphantly holding the gloopy, unshapely, croaking flesh of mammoth toad and informed us she would bring it to her family, who would be delighted to eat it. Twenty minutes later, having done a thorough check for any more lurking amphibians, which I was sure now were all out to get me, I crawled my crawly skin into bed and scratched myself to sleep. Believe it or not, when I eventually drifted off, I slept like a baby.

The following morning, I surveyed the damage. Calling out to Mark and Gerry from my bed, I told them I counted seventy-nine bites on my body. My shoulders, back, legs and bum were destroyed. Mark and Gerry weren't too far behind me.

After breakfast, we helped Antonio load up two bags of flour and some filtered water that he was delivering to a Warao settlement downriver and accompanied him on his journey. It is estimated that the Warao have lived in the delta for around 12,000 years. "Warao" literally means "people of the canoes" and Antonio explained that the children are able to swim and paddle almost as soon as they can walk. "My people believe that a long time ago we lived in the sky with the birds. One day, one of my ancestors shot a bird so hard that the arrow broke the ground of the sky and created a hole. He looked through the hole and saw the earth with all its animals below. He attached a long rope to a tree and lowered himself down, followed by everyone else, who abandoned the sky world to settle on earth."

I spotted a tiny dugout canoe, less than two metres in length, being paddled in the shadows of the trees that leaned heavily out into the river bank. The child was no more than five and he looked at us warily under a thick fringe of black hair as we approached him. He had heard us coming and had been sent out by his family to see who we were. Then he recognised Antonio and seemed to relax. They spoke a few words in his native dialect and the child then seemed happy enough to paddle along beside us toward his family settlement.

Their family homes consisted of three huts on stilts connected to one central hut by a long walkway. There were no walls, just a thatched roof. The most outgoing and gregarious of the locals was a black hairy pig who snorted and squealed with delight at his new visitors as we stepped out of the boat with the supplies. The Warao are an intensely shy race of people and some say this is because of attacks from Caribbean cannibals in days gone by. There were about six threadbare hammocks hanging beside each other out of the roof. Three babies lay asleep in one and it looked like two grandmothers had claimed two of the others. The rest of the village sat in groups on the floor of the hut and so we sat with them. Antonio told them a little bit about us and they seemed perfectly content to sit with us in silence, none of them in the least bit concerned with having to make conversation with us, even through translation. Antonio told us that, before they had access to flour, they ate (and still do) the worms of the moriche palm trees and drink the fruit of the tremiche tree.

The women are renowned for their basket-weaving skills, the proof of which I could see hanging from the corner posts of the hut. I thought about some of the indigenous people I had met on my travels, where, when you enter a community, sometimes it feel like you are intruding and you have to gauge the situation to assure you won't cause any offence. Today, though, in the remoteness of the swampy delta settlement, these people in their silence made me feel at home. A newborn baby, whose remaining piece of umbilical cord was still shrivelled in his bellybutton, was passed to me by his fifteen-year-old mother for me to hold. He must have judged me to be an outsider because, just at that moment, with his eyes closed, he peed a golden arch all over my arm, much to the amusement of his village family.

We said our goodbyes and set off downriver again. It wasn't long before the monsoon rains came thundering down on top of us and we pulled in to try to get some cover under a big tree. While we waited, Antonio baited two homemade fishing lines with raw meat he produced from a plastic bag in his pocket. Handing one to me, he showed me how to toss the line gently into the water, bouncing it slightly, to attract the piranha. This is one of the defining moments of my travels. Standing up in a small boat, rain thundering in my ears, fishing for a tiny creature that feasts on human flesh. I caught nothing, but after five minutes, Antonio's line went tight and he pulled out a small silvery fish, about the size of an outstretched palm. In Antonio's grip, it looked completely innocent until it opened its mouth to reveal a set of razor-sharp teeth. Plucking a leaf from over his head, Antonio put it in front of the fish. It bit down on the leaf angrily, leaving a perfectly formed cut-out.

That afternoon as we journeyed through more of the delta, we saw hummingbirds, colourful toucans and watery pink delta dolphins, which were playfully swimming in the river. After just two days, travelling and living on the water began to feel surprisingly normal. Roads don't exist out here, nor are they needed by the water people of a water world.

The following day, after a smooth river ride, we made it back to Puerto Ordaz where, across town, a small eight-seater plane was waiting to take us to Canaima. This is the jumping-off point for Angel Falls and would mark the beginning of the next part of our adventure. The only other passengers on board were a honeymoon couple from Canada and a cargo of frozen chickens taking up the two front seats. While we were belting ourselves in, I could tell that the new bride was extremely nervous. Neither of them had ever been on a small propeller plane before. I reassured her, as we sputtered down the runway, that she would be absolutely fine and that these planes were as safe as any other. As soon as we were airborne, the pilot, wearing black leather fingerless gloves and oversized sunglasses, pulled his mobile phone out of the top pocket of his shirt and held it up to check if he could still get a signal. Leaving it on the dashboard, he put the plane into autopilot, spread out a newspaper in front of him and began to read the sports pages. The girl's mouth dropped open in absolute horror and she turned around to us for reassurance. We all smiled and said that it was normal while inwardly I was praying that at the very least my remains be found so I could be scattered out over Kenmare Bay. While I prayed for the duration of the flight, she vomited. But the noise from the propeller was so loud that I couldn't hear her retching, which, I suppose, was at least something. Finally, we touched down at a small airstrip in the Canaima National Park. It was only a short drive to Orchid Lodge, where we were to spend one night before travelling through "the lost world" in search of Angel Falls.

There was a fax from José to say that the permits he had organised were not the correct ones for the days we were supposed to be there and to call him as soon as we could. It turned out that there was something wrong with the application form and to process it again would take three days, by which stage we would be on our way home. The trip to Angel Falls was the whole reason we had come to Venezuela and we wouldn't have a story if we couldn't shoot this part of the journey. Gerry was raging. José felt the best thing to do was to keep Mark's camera hidden in a rucksack for the short jeep drive through the park in the morning, where there was a heavy guard presence. Once we were on the water with our guide Tony, who knew our predicament, he assured us that the area is so big, we would more than likely not have an issue.

So the following morning, with Mark's camera hidden in his rucksack on his back and Gerry and I carrying a small waterproof bag each for our overnight trip, we jumped into the back of a pick-up truck with Tony and headed down a dusty overgrown track for the river. Five minutes later, a jeep drove past with two armed guards in it. They stopped us and got out to talk to the driver and to Tony, who told them he was guiding us to the Falls. They asked us to empty our bags and I knew we were in trouble. As my toothbrush, togs and clean t-shirt spilled onto the grass, I dreaded the sound of Mark's rucksack being opened, revealing the contents. As soon as they saw the camera, they asked to see our permit, which we handed over, pretending nothing. "This is not a permit for filming today. This was for last week." He ordered us back to the police station at the airstrip, where the camera was taken off us. We explained to them that we had been given the wrong permit, that we were here making a television programme to promote tourism in Venezuela. The six guards disappeared into another room and after a fifteen-minute deliberation came back with an offer. "You can take small video camera and make television with that but you cannot take this," he said, holding up Mark's camera. "You want to use this, you have to pay us $5,000 American dollars in cash."

The whole thing was turning out to be an absolute nightmare. We didn't have the money and even if we did, Tony assured us it would not get into the right hands. Gerry decided the only thing we could do was to shoot on his small Sony video camera, which he had luckily packed for his own personal use. Mark had kept one radio microphone which they hadn't confiscated, and that would have to be the sum total of our filming equipment. The guards assured Mark that they would look after his equipment until we returned the following day. He didn't trust them, but there was nothing he could do. He watched them lock it in a safe and got them to sign an agreement of return.

We couldn't wait any longer if we wanted to make base camp before dark. With nothing but a few essentials and our entire filming kit inside Mark's bum-bag, we jumped on board our canoe, with its forty-eight-horsepower engine hanging off the back, and took off down the Rio Carrao. We motored flat-out for about an hour until we reached the Mayupa lagoon and then, shortly after that, the bubbling white froth of the Arautaima rapids came into view. Tony manoeuvred the boat through them as best he could and Mark even managed to film and keep the camera dry, even though we were all soaked and there was about three inches of water in the bottom of the boat. Eventually, we had to pull in and walk twenty minutes overland while Tony took the boat through the more treacherous rapids on his own. We lost sight of him a couple of times in an effort to keep up with him. We finally made it to the Churn River, a much narrower channel with huge boulders and more rapids, and entered the incredible Devil's Canyon.

Arthur Conan Doyle wrote a novel called *The Lost World* in 1912, where he described a forgotten prehistoric world, left isolated and unchanged for millions of years, where strange plants grew and dinosaurs roamed. Although he had never been to South America, he created this world in his mind after hearing descriptions of Gran Sabana in Venezuela. I had never read the book and really wasn't prepared for what I saw.

Towering above us, standing side by side, were enormous flat-topped mountains, which the Pemon Indians called tepuis. These giant singular mountains used to be one large plateau, before erosion carved out crevices creating rugged walls, turning them into massive biological islands, some measuring over 6,000 metres in height. The tepuis are made up of 1.8 billion-year-old blocks of sandstone that predate the drifting apart of South America and Africa. I was totally blown away, realising that hidden deep within the Gran Sabana Valley, landscape as wonderful as this existed, unknown to the outside world for such a long time. Water cascaded over the top of some and disappeared, only to re-emerge from a hole in the rock halfway down. Trees and plants grew haphazardly at various points along the rugged walls, like some sort of supernatural oasis that didn't need the ground or its soil to let them grow. Standing there defiantly, these huge monuments seemed even more vast in contrast to the wide flat river and plains at their base. It was one of the most beautiful places I had ever been. As it is one of the most thinly populated places on the entire South American continent and because it had been such an adventure for us to get here, it truly felt like a lost world.

And then I saw it: my first glimpse of Auyan-tepui, from which plummeted the mighty Angel Falls. It was so beautiful and I wanted to get closer immediately, to really appreciate the sense of scale. We were so near, yet so far. Because of our delay earlier in the day, we had to put our hike off until the following morning and head straight for base camp. Just at that moment, the battery in the camera died and we all just prayed that there was a power supply where we could charge it up.

There were already nine other canoes tied up at the base camp's small jetty and, just as we were arriving, everybody else was returning from the viewing point of the falls, talking excitedly and flicking through photos. "Amazing", "incredible", "exhilarating" was all I could hear and I could barely contain myself until the following morning.

A couple of the boat drivers were preparing dinner. About forty chickens, skewered onto long poles, were sticking out of the ground at a forty-five-degree angle, leaning in over big crackling fires. A huge pot of rice was also on the boil and, having not eaten properly all day, we sat around a huge table with everybody else and tucked in. There were tourists from Japan, Australia, Sweden and the US, most of whom were travelling around South America. Without question, this had been the highlight of everybody's trip so far.

There was one generator and Mark explained that he needed to charge his batteries.

"Join the queue, mate," piped up an Aussie voice with a mouthful of chicken.

"No, but you don't understand, you see we are a television crew from Ireland. We are working here."

"You are a television crew and that is your equipment?" the Japanese man said, pointing down at our handy-cam, which, having been bounced around all day, was held together with the gammy bandage from Mark's leg. Beside it was a miniscule tripod for a stills camera, which measured exactly four inches in length. "Haw haw, that even tiny for Japanese crew," he chuckled, clearly delighted at his humour. I swooped in to defend Mark. "Well, I have this, so they can hear me." I pulled out the radio microphone, which was clipped inside my t-shirt and only at that moment remembered that we had gaffer-taped it inside a condom to protect it from getting wet in the river. So while I sat there holding a limp condom in my hand, nobody seemed to want to question us anymore and they let us charge our batteries.

That night we all retired to bed. Sleeping quarters were two rows of hammocks strung up under a thatched roof. We resembled carcasses slung from hooks behind a butcher's counter. They were the type of hammock where, if you moved too quickly, you ended up in a tangled heap on the ground. Eventually, when we were all comfortable, Tony, who was two feet away from me, whispered, "You know what . . . it's probably better that we don't get there until tomorrow. These guys will be leaving, other tourists won't have arrived and we will have Angel Falls all to ourselves."

He was right. The following morning, everybody rose at six and after a rough-and-ready breakfast of tea in a tin cup with a piece of bread and butter, we left Isla Raton camp and set off through the jungle while everybody else decamped and prepared to travel back upstream. At first, the walk through the jungle was fairly flat terrain. Exquisite colourful butterflies danced in the leaves above our heads. Poor Mark – every time he went to point the camera at them, they disappeared. We would stand still for about ten minutes and when he finally had one framed up, it would fly away.

It is fortunate that the falls were found by and named after an American bush pilot called Jimmy Angel. Imagine if it had been Jimmy Smith or Jimmy Bloggs. But no, it was found by a man with the best name on the planet! Of course, the local Indians had known for thousands of years that it was there and it is thought the first white man to ever see it was an Ernesto Sanchez La Cruz. But it was Jimmy Angel who brought the falls to the attention of the world. The story goes that he met a gold prospector named McCracken in a bar in Panama and, after a few pints, Jimmy agreed to fly them to the top of a mountain where there was a river rumoured to have a gold ore bed. They reached Canaima and landed on one of the tepuis, where they found what they were looking for, riverbeds of gold ore. Having filled up the plane, they took off in bad conditions and couldn't return. McCracken died shortly afterwards and Jimmy spent the next thirty-three years trying to find the exact spot again. In 1933, on one of these searches, he discovered the falls that now bear his name. He returned again in 1937 with his wife, Marie, his friend Gustavo Heny and Heny's gardener. Their plane crash-landed in the marshy ground on top of Auyan-tepui and although they all walked away alive, it took them eleven days to walk down the mountain to the valley floor and back to civilisation. His plane sat at the top of the mountain island for another thirty-three years before it was lifted off by helicopter.

As we climbed higher into the jungle, hidden under the canopy of trees, I was surprised that I couldn't hear the thunderous sound of the falls, but Tony explained that because it is so high it doesn't have the roar that you would expect. The farther we climbed, the wetter and slippier the rocks became due to the mist from the falls. My hiking boots weren't gripping the damp rocks and three times I fell hard on my knees, both of which were swollen and trickling blood. Gerry needed me to deliver my pieces to camera at very specific points, as the camera wasn't good enough unless we were in the right light. This proved tiring for everybody, especially knowing we had professional equipment locked in a safe, which should be capturing this revelation. I tried to keep my spirits up but I was getting frustrated.

Eventually we made it to the top of the climb. I purposely didn't look up until I made it right out onto Laime's viewpoint. I steadied myself, holding onto a rock, and looked up.

And there she was; the white angel. Cascading down a canyon, etched out over millions of years, sheets of water pouring from the heavens. From where I was standing, looking up, the view reminded me of the gothic façade of an otherworldly cathedral. On either side of the waterfall, the vertical rock protruded slightly, creating a sort of heart-shaped mountain. In some places, by the time the falls had reached halfway, the water evaporated and had turned to mist. In other places, the water gushed down the steep straight mountain-side, dancing off the rocks into the lagoon below. It was beautiful and powerful and demanded my full attention as it roared loudly and sprayed me in the face as I admired its beauty. Standing there, I felt like our little group were the only people in the world to have seen it, that we had made this incredible discovery. I drank it all in and it seemed right that our Venezuelan journey of discovery culminated here. I was tired, damp, stiff and sore after our last few days in the Orinoco Delta and the jungles of Canaima. But I took a moment and smiled. Admiring the eighth natural wonder of the world, I decided that sometimes amazing places should not be easy to get to.

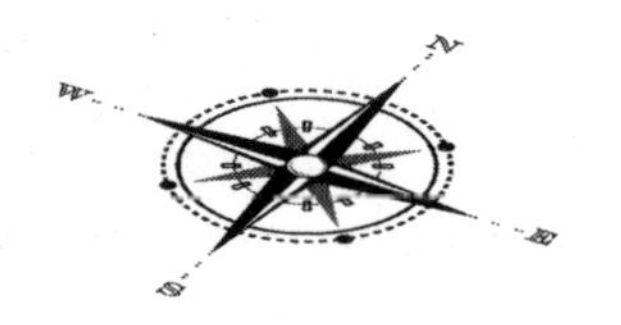

Venezuela Fast Facts

Population: 27 million approx.

Capital City: Caracas.

Official Name: Venezuela's Constitutional Assembly approved a name change for the country in 1999, to the Bolívarian Republic of Venezuela.

Languages: Spanish (official), numerous indigenous dialects.

Size: 912,050 square kilometres. Venezuela borders Guyana to the east, Brazil to the south, and Colombia to the west.

Climate: Venezuela's dry season is from late November to early May, with a wet season for the rest of the year, with rainfall peaking around October. The mountains can be quite cooler at any time of the year. Average temperatures are 24°C to 27°C.

Best time to go: The best time to visit Venezuela depends on your possible itinerary. The tourist season runs year-round, with the dry season certainly more pleasant for travelling, hiking and outdoor activities. Bear in mind that some tourist attractions in Venezuela like waterfalls are more impressive in the wet season, and may even be inaccessible by boat in the dry season.

Time Difference: –4 hours from Ireland.

Where I went: Caracas, Canaima National Park, Angel Falls, the Orinoco Delta.

Who to go with: Beacon South America, Trailfinders

Visa Requirements: Irish passport holders do not need a visa to travel to Venezuela as tourists for up to ninety days, *if entering and leaving the country by air*. A Tourist Entry Card (TEC) is valid for ninety days and is available at no cost from your airline. Contact the Embassy in London for more information.

Currency: The local currency for Venezuela is the Bolívar Fuerte, since January 2008. The US Dollar is also widely accepted in the major cities. ATMs are widely available and credit cards are accepted in most hotels, restaurants and guesthouses.

Tipping: Some restaurants automatically add a ten per cent service charge. If they do not add the service charge, you should tip as you would at home. Similarly, tip the hotel staff as you would at home. As most taxis do not use the meter, it is not customary to tip taxi drivers but it is up to you if you feel the service was good.

Vaccinations Needed: It is recommended that you consult your local Tropical Medical Bureau or GP before travelling to Venezuela for all relevant vaccines. The WHO report malaria transmission in certain parts of the country.

Emergency Numbers: Venezuela has an integrated emergency network similar to ours (fire, police, ambulance). You can call 171 from any pay phone without using a call card, but do not expect the operators to all understand English.

Electricity: Electric current is 110 volts AC (60 cycles). US-style flat-prong plugs are used.

Other Highlights: Venezuela, although a Caribbean country, enjoys a wide variety of climates and landscapes and has something to suit all travellers.

- Caracas: Take a tour of the numerous historical museums.

- Visit the Andean Range: This region offers extraordinary views and picturesque spots which make it a prime area for hiking, trekking and a wide range of adventure sports.

- A visit to Los Llanos: Located on plains below the Andes, with a variety of wildlife visible that is truly phenomenal – anaconda, caiman, capybara, deer and many more. It is also reported as being one of the top spots on the planet for bird-watching.

- Visit the Caribbean Coast: The largest of the islands, Isla de Margarita, is Venezuela's most popular tourist destination, offering wide beaches and an extensive range of water sports and fishing.

Fun Facts

- **The world's largest rodent, the capybara, lives in the grassy plains (llanos) of Venezuela. But recently, the fossil of a giant rodent was found in Venezuela that looked very similar to a guinea pig. It would have been a foot long and roughly 700 kilograms.**
- **The most powerful electric eel is found in the rivers of Venezuela and produces a shock of between 400–650 volts.**
- **The Venezuelan brown bat can detect and dodge individual raindrops in mid-flight, arriving safely back at its cave completely dry.**
- **Venezuela's favorite sport is baseball.**

Useful Contacts:

- Venezuelan Embassy, London: www.venezlon.co.uk – this website also has an extensive section on tourist information.
- *No Frontiers*, where you can watch my journey to Venezuela: www.rte.ie/nofrontiers (Archive Section)
- Tropical Medical Bureau: www.tmb.ie

Vietnam

Strangely, one of the most exhilarating and adrenalin-fuelled afternoons I've ever had was walking around the Vietnamese capital of Hanoi. The simple act of putting one foot in front of the other, attempting to cross the road, is an adventure sport in itself.

The narrow streets are thronged with bicycles, rickshaws, cyclos, cars, taxis and mopeds, all moving in the one direction. A sea of curious faces coming towards you, camouflaged behind black sunglasses and white cotton facemasks. Moving carts with piles of shoes, rolls of cloth, flowers and leafy vegetables, so high as to defy the laws of gravity. Women weave in and out of the traffic balancing long sticks on their shoulders laden down with suspended bowls of produce. Whole families of four and five people balance on one motorbike like a circus act.

Here, the green cross code does not exist and looking "left and right and left again" before you step out will almost certainly mean you will be stuck on the side of the road for your entire holiday. You just take a deep breath, look straight ahead, close your eyes if you have to and plunge into the oncoming traffic. As if by magic, the traffic parts and you just become another obstacle that they have to avoid. The noise buzzing around you is deafening – horns beeping, radios blaring, phones ringing, people shouting. As you walk, the space you created is quickly swallowed up behind you. When you eventually reach the other side, you breathe a sigh of relief, look back over your shoulder and have the urge to do it all over again. Well, I did anyway and that was how I spent my first few hours in Vietnam.

It is one of the few countries in the world that everybody knows of, yet knows nothing about – except, of course, for one thing. The Vietnam War, the Conflict or the American War, as it is called by the Vietnamese, put this country on the world map, for all the wrong reasons. Although now firmly on the backpacker trail, the country and its tourism industry has struggled to shake the stigma of its recent history. I got a phone call one day from a friend of mine in Carlow who was thinking about a holiday in Vietnam. Her husband's company had offered to take them there on a golfing trip, but she was so frightened she genuinely didn't want to go. The image and perception that she had in her head of Vietnam was not where she wanted to spend the two weeks she had off work. She knew I had been there and had even seen the piece on *No Frontiers* but had convinced herself that what we had shown was only one side of the story. Was there something we were not telling her? Were we just showing a part of the country that had smiling children, bustling streets and beautiful landscapes? How could the fallout of such a recent war, ending only in 1975, a war which saw such unspeakable atrocities and tragedy, still not be felt, up and down, North and South of this country?

To be honest, before I got there, I had wondered this myself. Although now a peaceful country, would it not be etched on the faces and felt in the hearts of the nation who had been witnesses to such horror? I had travelled to countries that had, as recently as Vietnam, suffered the ravages of war – places like Cambodia, Croatia and parts of Africa that are stable now and I found that overall, the attitude of the population is a desire and a need to look forward and not back, in order to move on.

I will never forget having a conversation with a man outside the temple of Angkor Wat in Cambodia. As I sat in the sun, slurping on a Coke, wondering why it never tasted the same through a straw, he sidled up to me on his knuckles, the two butchered stumps of his legs sticking out from a rag that covered his modesty. My initial thought was that he was going to harass me by begging, hoping I would take pity on him. Instinctively I drew my backpack closer to me while at the same time rummaging in my pocket for some small notes.

"Have you got a lighter?" he asked.

"No, sorry, I'm afraid I don't." I smiled, trying not to wince at his crudely amputated stumps.

"Ah, you are Irish! Are you enjoying your holiday?" I couldn't believe he had deciphered my accent so quickly. His name was Munney. He was twenty-seven and both his legs had been blasted off when he had walked on an unexploded landmine. He had been orphaned at the age of ten when both his parents were killed by the Khmer Rouge. After he spoke a little about himself we sat in silence for a moment. "But I know you have also had a difficult history in your country. You have seen terrible suffering. It is great that you now have the ceasefire and there are no more bombs in Belfast. I am happy for you and your country."

I told him I was also happy that I now lived in a peaceful country and that I was proud of that, but that, unlike him, I had only ever witnessed Ireland's troubles on television. I was very fortunate not to have been personally affected as many others had been. Belfast, as far as I was concerned at the time, might as well have been at the other side of the world, I told him, thousands of miles away, if it had not been for television.

He thought for a second. "Yes, but your *country* saw it, you carry it with you in your heart and now you, like me, must look forward to the future." I agreed and after we talked a little longer about everything from Buddhism to Asian pop, we shook hands and I was glad that I felt no pity, only pride for him as he dragged himself down the dusty street.

I was born in 1979, four years after the Americans pulled out of Vietnam, and so I don't remember the television images of the war and of the protests as my parents and their generation do. As Canadian writer Marshall McLuhan famously wrote, "Television brought the brutality of war into the comfort of the living room. Vietnam was lost in the living rooms of America – not on the battlefields of Vietnam."

For my first trip to Vietnam, we would be bringing home television images of a different kind. We would be reporting on the bustling city of Hanoi, finding out how this fast-paced city is moving into the twenty-first century, and hiking along the lesser-known Limestone Track in the Hoa Binh province to meet the people of the highland villages. I had heard so many wonderful accounts of people who had travelled to Vietnam – of the people, the scenery, the food and most of all of a country that now genuinely welcomes foreigners with open arms.

We set off in late November and the crew for this trip was Ingrid, Mark and myself. My Mum had never been to Asia before and so her Christmas present from the whole family was a place on the trip. It turned out to be quite the family affair – my sister Linda and her boyfriend Rob, on the final leg of their round-the-world adventure, were already in Cambodia and planned to meet us in Vietnam when we had finished shooting; and my brother David was also going to fly in to meet us. He was off to work in Australia for two years and made Vietnam his first stop-off. I couldn't believe we had managed to organise an Asian reunion with just a couple of phone calls and emails. Amazing, considering we are usually the family who couldn't organise a get-together if we tried! Ingrid's husband Chris was going to fly out and Mark was going to take a week's holiday with all of us when we'd finished shooting too. So, with bags packed and a mother in tow for the first time, we set off.

Ingrid, Mark, Mum and I arrived into Hanoi at 6.00 a.m., just in time to get stuck in the frenzy of rush-hour traffic. We had taken an overnight flight from Bangkok and were a sorry-looking sight when Dan, our smiling local fixer, met us at the airport. He suggested that, when we got to the hotel, we lie down for the afternoon, as we had a busy day sightseeing ahead of us before heading south on our trek. "We will just walk around tomorrow or take motorbike, no point in driving, always too slow."

When we eventually got to the city centre, although the traffic was intense and the noise of the horns incessant, it felt different to the frenzy of Bangkok and the other Asian capitals I had visited. The small, tight streets of the old quarter had a real sense of intimacy. The lanes were a hive of activity, everyone with a purpose and a job to do – opening stalls and wooden shutters, men and women selling big sticks of French baguettes to passers-by, peddling bikes laden down with huge bunches of flowers, stirring big steaming cauldrons of "pho" or noodle soup on every street corner. But these people with their gentle manner managed to give the whole chaotic scene a sense of calm. All of them were smiling at nobody in particular as they went about their business. I tried to pick out one of Hanoi's 3.5 million inhabitants who was standing still, doing nothing, just shooting the breeze. I failed.

We arrived at the Hong Ngoc Hotel on Cu Long Street. I was sharing a room with Mum and after an hour looking at the ceiling, listening to her snoring contently, I decided I couldn't ignore the excitement of the city below me any longer and I slipped out. In the creaking elevator, an old laminated page with curled-up ends was taped to the wall: "Good massage. Good price. Good time in basement." I wondered if we were staying in a Happy Endings hotel and made a note to self to send Mark down to find out! As I walked across the air-conditioned lobby, I decided there was no way that this hotel, with its dark wood, gold gilt and shiny polished floor would condone any love-you-long-time-hanky-panky in their basement.

A mixture of diesel fumes, spices and hot city smells greeted me as I stepped out onto the footpath. It took about ten minutes observing the locals before I could work up the courage to step out onto the road. After that, I was hooked.

After a couple of hours of playing in the traffic and poking around, I came to the conclusion that Hanoi is an easy city to get your head around. It is divided into three main districts: Hoan Kiem, Ba Dinh and Hai Ba Trung. Hoan Kiem is downtown, centred around the lake and the old quarter, and is where most of the sights and hotels are. This is where you'll spend most of your time. There is no mistaking that the French were here; they occupied from the 1850s to the 1950s. The city's colonial past can be felt everywhere – in the architecture, decorative latticework and ornate window shutters – giving the place quite a grand feel, which I really wasn't expecting. Some of the quieter tree-lined streets were remarkably like suburban Paris.

Wandering around the old quarter, I really felt the history of this thousand-year-old city. Although there are about seventy streets in all, it is known as the area of "thirty-six old streets"; this is probably because there were originally this number of specialised trading areas and these original streets were named after the trade that was carried out on them. The silversmiths all established their business on one street, Hang Boc Street; the silk merchants on another, Hang Gai Street; the bamboo raft-makers had every inch of Hang Be. There was an area for every trader, whether they were in the line of coffins, pickled fish, paper-making, salt, clam worms, bottles or baskets.

What makes it different to the hutongs of Beijing or many other cities' old quarters are the long traditional tube houses. The average dimensions of these houses are just three metres wide but sixty metres long. This was because shops were taxed on the width of their shop fronts, so all storage and living areas were moved to the back. While a lot of the original trade can still be seen, some of these narrow houses have been made into modern cafés and boutiques.

I had heard that clothes-shopping in Hanoi was unbelievable value but what people omitted to tell me was that you had to be under five foot five and weigh less than eight stone. In one shop, I got stuck in a dress, my arms over my head and the material stretched to bursting point. I thought I would have to get it surgically removed as three Vietnamese shop assistants struggled to release me. Finally, they took the scissors to it, smiled sweetly and handed me the bill. I gave what was left of the dress to a woman outside so she could clean her pots with it. After traipsing from shop to shop for an hour, finding nothing that fitted me, I decided to give up and told myself I would not try on anything else until I got to Hoi An, where I could get my clothes tailor-made. My only purchase of the afternoon was a plastic cat with a mechanical waving arm. This certainly could not be classed as retail therapy. Feeling like a giant in a land of petite people, I wandered down towards Hoan Kiem Lake and did what any normal girl with a complex would do: ordered three massive scoops of lime and passion fruit ice-cream and watched the world go by.

Wandering around the northern side of the lake shore, I found a rather upmarket beauty salon and went inside to see if I could get a facial. I knew I would be roughing it for the next few days and decided to treat myself before setting off. Inside, the salon was serene and calm and a welcome break from my morning of "extreme road crossing" and "death-by-embarrassment clothes shopping". Three ladies behind a bamboo counter beamed up at me. "Hello, lady, what you like? We do nails! You want man-cure, ped-cure. We do very good massage, strong hands." They all waved them at me to prove her point. I smiled. They giggled and then I giggled. "Anything you wan', no problem."

"I would love a facial."

"Very good, I aw-so gi' you Brazilian ha' pri'. No pai'. No pai'. Me very good. No crying."

"Em, no a facial will be just fine, thank you."

"Okay, Okay. Come this way."

She led me into a beautiful room, with soft towels, scented candles and piped music emanating from the ceiling. I could have been in any upmarket beauty salon in Dublin. "Take everything off, I give you massage, then facial." So I followed orders and, lying face down, I received the most wonderful back massage.

By the time I got back to the hotel that evening, the guys were all in a little café across the road. I filled them in on my day's exploring. Ingrid told me she had gone downstairs in our hotel to have a massage and confirmed that we were definitely not staying in a den of iniquity. The lovely lady smiling down on her had asked when she was expecting her baby.

"I'm not having a baby."

"Ahh, sorry, me sorry, you have nice soft belly. You very beautiful."

Needless to say, I advised Ingrid to hold off on the shopping front if she didn't want to sink into the depths of depression.

Mum had convinced Mark to join her at a traditional water puppet show, which they had received last-minute tickets for down by the lake. Stories from Vietnamese history are told using wooden puppets and dragons splashing around in the water in a dark theatre. Mum raved about how good it was while Mark told me under his breath that, even though he was wedged into a seat the size of a cat flap, he slept through the whole one-hour show, waking only when Mum clapped loudly with enthusiasm beside him.

With most of the group feeling rather "large" we decided the best thing to do was to head to the community of Le Mat, better known as the Snake Village, where all the restaurants specialise in cobra dishes. Huge snakes are on display and drinking snake blood to wash down a still-beating cobra heart is a delicacy akin to our coddle and crubeens. We decided not to rush into ordering straight away as we had read about another delicacy, "thit cho" or dog meat. This is widely available in street stalls and roadside cafés. We watched an English guy tuck into a "Fido" kebab and took his word that the meat had a slightly gamey flavour. After an hour of failing to work up an appetite, which was the original plan, we sat on miniature chairs on a dimly lit street corner and ordered steaming bowls of pho which we ate out of plastic bowls. The spicy noodle soup mixed with chilli and lemon was unsurprisingly easier to digest, having seen what else was on offer in town.

The following morning we re-traced my steps in and around the old quarter before moving on to get a shot of the Ho Chi Minh Mausoleum on Hung Vuong St. The big grey ugly building is a copy of Lenin's tomb in Moscow and apparently not what Uncle Ho had outlined in his will. He wanted to be cremated, citing that "not only is cremation good from the point of view of hygiene but it also saves farmland". Unfortunately, Ho at the time of our visit was in Moscow being restored on his annual three-month recovery programme. He is only laid out nine months of the year. Even still, there were hundreds of people queuing to get a glimpse of where the great leader normally lies, tourists and locals alike. It is quite clear from the number of Vietnamese queuing that he is still revered and loved as the man who united Vietnam and gave her independence. There are rules to follow: complete silence, no photography, no mini-skirts, no singlet tops, no caps, no shorts, no laughing, no hands behind your back. No fun, essentially. I felt I got more of an insight into what Uncle Ho was about by visiting the basic little wooden stilt house he lived in for ten years before he died, only a short walk away from the austere mausoleum, than I would have looking at his preserved body. So, in a way, I was delighted he'd gone on his holidays to Russia.

Dan collected us the following morning and we left Hanoi behind at sunrise. Accompanying him was Quan, a government official required to come along to make sure everything we filmed was above-board. Quan looked no older than fourteen but carried a very official-looking brief case. As we introduced ourselves, he repeated our names: "Hello Mr Mark; hello Miss Anne; hello Miss Kat-reen; hello Miss Ingrid." We found out in less than thirty minutes that he wanted to learn more English in these two days, that he loved Westlife, and that he knew the words to Ronan Keating's "When You Say Nothing at All", which he sung in its entirety with his eyes closed. Every time Quan opened his mouth, Mum began correcting his English and the two of them immediately struck up a close relationship of teacher and student. We headed southwest toward the Mai Chou valley, where we would begin our two-day hiking adventure. I drifted off into a light sleep punctuated with "Yes, Miss Anne; No, Miss Anne".

Most tourists who come to Vietnam to go trekking do so in the northern district of Sapa, but we wanted to experience a less-travelled route and meet some of Vietnam's ethnic minorities along the way. Vietnam is home to fifty-four recognised ethnic groups. The Hmong and White Thai populate the area around Mai Chou and these hill tribes still live very traditional lifestyles.

Three hours after setting off, our minibus rounded a bend and we were given an incredible view of the Mai Chou valley below us. The village was nestled between two steep cliffs, surrounded by a patchwork of waterlogged emerald green rice paddies glistening in the sun. In the distance, massive limestone karsts jutted into the sky cloaked with thick forests of green bushy trees. We wound our way down the mountainside to the valley floor and at the bottom met the rest of our hiking team. Viet and Hu'ng were our local guides and Thang was the driver of an old Russian army bus, which would transport our gear and supplies as we walked.

Poom Cong village was where we were to spend our first night. The short walk to Poom Cong took less than two hours on unsealed flat dirt tracks, through bamboo forests and across low-lying terraces and farms. It was incredibly serene, as were the people we met along the way – women carrying huge baskets of sticks on their backs; others stooped knee-deep in the brown waters of the paddy fields; the most beautiful children I have ever seen washing their trusty bicycles in the rivers. Everyone smiled and stopped what they were doing to wave hello.

It was getting dark when we arrived at the village and our host family was there to greet us. Our home for the visit was their traditional one-roomed stilt house, of which there were about thirty in the village. They are made entirely from natural materials, with a thatched banana or palm-leaf roof, and it is customary that the entire extended family all live under one roof, essentially in one room. Some houses have a small woven partition at one end where the women prepare and cook the food, but otherwise everyone sleeps and socialises in the one main room. There is no furniture, as everybody sits on the floor.

We climbed up the rickety wooden ladder into the stilt house, three metres above the ground. Underneath, all the family's animals were penned in: chickens, pigs and water buffalo. In the corner of the long darkened hut, two elderly men with wizened faces sat huddled in the corner puffing on rolled-up cigarettes. Smoke from a small fire snaked up and over the partition at the end of the room, behind which I could hear and smell strong spices being fried. The room was bare except for our rucksacks, which had been lined up neatly against the far wall, and our thin foam sleeping mats, which had been unrolled next to each other. Over them, mosquito nets hung from the ceiling, ghostly pale in the fading light, giving that end of the room an eerie, enchanted feel.

Looking out the window, I saw Thang and Qu'an offload a white porcelain toilet, which they placed strategically over a hole in the ground before erecting a red plastic sheet around it. I couldn't believe my eyes – we were transporting our very own toilet in the back of our van! Miss Anne made it very clear to Mark and me that she would rather throw caution to the wind (for want of a better expression) and preferred to have her quiet time in the jungle.

We sat in a circle on the floor in our socks and as dinner was served, the room slowly filled up. I counted seventeen people in the house, seven of us and ten family members. Three women, whom I assumed to be the grandmother, mother and daughter, served up piping hot plates of spring rolls, steamed rice, fried pork and chicken. It was absolutely delicious. Animated after our day, we talked and laughed loudly amongst ourselves as they spoke in hushed tones and smiled. I could sense that they were inquisitive but seemed too shy and polite to ask about us, so I got Dan to translate. We told them about our work and the programme and about Ireland. They in turn told us about their quiet day-to-day lives in the village. Looking at the older faces in the dim light, there were so many questions I wanted to ask them about the past. What had they seen? How had it affected them up here in these remote hills? But it didn't feel right and never once did anyone mention the war.

That night, we were all too tired to rummage for stuff in our bags and, considering that everybody else in the room just picked a spot, lay down on the floor and went asleep, we decided we could stay as we were until the morning. As I lay down, with Ingrid on one side and Miss Anne on the other, I looked through the thin bamboo slats on the floor. I could make out the bulky shadows of four water buffalo beneath us. The smell of dung and farmyard was more noticeable now that the cooking smells no longer filled the hut. The three of us lay side by side on the floor in the dark, suppressing uncontrollable fits of the giggles as we listened to a cacophony of dogs barking, pigs snorting, buffalo shitting and farting, and men snoring. I reminded Miss Anne that her last holiday had been to the five-star Aghadoe Heights in Killarney. In between stifled laughs, she whispered, "I never thought that, at my age, my holidays would consist of lying on the floor of a farmyard house in a remote corner of Vietnam and that I would see it as an absolute privilege." I looked at her with a new-found respect – my mother, who, to be honest, I thought wouldn't be able for the rough-and-ready nature of the trip, drifted off into a deep sleep not long after and gave the rest of the midnight snorers a run for their money.

It was still pitch dark when we were all woken by unmerciful squealing. It took a disgruntled Dan to explain that the probable cause was one of the buffalo standing on a pig, who had then woken the cockerel, who had in turn become confused and began his usual alarm call three hours before sunrise. There was no shutting them up, so people began to rise and the day began in the dark.

By 8.00 a.m. we had all been up for hours, had eaten breakfast and climbed the steep mountainside, where our van was waiting to take us twenty kilometres down the road to Cu Long. There we boarded two longboats with small outboard engines and set off down the river. Tall tropical palm trees stood in front of huge limestone cliffs that flanked the water on both sides. The air was heavy with humidity but it felt good to be motoring downstream with a breeze on our faces, watching the world go by. Women washed clothes in front of their tiny huts on either side of the river bank. These were then strewn up on low branches to dry. We passed a small man with long white hair and matching flowing beard, who took a break from stuffing a scarecrow in a field to wave us on our way. I had seen quite a few of these scarecrows the day before and it only dawned on me then as I looked up at the sky that I had actually seen and heard very little birdlife. Dan explained that Mai Chou's bird population is very low, as most villagers have homemade shotguns and over the last twenty years, when times were hard, birds were an extra source of meat.

An hour later, we came to a jetty which was our jumping-off point and set off down an unsealed road. We passed through villages made up of no more than five or six houses. The women sat in the open windows of their elevated houses, making the most of the available light for their weaving. We saw many of the industries essential to the survival of these villages – well-digging, coconut-harvesting and, of course, rice planting.

Today there was no wind and as the sun beat down on us, the inclines seemed to get steeper; at times, we were climbing at almost vertical angles. We would reach the crest of a hill only to be met with another.

Every now and then on the remote mountain track, women would pass us, sometimes in their twenties and sometimes in their sixties, each woman laden down and almost entirely hidden by a massive basket of sticks on her back. The basket was held in place by a bark strap which dug into the forehead. These tiny women with thin legs and ankles seemed tireless and I couldn't fathom how the vertebrae in their necks allowed them to hold their load while walking, let alone climbing. Every one of them managed to lift her head from her stooped position, visibly shaking under the weight of her load, to smile hello as she walked past. Dan told us that not only was it the women's job to collect the wood, they had to find it and chop it down too.

Word seemed to spread from village to village that we were on the way and by the time we approached, groups of children were running down the dirt roads to greet us.

We trekked for nineteen kilometres before we got to Hang village, arriving tired and sweaty. Almost instantly, we were led down a path by a group of about twenty children to a dammed river reservoir. The dam and the water flow seemed quite strong, but it didn't bother them, not even the youngest ones, who were only about five. They pleaded with us to get in and play and, as it was our last filming day, Ingrid, Miss Anne and I held hands and jumped in fully clothed, much to their delight.

Back at the village a big blue bucket of hot water was left on the ground outside the house so we could rinse ourselves. As I washed I surveyed the scene: the porcelain throne being dragged out of the van; three playful children sitting on top of a buffalo's head; and the old man of the house proudly showing Mark his rustic coffin, which had been delivered to him that morning. Not that he planned on dying any time soon. The village carpenter had done him a good deal and now the coffin was to rest against the wall of his house until he was ready to rest in it.

We celebrated the end of our highland trek with Dan, Quan and everyone in the village with numerous bottles of homemade rice wine. Needless to say, it wasn't the buffalo keeping everybody awake that night.

Back in Hanoi, lunchtime the following day, I stood under a hot steaming shower for twenty minutes, the first proper wash I'd had in days. It took until then for the water to run clear. I was feeling horrendous and, rice-wine hangover aside, I was beginning to think that I had picked up some bug from swimming in the water at the reservoir. Ingrid's husband Chris had flown in to have a week's holidays and we were expecting my sister and her boyfriend that night. I had emailed her to meet us in the Jazz Club on Luong Van Can, down the street from our hotel.

I dragged myself out of bed and was so disappointed that I felt so awful, as this was to be our reunion night. I hadn't seen Linda in nearly a year and as I sat in the dark bar, shivering, waiting for her to arrive, all I wanted to do was crawl back to bed and curl up in a ball. I decided that if a beer or two wouldn't kill me, it might cure me. Eventually, the two tanned travellers arrived, having been to three different Jazz bars before they finally found us. They had spent two days at the border trying to get out of Laos as their visas hadn't been processed to enter Vietnam, and they then had to endure a twelve-hour bus journey to get to Hanoi.

Hearing their horrendous tales of endurance, stolen passports and money made me feel less sorry for myself. I began to feel better and, against Miss Anne's better judgement, by midnight Mark and I, Linda and Rob were on our way to the New Century nightclub. On the steps leading down to the club, we passed two Irish guys who looked suitably bored and, before they uttered a word, I knew by their Leinster jerseys and gelled fringes that they were dying to be back in Kielys of Donnybrook. "Hey man, its Kathryn Thomas! No way, like, that is deadly. Hey, Kathryn, I wouldn't bother going in there. There's, like, nobody really there except like locals and stuff. Where are all the hot backpacker birds at?"

Against the advice of Ross O'Carroll-Kelly and his brother, we went in and had a great night.

So, having roughed it in the mountains and immersed ourselves in the bedlam of Hanoi, we decided it was time to leave town and spend some "R and R" time on the coast. We chose a beautiful and affordable five-star hotel on the beach at Hoi An, famous for its ancient buildings and expert tailors.

Leaving Ingrid and Chris to their own devices in Hanoi, Miss Anne, Linda, Rob, Mark and I headed for the train station to catch the overnight train to the town closest to Hoi An, Danang. The station was manic by the time we arrived at 9.00 p.m. Crowds of people shuffled in every direction, people carried cages of squawking chickens, Vietnamese announcements rang over crackly speakers. The information desk was closed and nobody could tell us what platform our train left from. Eventually, we found one of the station masters, who pointed us in the direction of an ancient train. We walked toward the front of the train looking for the first-class berth we had booked. We eventually found the six-berth cabin that had been allocated to us at the end of the carriage. It was less than two metres wide with six foldaway beds, resembling bread racks, sticking out of the walls, three on either side. With all our rucksacks piled onto one bed, the five of us just about fit in, standing upright, unable to move. It took us ten minutes to stop laughing. We double-checked with a frustrated looking conductor if we were in the right part of the train; with a fierce nodding of the head he assured us that indeed this was where we were supposed to be.

Mark, who was closest to the door, squeezed out, jumped off the train and disappeared into the sea of moving conical hats on the platform. He was followed in hot pursuit by Rob. For a split second, we thought the idea of spending thirteen hours in a confined space with the Thomas women was too much for them. As it turned out, it probably would have been, if they hadn't stocked up on some essential supplies. We watched them wind their way through the crowd to a small shop where they bought up a large supply of drink – six bottles of wine and six cans of beer. As they were haggling over the price, the whistle sounded on our train. In a flurry of panic, people stubbed out cigarettes, handed food parcels and bags through windows and doors and jumped aboard. We were not meant to be leaving for another ten minutes, but with a sudden jolt our train began to move. Linda, Mum and I began shouting out the window at the guys to hurry the hell up. Carrying their wares over their heads, they ploughed through the crowd toward the train. "Wait, wait, we're coming!" But this train was waiting for nobody, not even very important first-class travellers! The small conductor, in his faded but immaculate green uniform, was standing at the open door with a smile on his face, clearly enjoying the unfolding disaster. It was like a scene from a film, the two boys running alongside the train, imploring somebody, anybody, to stop and wait for them. Mark threw the bag of beer cans onto the train, which scattered everywhere, leapt on board and, leaning out, holding on for dear life, pulled Rob, who had held onto the bag of wine bottles like his life depended on it, up after him just before the platform ran out.

Everyone was silent until Linda, who had just witnessed her boyfriend's near-death experience, asked with grave concern, "Did you not get a bottle opener?" We were all in fits of giggles except Mark, who went off down the carriages with a look of sheer desperation on his face, clutching the wine bottle, indicating to anybody he met what he was looking for. Twenty minutes later, he came back, unsuccessful.

Further up the track the train stopped at a small station, where women selling baskets of fresh fruit, warm pastries and spring rolls sold their wares to desperate, outstretched arms through the windows. Mark, waving his bottle of wine in the air, made eye contact with a young boy who understood his needs and came back with an opener. He held it up in the air: "Twenty dollar." The wine itself had cost the equivalent of $2 in dong, but this savvy eight-year-old businessman, smiling up at Mark, knew he was our last hope. Mark handed ten dollars out the window of the train, knowing that even at that he'd been had. There was a stand-off as the boy insisted "Twenty dollar." Then the train began to move and, at the last minute, the transaction was completed and both parties whooped with joy! Our thirteen-hour slumber party in close confines began. With our iPod playing and not enough room to stand up, we all danced lying down on our bread racks. Miss Anne didn't complain once about her situation, even when the overflow from the toilet right next to our cabin filled our little enclosure with the foulest of smells. We laughed, held our noses and enjoyed the first-class experience as much as we could.

We disembarked at Danang the following morning, slightly the worse for wear. We had arrived into what felt like a different country. The weather had taken a sudden downturn. Howling winds whipped around us, making it difficult to walk, and sheets of torrential rain meant that we were soaked to the skin in a matter of seconds. There was no sign of any taxis. Groups of men stood around in giant plastic ponchos waiting to give people lifts on the back of their mopeds. It didn't make sense that the taxi drivers had gone home in the bad weather, yet the moped drivers were willing to brave the elements.

At first Miss Anne, Linda and I refused point blank to take the thirty-minute suicide drive on the back of the bikes. But the owners were working hard, trying to convince Mark and Rob that the roads, which had literally turned into rivers, were not going to be an issue for the mopeds. "150,000 dong, very good price. Thirty minute to Hoi An. Safe, no problem. We have raincoat for every people." The longer we stood there, the heavier our bags got and the more our frustration grew. Finally, we had no choice but to pull on large plastic ponchos, strap our bags on firmly and head off into the storm.

The rain was so heavy I could just about make out Miss Anne on the moped in front of me, clinging on tightly. I could do nothing but laugh. Our expectations had been so wrong. I thought to myself, this was meant to be the luxurious part of our Vietnamese experience. Yet, after roughing it in the highlands, here we were like five drowned rats on a suicide mission!

My driver turned around to face me, never easing off the accelerator. "Ty-hoo," he yelled, smiling, rain and snot streaming down his face. "What?" I screamed back at him. "Ty-hoo, Ty-hoo." I couldn't understand what he was saying but wanted him to look where we were going, so I just nodded and smiled. As I later found out, he was trying to explain that we were experiencing the onslaught of Typhoon Durian, which had wreaked havoc in the Philippines, killing hundreds of people in the previous few days, and was making its way toward Vietnam.

Half an hour later, we pulled up at the front door of our five-star hotel. It was clear from the stunned look on the concierge's face that the majority of guests arrived in air-conditioned cars or, at the very least, in taxis. Instead, we got off our mopeds, soaked to the skin, and squelched through the lobby trussed up in our plastic ponchos. The concierge enquired rather curtly if our party was in the right place. I stopped, long enough for my shoes to create a little puddle on the floor, and smiled at him. "I hope so, because I couldn't go much longer without a shower. I stink." Miss Anne was mortified. That evening, my brother Dave arrived in the same style, on the back of a moped, also soaked, with a year's worth of worldly possessions on his back, ready to begin his adventure.

We spent the afternoon catching up and that evening hopped in two taxis and headed into Hoi An. The rain had eased off. Once upon a time, Hoi An had been south Vietnam's most important port. It attracted traders from Portugal, Holland, England, France, Japan and India. But it is the Chinese influence that is most prominent along the waterfront and in the narrow streets behind. The town was the first Chinese settlement in south Vietnam and they now make up one quarter of the population. Eventually, trade moved north toward the bigger and more industrial town of Danang and now Hoi An's main industry is tourism.

Some people say that it has become a bit of a tourist trap, but certainly walking along the streets in the evening light that first night, I thought the place was magical. Red lanterns lit up the dark nineteenth-century wooden houses, decorated with writhing dragons and colourful glazed roof tiles, nestled snugly between French colonial buildings painted bright yellow decorated with their beautiful window shutters. While bars advertised happy hour and two-for-one cocktails, it still felt very old and it was easy to imagine what the bustling port would have been like in its heyday. We walked down by the old Japanese bridge, which connected the Japanese part of town with the Chinese one. The beautiful structure, with a decorative wooden pagoda covering it on one side, is even more interesting when you think that it has survived the elements since 1593. We had been here one day and already Typhoon Durian was affecting our holiday spirit!

The following morning, the typhoon continued to batter the coast of Hoi An and for two days we were essentially hotel-bound. All we could do was look out the windows at the beautifully manicured hotel gardens and huge blue pool with the beach in the distance. The waves were angry, trees had been uprooted and the whole scene looked like it could be blown away at any moment. Poor Miss Anne planned an itinerary every morning at breakfast – a visit to the temples of My Son, a tour of Hoi An's museums, a boat trip on the Perfume River – but all we could do was read in our rooms and empty the mini-bar.

Finally, the rain stopped on our last day, allowing us to go into town, which had been completely flooded and turned into a mini-Venice. Luckily, because most of the shops and cafés were built on steps, they didn't suffer any water damage, and the people of Hoi An went about their business as normal. Boat drivers and fishermen became taxis ferrying people up and down the main street.

Miss Anne had read a lot about a great patisserie in town and was determined to taste as many of the buns and tarts as possible, come hell or high water! Linda and I busied ourselves getting a new wardrobe made while Dave, Mark and Rob explored more of the old town, knee-deep in water, spotting giant rats as they went.

Laden down with bags of Christmas presents, we all converged at Tam Tam's café. We whiled away the afternoon, sitting in damp clothes on damp chairs drinking inexpensive bottles of wine, and none of us could have been happier. It hadn't been the ideal way to end our trip – getting caught up in a typhoon. But it was wonderful to spend time with my family before we all took off in different directions. We agreed that Vietnam and her people had shown all of us a good time and that we were leaving, not with a country's tragic history in our minds, but with memories of an incredible travel adventure.

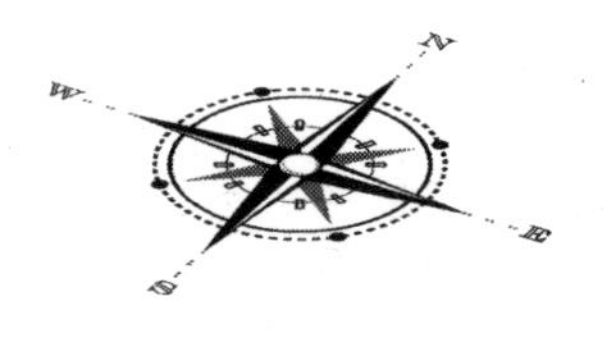

Vietnam Fast Facts

Population: 84 million approx.

Capital City: Following the end of the war, Hanoi became the capital of Vietnam, when North and South Vietnam were reunited on 2 July 1976.

Languages: Vietnamese (official), English, French, Chinese, and Khmer; mountain area languages (Mon-Khmer and Malayo-Polynesian).

Size: 331,114 square kilometres, and borders alongside China, Laos and Cambodia. It stretches 1,000 miles north to south but is only about twenty-five miles wide at its narrowest point.

Climate: Vietnam's weather is tropical in the south, more monsoonal in the north, and has two distinct seasons – the hot rainy season from mid-May to mid-September; and the warm dry season from mid-October to mid-March. Occasional typhoons from May to January may cause flooding. The average summer temperature is 23°C - 28°C, and winter is 17°C - 24°C.

Best time to go: The best time to visit Vietnam is between October and January, when the weather is most temperate in the south, with the north being a bit cooler. The mountains can be quite cold any time of the year so bring along a sweater for cooler nights.

Time Difference: +7 hours from Ireland.

Where I went: Hanoi, Ma River, trekking in the Mai Chou district and Hoi An.

Who to go with: There are numerous companies that offer tours to Vietnam and therefore you should shop around for the best option. Some of the larger tour operators to Vietnam include: Trailfinders, Twohigs Travel, Sunway Holidays, Destinations and Tropical Places.

Visa Requirements: You do need a visa to travel in Vietnam. This can be obtained through the Vietnamese embassy in London prior to travel. A visa upon arrival can also be obtained, but only if you arrive into the country by air, and you will need an approved travel service in Vietnam to assist you with this process.

Currency: Local currency is the Vietnamese Dong, but the US dollar is widely accepted in most major cities. ATMs are widely available, and credit cards are accepted in most hotels, restaurants and guesthouses in big cities.

Tipping: Tipping is not customary in Vietnam and is something you may or may not wish to do. Bear in mind that five to ten per cent may be a day's wage for some workers. Avoid tipping too much as this will set a precedent for others.

Vaccinations Needed: Vaccinations are required for travel in Vietnam. The WHO also report malaria transmission in certain parts of the country. You should consult your local Tropical Medical Bureau or GP before travelling to Vietnam.

Electricity: 220V

Water: Drink only bottled water and beverages without ice.

Emergency Numbers: Nationwide emergency numbers are as follows: for police, dial 113; for fire, dial 114; and for ambulance, dial 115. Operators speak Vietnamese only.

Other Highlights:

- Ho Chi Minh City: This is the largest city in Vietnam.

- Mekong Delta: One of the world's largest deltas winds its way for 4,500 kilometres through China, Burma, Laos, Thailand, Cambodia and southern Vietnam.

- Hue: One of the main tourism sites of Vietnam with its splendid tombs, several notable pagodas as well as the romantic Perfume River.

- Halong Bay: Has fascinating limestone formations, coves for night-time excursions, sheer cliffs, grottoes, arches and scores of small islets.

Fun Facts

- **"Nguyen" is the most popular surname in Vietnam.**
- **Vietnam is the second-largest exporter of rice and coffee in the world.**
- **Vietnam's Communist leader Ho Chi Minh's nickname was Uncle Ho.**
- **Ha Long Bay consists of 1,969 islands and islets situated in the Gulf of Tonkin.**
- **In Vietnamese schools, instead of bells, gongs are used to call children.**

Useful Contacts:

- Vietnamese Embassy, London: www.vietnamembassy.org.uk/consular.html
- Vietnam Tourist Board: www.vietnamtourism.com
- Tropical Medical Bureau: www.tmb.ie

Books to Read:

All the relevant travel books –
Lonely Planet, *Frommer's Guide*, *The Rough Guide*

Ethiopia

The evening was still warm and I was in the lead with thirteen tadpoles in my bucket. I could hear Mum somewhere in the distance calling me in for dinner but the fervour of competition had suppressed my appetite and I wasn't hungry. I threw the jam jar into the river one last time, holding on tightly to the string and, for a second, the sound of it sloshing into the water drowned her out. I could hear my cousin Alan counting his new catch out loud beside me: "One, two, three. That gives me a total of nineteen. Woohoo! I'm winning!" I carefully lifted my jam jar out of the river and peered into the murky water. Nothing swam inside but silt and mud. I had to admit defeat for now.

We ran across the field toward the house where dinner was waiting on the table. Alan obediently sat and ate while I pushed the food around my plate, eager to get back to the river to restore my title as "Tadpole Queen". But Mum signalled the end of the competition, "You may forget about going back down to the river, Kathryn. It's too late now and you are not getting up from the table until you eat every last bit on that plate." Unbeknownst to her, she had crowned Alan the tadpole king. He smiled at me from across the table, delighted with himself.

Finally, when I had finished and washed my plate, I skulked in to join the rest of them in the sitting room where they were watching the news. This was the first time I ever saw images of Ethiopia. Crying babies with protruding malnourished bellies, clinging to skeleton mothers in a hot dry place where there were no rivers or fields, or tadpole kings and queens – just flies and sand and sadness.

Bob Geldof's efforts, culminating in Live Aid and the donation of $100 million in foreign aid, had taken place two years before in 1985. Ireland was the highest per capita donor in the world and every nation was sitting up and taking notice of Ethiopia's plight. Twenty-one years later, Ethiopia is still one of the poorest countries in the world and still relies heavily on foreign aid.

When I announced to my friends and family that I was heading off to Ethiopia with *No Frontiers*, the general reaction was one of confusion, shock and disbelief. Why in the hell would anybody want to go on holidays there? But six weeks' research confirmed what I had been told by anyone who had been there: this country, the size of France and Spain combined, is Africa's best-kept secret.

I knew that travelling in Africa can sometimes be a challenge but I had always been so rewarded by my experiences and knew that this was going to be an amazing adventure. Our itinerary was going to take us to the incredible rock churches of Lalibela and onto Gondar, the Camelot of Africa. From there we would explore the Simien mountains before finishing our trip in Bahir Dar, exploring the island monasteries of Lake Tana. Joining me were Dan, who was directing, and Stu on camera. So, packed up, briefed and ready, we set off on our African adventure.

I love saying Addis Ababa. Like Timbuktu, it rolls off the tongue beautifully and I was still saying it under my breath as we flew into the capital on the overnight flight from London.

We were greeted by our friendly guide and driver Abeje, who had brought his six-year-old son with him to say hello. We had booked with a small adventure company called Ethiopian Quadrants, run by an Irishman, Tony Hickey, who has lived in Ethiopia for fifteen years. "Mr Tony will be here presently to take you all to the police station. You will only have to stay one night," said Abeje smiling and nodding at us.

We all did a double take. He erupted into a fit of giggles, as did his young son, who quite clearly did not even speak English but obviously enjoyed his father's infectious laugh. "Have no worries. I am joking, joking, joking. Ethiopian people always joking. We like to laugh a lot." Finally he stopped laughing long enough to tell us, "You must go to the police station just to collect your filming permits." We all breathed a collective sigh of relief and laughed along with him for the first of many times on the trip.

I heard Mr Tony before I saw him and turned my head in the direction of the booming, rather posh English accent. He was on the phone sounding rather frustrated with somebody on the other end, who I was glad was not me. Dressed in a black leather jacket and sunglasses, standing at about 6'6", with grey hair and a matching thick moustache, he was definitely someone who commanded your attention.

We all said hello and shook hands, mine crushed in his huge grip. Then he stood back with his hands on his hips. "Right, have we got everything? We need to go to the police station." He turned on his heel toward the door. I looked at the lads who looked back at me and I knew they were thinking the same thing: *Oh dear, this is going to be a long week*. Abeje scurried behind him with the bags.

To be honest, my first impression was that Tony had taken the colonial attitude to living in Africa, barking orders as if he had more of a right to be there than anyone else. I thought at this stage that we might not see eye-to-eye and decided I needed to be assertive. I suggested the boys go back in the van with Abeje, check into the hotel and get some sleep. I would go to the police station with Tony in his car and sign the clearance forms for the filming permits. Dan and Stu looked at me as if I had two heads and Tony as if I had four. "I assume we are not all needed to sign one form?" Tony nodded and so, leaving the boys to pack the gear into the van, I disappeared in a cloud of dust into the thick city traffic.

With the window down, I took a deep breath in the dusty heat and was happy to be back in Africa. My first impression of Addis, like so many other African cities, was one of chaos, cars and crowds. Driving from the airport down Bole Road, Tony explained that the city, with a population of five million, is divided into three parts: the east, which is the government and educational sector; the commercial sector in the centre; and the west, where all the trade, including Africa's biggest open air market, the Addis Mercado, is done.

We pulled up on a wide street outside a police station in the commercial district, which even on a Sunday was fairly busy, and waited outside for a few minutes until we were called. There are a lot of ex-pats living in Addis, so even though men stared as they walked past, they would smile and say hello. The whole vibe was far less threatening than any other African city I had been to and I began to understand why they call Addis the safest city in Africa.

We were in and out of the police station in five minutes and finally we made it back through the horrendous traffic to the hotel. The Ghion chain of hotels is owned by the government and they are probably the most upmarket places to stay when travelling around Ethiopia. There are certainly more expensive places to stay in the city, like the Sheraton and the Hilton, but the Ghion is the best value. It is quite basic but has a huge pool and quiet gardens. The interior is dated but the room was clean and the beds were comfortable. (Mind you, I was so tired, I could have slept on a bed of nails.) I was amused to find a note in my room citing restrictions on unmarried couples sharing rooms.

Later that afternoon when we were rested, Abeje took us on a whirlwind tour of the third-highest city in the world. Addis stands at between 2,300 and 2,500 metres above sea level and is built at the foothill of Mount Entoto, which itself stands at an impressive 3,200 metres, the summit of which was to be our first stop. On the drive up, passing lines of eucalyptus trees, the air got noticeably colder but it was well worth the journey when we took in the panoramic view of the city from the top. This was the site of the first palace of Emperor Menelik II, who founded Addis Ababa in 1881. But because of the cold and the difficulty of supplying provisions, the capital was later moved down the valley and re-named Addis Ababa, meaning "new flower".

Abeje was keen and proud to tell us everything about the history of his country, the only one in Africa never to have been colonised. “The Italians under Mussolini did try but only could occupy us for six years until 1940, not long enough to leave any sort of influence on the country as a whole. What were they thinking? This is the birthplace of civilisation. We know nothing about being anybody else except Ethiopian and we are proud for that.” As we drove back down the mountainside, Abeje chatted away, pointing out the City University and the National Museum of Ethiopia, where the bones of Lucy are kept. Lucy is one of the oldest hominids known to man. Her skeleton was found in Harar in 1974 and is estimated to be 3.18 million years old. “She was pretty like you, Miss Kathryn, but I do not think you are so old,” he chuckled.

Later that evening, Tony picked us up from the hotel to take us for dinner in the Old Milk House in town. We pulled up outside what looked like a grotty apartment block and walked in pitch darkness across the car park until we came across two men guarding a dimly lit elevator shaft. Feeling rather unsure, we all squeezed into the lift, not sure whether we would get to the top at all. When the doors opened we emerged into a colourful and atmospheric restaurant on the top floor where we were shown to a table in the middle of the room and ordered a round of beer. There was a band playing traditional music in the corner. The place was buzzing and not at all what I had expected. We let Tony order dinner for us and while we were waiting, he gave us the low-down on Ethiopian cuisine.

He told us that the Coptic Church dictates many of the country’s food customs. Wednesdays and Fridays are fasting days when people don’t eat meat and no one is allowed to eat pork at all. Ethiopians eat with their right hand only. In general, Ethiopian food is the hottest and spiciest in all of

Africa, with dishes specially prepared in red pepper and berberis.

Fifteen minutes later a huge flat round metal tray was brought to our table and sitting on top of a massive pancake were different coloured piles of stew. Another plate of pancakes accompanied the huge dish. Using our right hands, we tore off strips of pancakes and dipped them into the puddles of spicy vegetable and meat stews. It tasted fantastic. The sour pancakes are made from injera, which is fermented teff flour and is the staple food of the country. They have a greyish complexion, full of holes and somewhat resembling tripe but, covered and stained in rich globs of colourful sauce, they were a pleasure to eat.

The next morning we were back at the airport again for a short flight north-east to Lalibela. The propellers of the Ethiopian Air Fokker spurred into action and soon we were flying over huge canyons and gorges below. My first of many surprises on this trip was of how green and mountainous the country is. I was so excited about visiting the ancient rock churches of Lalibela, considered to be the eighth man-made wonder of the world. King Lalibela, in the late twelfth or early thirteenth century, was so impressed when he visited Jerusalem that he decided he would return to Ethiopia and build a holy city of his own.

We landed in Lalibela and were greeted by Solomon, a good friend of Tony, who owned the Jerusalem guest house in town. Although we weren't staying there, they greeted each other warmly and suddenly I was starting to see a whole other side of Tony. It became quite clear, as all of us piled into Solomon's old van for the windy, twenty-three-kilometre drive over the mountains, that they were firm friends. Tony had been working in this business and had been encouraging tourism here for years. He could see Ethiopia's potential and as we passed through small roadside villages with their round stone houses and thatched roofs, Tony waved at everybody, who waved back in recognition.

We arrived at the Ghion Roha in time for lunch. This hotel with its adobe mud front was much nicer and more traditional than its sister hotel where we had stayed in Addis. The rooms' exposed brick walls and ethnic interiors gave them a really homely feel – not that we had much time to relax and enjoy them. After a brief lunch, we were back in the van again. It was so hard to believe that Lalibela was home to Ethiopia's main tourist attraction, because it felt like a place where time had stood still for centuries. We drove past children coming from school carrying umbrellas to shade themselves from the sun. Women with huge bundles of firewood on their heads stopped and smiled as we trundled by. They were so beautiful; I still maintain that Ethiopian women are the most beautiful I have ever seen. With their high foreheads, wide eyes and incredible smiles, they exude grace, intelligence, humility and pride, all at the same time.

The first church we visited is the most famous of all the churches, Bete Giyorgis. What is so incredible about these twelve man-made churches is that each one is hewn and carved out of one piece of solid rock, inside and out, an incredible feat of architecture in any era. It is estimated that it took twenty-five years for the construction of the monolithic churches to be completed, which proves that it was a very wealthy area to have been able to keep such a huge workforce engaged for so long in economically unproductive labour. According to legend, they had help from the angels, who did double the amount of work while the men slept at night.

Bete Giyorgis, one of Lalibela's famous rock churches

Ethiopia

Above:
Salubrious departure lounge at Lalibela airport!

The Ethiopian smile that never fails to cheer me up when I'm feeling down

My two new friends in Lalibela were certainly not camera shy

The sight that greeted our eyes when we woke in Simien National Park

Gelada baboons heading off the beaten track in Semien

A local ferryman paddles his tankwa across Lake Tana

Success in reaching the summit of Mount Wilhelm in Papua New Guinea
PHOTO COURTESY OF AND © *RTÉ 2008*

The villagers of Waim

Above:
A Waim man wearing traditional Papua New Guinea piercing

Taking ceremonial duties very seriously

PHOTO COURTESY OF AND

Giving Philip Treacy a run for his money!

Below:
Having a laugh with your friends is always fun

Papua New Guinea

The four wise women of Waim

This was just the start of a difficult and dangerous trek in the Gulf Province of Papua New Guinea

Built in the shape of a horizontal crucifix, with the roof at ground level, it's only when you walk through a series of trenches thirty metres into the ground below and look up that you truly appreciate the magnificence of Bete Giyorgis. Dwarfed by its size, it is almost inconceivable to imagine how the workers carved into the rock, leaving the freestanding cross, measuring twelve metres by twelve metres, without a single seam or join.

The Father of the church greeted us at the door and we followed him inside. Again I was speechless as I looked up and around. Although the floor space was small, the symmetry of the architecture was incredible. Tiny windows carved up along the thirty-metre height allowed shafts of light to reflect and bounce off the walls, casting beautiful shadows inside the church. The father who sat by the altar in the dim light smiled as we filmed and then called on me to be blessed. I bent down in front of him and he placed his brass staff against my forehead and prayed in Amharic. Tony later told me that most men in the village have their own staff because services can be anything up to five hours' long. There are no seats so they have mastered the art of sleeping standing up, leaning on their staffs much like our county council workers with their shovels.

Outside in the deep courtyard that surrounds the church, I noticed small holes dug into the steep wall. On closer inspection, I realised that inside was a partially mummified skeleton of human remains. There was still skin on the foot and the leg and Tony explained that it was and still is the wish of many pilgrims to be laid to rest in the holy city.

Afterwards we headed across the River Jordan to look at the churches of the western cluster. There was a totally different feeling here, more of a community as six of the churches are linked by tunnels, underground passageways and massive courtyards below the ground. The largest is Bete Medhane Alem; measuring thirty-three metres by twenty-three metres wide and eleven metres high, it is surrounded by huge columns, taking the weight of the low roof. Inside there are five aisles, a barrel vault with eight bays and a further twenty-eight massive columns.

Although Lalibela is listed as a UNESCO world heritage site, I couldn't fathom why more people, including me, had not heard of these incredible buildings sooner. Everywhere we walked, life was going on as normal, almost as if we were part of a movie set. Children with sticks ran after goats, women carried huge flat baskets of grain and vegetables on their heads and old men in full-length cotton robes sat in shaded corners, fanning the flies away. All the while, small groups of tourists wandered around, removing their shoes before entering each of the churches, which were then lined up in a very orderly fashion by the shoe boys outside. The atmosphere was one of peace and quiet satisfaction that everything happened just as it should.

We filmed until closing time at 5.00 p.m. and left in a sea of red light, the evening sun reflecting off the imposing rock walls.

That evening, Solomon invited us to dinner and a traditional Ethiopian night at his guest house. We all showered back at the hotel and then drove down the long winding hill to the Jerusalem guest house. The temperature had dropped dramatically and it was cold even as we sat wrapped up in blankets around a huge open fire in the courtyard outside the round mud dining room. A beautiful woman came out with a tray of beer and we chatted and listened to Tony and Solomon telling stories that covered their years of friendship. Finally, the pretty waitress called us in for dinner, which was a basic meal of chicken and rice. Solomon joined our table and produced a bottle of White Horse whiskey. As an Irish person, I believe it is an insult to refuse whiskey, even if it is something called White Horse, so the bottle was passed around and we all drank it neat.

After dinner, the waiting staff sat on the ground in the middle of the room with their instruments for a performance of traditional song and dance, which to be honest I suspected was going to be a little bit like Jury's cabaret. Tony had told us that Eskista is the traditional Ethiopian dance. If dancing as we know it is all about the hips, then in Ethiopia, it's all about the shoulders. Men and women dance together very seductively and sensually, shimmying their shoulders and necks in a way that makes them look disjointed from the rest of their bodies. Like so many other African dances, there is a feeling of celebration about it. In every town and village in Ethiopia there is a place called an Azmari Bait where people go to dance and Tony assured us we would visit a few on our trip where we could take some footage; but this night it was nice to be able to sit back and enjoy it.

It was incredible to watch and in the dim light, lubricated with White Horse whiskey, with the high-pitched singing and the music of the masenko and a six-stringed lyre called a krar, it was almost mesmerising. It wasn't long before we were all out dancing, including the staff of the guest house. Dan was trying to play one of the instruments and Stu was already trying to impress the waitresses with his shoulder action. Attempting a few Irish dancing steps sent them all into convulsions, as they had never seen or heard of a dance where the shoulders stayed absolutely still. In hindsight, they were probably laughing at our very bad attempt at both Irish and Ethiopian dancing.

God knows how many shots of White Horse later, Solomon was asleep at the table and certainly in no fit state to drive us. We decided the walk back to the hotel would do us good. It was pitch black and we estimated that it was at least a twenty-minute uphill walk along the road back to the Roha. If we could just find the road. We wandered out of the car park, trying to find our way out of the blackness. The ground was so uneven it felt like we were navigating the surface of the moon as we walked in and out of huge dry craters, in what we thought was the general direction of the road. I had linked arms with Dan and at first the whole thing was rather amusing, until we took a step into nothingness and ended up in a heap on the ground. I could feel blood coming out of both my elbows and the palms of my hands. We crawled out of the large hole and could hear Tony talking to somebody in the distance. He had found the road, and more importantly somebody to drive us home, and it felt like we had been rescued as two huge bright headlights came toward us.

I woke the next morning feeling great, apart from two sore arms which I lathered with antiseptic cream. At breakfast the guys weren't looking too hot and admitted to heading back into town in the van after they had dropped me off! Luckily, "Le Pub" in town didn't stay open all night but it was a long walk home after a long night.

It was time to move on from Lalibela. Solomon arrived to pick us up. On the way to the airport, Tony got a phone call to say that our flight to Gondar had been delayed. When we got to the airport, Solomon suggested we should all go to the waiting lounge. We thought he was joking when he headed off across a rugged field to a hut about thirty metres from the airport building. There we sat on stumps of logs, drinking Cokes and eating peanuts. Although the sun was baking down in the wide open space, under the shade of the thatched roof, a gentle breeze kept us cool. Our spirits were high, although we were slightly worried about our schedule. Our plan had been to arrive into Gondar and drive for four hours into the Simien Mountains National Park, where we would pick up our guides and porters and set up camp for the night. Unfortunately, we were not allowed to drive in the National Park after dark and if our flight was going to be any further delayed, we would not arrive on time to enter the park and would have to change our plans.

I had learnt with the job at this stage that the schedule will change nine times out of ten due to unforeseen circumstances, so we weren't that stressed. Besides, sitting where we were, there was no way anybody could get airport stress; it was the best waiting lounge I have ever been in. Solomon was in flying form as we all recounted the previous night's festivities. I came under particular scrutiny for my attempts to line everybody up for an Ethiopian *Riverdance*.

An hour later, a plane flew over our heads and landed on the runway. A small boy came racing out to our shack looking for the passengers for the flight to Gondar. We said our goodbyes to Solomon, thanked him and cursed him for his hospitality and took off for Gondar.

We arrived two hours later than planned at 4.00 p.m. We knew we would not reach the National Park, 100 kilometres away, before dark but Tony decided that the best thing to do was to drive as far as we could in daylight and overnight in a village close to the park's perimeter.

I dozed off and woke up when I heard voices outside the window. I realised we had stopped and I stretched and rubbed my eyes. I could see Tony's silhouette in the evening light talking to two men who were wrapped up in large coats and woollen hats. Now that we were farther up in the highlands, you could really feel the change in temperature. The door of the jeep opened and one guy with a small rucksack jumped in and sat beside me, followed by another guy armed with an AK47 who jumped in and sat beside Stu! Back in the van, Tony slammed the door but we still didn't move. Then there was another knock on the window and a dark figure handed what looked like a bottle wrapped in a paper bag through the window to Tony. He thanked the man in Amharic and barked an order to "drive on". For the first couple of minutes nobody said anything. Looking at the row of seats in front of me, all I could see was the silhouette of Stu's head and the outline of an AK47.

"I think we'd all be a little more comfortable if you introduced us, Tony," I ventured to the back of his head in the front seat.

"Oh sorry! This is David, our guide, and Ben, who will be making sure we come to no harm. They feel that if we play our cards right, we should be able to get past the guard on the gate of the park. We then have another hour to drive to get to our camping spot, so it will save us time in the morning if we can get through tonight."

I wasn't sure whether Ben "making sure we come to no harm" meant protecting us against any wild animals we might encounter on our trek the following day or protecting us as we drove at night farther into the remote highlands. Roadside bandit attacks were not uncommon in Ethiopia. I looked out and up to the stars as our jeep climbed higher and higher into the hills. It was a moment that made me smile as I thought of my Dad and all the situations he had warned me not to get myself into. There I was, in the middle of Africa, squeezed into a jeep with seven men, one with a machine gun, in the pitch dark, with no real clue as to what was about to unfold. I trusted Tony completely and knew everyone was working for us and for the benefit of the show, so I sat back and enjoyed the adventure.

We finally made it to Debark, the entrance to the National Park. A barrier and two men with machine guns blocked our way. Our armed guide, having looked closely at the two figures in the headlights of our jeep, quite obviously recognised one of the official guards and jumped out with his gun slung over his shoulder. I didn't see whether money changed hands or not, but five minutes later we were continuing our windy twisty journey uphill. I wished I could see where the hell we were; with all this weaving uphill, it felt like we were driving to the top of the world.

An hour later, we could see fires and the headlights of the rest of our team in the distance. We pulled up alongside two other jeeps. There were five men scurrying around by the light of torches, some setting tents up, some carrying boxes and one tending to the roaring fire. We had dinner sitting on fold-out chairs in a large tent that had already been pitched. We ate the hot meal by the light of our torches. We were not sure at this stage whether we were sharing tents or not. I had no objection if we were, as I knew it would be a guarantee of warmer surroundings. Eventually, Tony signalled to our three tents that were pitched in a row, equipped with thermal sleeping bags and blankets and, after a quick pit stop in the long grass, we turned in for the night.

The following morning I unzipped my tent to the most incredible view of the "Roof of Africa". Huge peaks and flat-topped mountains, some above 4,000 metres, jutted into the sky as if they were trying to touch the heavens. They towered over the deep gorges and rivers of the lowland valleys that spread out on the horizon, all the way to Eritrea, with vistas up to 100 kilometres away. It was green and lush and about as far from the stereotypical images of Ethiopia I had always known. Stu was already out with his camera, eager to capture the dramatic beauty in the early morning light.

After breakfast, eight of us, including two donkeys, set off on our trek. David was so charming and had worked as a guide here for two years. As we walked he told us of the endemic gelada baboons, walia ibex and Simien wolf that could be found in the area and was quick to point out the endemic birds such as the thick-billed raven, white-collared pigeon, spot-breasted plover and the white-backed black tit. We passed through rural villages of local people still living within the park. David explained that Ethiopia's highlands are some of the most densely populated agricultural areas in Africa. Originally there were 2,500 Amhara people living in the park. In 1978–79 and 1985–86 the population was reduced by forced relocation of 1,800 people but following the civil unrest between 1983 and 1991, visitors were banned and a massive number of refugees moved back into the park. UNESCO have listed it as a world heritage site in danger with several species set to become extinct. I couldn't help thinking to myself, though, that if I was a poor farmer who had witnessed the atrocities of the 1980s and had moved back into the park because it was the best place to grow food for my family, how much would I really prioritise the decline of the Simien wolf?

We finally came upon a troop of gelada baboons who were making their way across the valley. There were hundreds of them and it seemed like they were playing with us because every time we got close enough to set the camera up to take a few shots, they would up and scatter across the hillsides. We must have walked for two hours after them and covered a lot of ground. Eventually we took the chance of going ahead of them and hoping they would pass close enough to us. I had read in the *Lonely Planet* that there had been recorded instances of baboon attacks on locals, where they tried to rape and, in one case, even kill a local child, so we were all a little tense lying flat in the grass as hundreds of them came over the hillside toward us. We got great shots as they thundered past and not one of them looked the least bit interested in any of us.

When we had everything we needed, we packed up the jeeps and headed down the mountain road to Gondar. I couldn't believe that we had travelled the same road in the pitch dark the night before. At one stage, there was a sheer drop of 1,000 feet on both sides of the car.

Later that evening, we checked into the Goha Hotel in Gondar. As well as being known as the Camelot of Africa, with its beautiful fairytale castles, the city is also renowned for its great Azmari nightlife. We had arranged to meet David, who assured us he would take us off the beaten track to the best Azmari Bait in town, Balagerua. We parked up on a deserted backstreet and followed him in single file down a labyrinth of narrow muddy alleyways. I had my radio microphone on and Stu held his camera as tightly as was physically possible. All of a sudden, we were standing in front of a torn strip of curtain, which David pulled aside, and we entered another alley.

At this stage we could hear the music from inside the little house and when we opened the door, the room was absolutely packed to the rafters. People sat on wooden benches against every wall. The azmari stood in the middle of the room with four people dancing wildly around him, their shoulders gyrating at what looked like ninety miles an hour. Traditionally an azmari was like an English bard, a wanderer who travelled far and wide telling stories and singing for a few birr. Nowadays, the entertainment mostly consisted of him slagging off members of his audience, who in return laughed at this hilarity and stuck money to his head with spit.

It was hot and damp and dark and the smell of sweat added to the intense atmosphere. The sexual energy in the room was electric. Once we had everything on camera, we put the gear away and joined in the party. The dancing was incredible. A young guy wearing a Puma tracksuit stood up and shook his shoulders until I thought they would become detached from his body. I looked around in utter disbelief at Tony and Dan. There was no sign of Stu. After Puma King had finished, the band started up again and, all of a sudden, in bursts Stu shaking from head to toe like he was having an epileptic fit, attempting to give Puma King a run for his money. The whole room cheered and I didn't know whether to laugh or cry with embarrassment. All of a sudden there was an Azmari dance-off. Everybody circled them and the shrieking and laughing reached deafening levels. The look of concentration on Stu's face meant business but, unfortunately, to everybody else he was a lost cause. When he couldn't hold it in any longer, he burst out laughing, admitted defeat and all of a sudden his head was covered with money, stuck with gobs of saliva, and the whole room was clambering to buy him a drink. In a way it was like a good Irish session and we left everybody in high spirits.

We were back on the historical route again the following morning, still laughing at last night's antics as we pulled up to

Fasil Ghebbi or the royal enclosure, which was the imperial capital from the seventeenth to nineteenth centuries. The seven-hectare site, built by Emperor Fasilides, contains six compounds of castles, churches, raised walkways and connecting tunnels surrounded by a 900-metre-long stone wall. To me, it's like a European medieval citadel, where you can imagine huge banquets and tournaments of chivalrous knights taking place.

We then drove to the north-west of the city to see the famous images of the angel faces of the Church of Debra Selassie. It was built by Fasilides's grandson and from the outside it looked like any other building on the outskirts of town, a plain, thatched rectangular building; but the roof inside is painted with the faces of hundreds of beautiful angels peering down on you, all with different facial expressions.

The tree-lined town of Bahir Dar was the last stop on our historical route before heading back to Addis. It is built on the shores of Lake Tana, Ethiopia's largest lake, measuring 3,600 square kilometres. The lake is the source of the Blue Nile river, which starts its journey here before entering the Sudan and finally Egypt. I was astounded to find out that, for a river that's so synonymous with Egypt, ninety per cent of the main Nile flow is actually from Ethiopia. The lake is dotted with thirty-seven islands, on many of which are found churches and monasteries dating from the thirteenth century, which were the main reason for our trip.

On the shores of the lake we met Fanta, our local guide and boat driver. When we were all aboard, he headed for the islands of the Zeghie Peninsula. He was a student at the town's university and his English was excellent. He told us he was a former deacon, which surprised me because I wouldn't even have put him at thirty. He was intrigued about how we filmed everything and was eager to help in any way possible. He even suggested taking me for dinner later that evening so we could film him telling me about Ethiopian cuisine. We signed him up for a starring role straight away!

As we motored gently out into the lake, we passed locals traversing the waters in papyrus boats ("tankwas"), the same kind as have been found in the tombs of the Pharaohs in Egypt. Men fished on the lake or gathered wood and coffee beans from trees on the islands and rowed them back to the mainland.

Fanta explained that, because of their isolation, the islands were used as secret hiding places to store relics and treasures from all parts of the country, including, supposedly, the Ark of the Covenant when the city of Axum was under siege.

Stepping out of the boat, we walked through a forest along a narrow path which was lined with coffee trees. All of a sudden I felt something bite the back of my calf. I looked down to discover that my feet and legs were crawling with huge ants. I freaked out and frantically started slapping at my legs to try to get them off. But they were biting ants that resisted being flicked off by sinking their jaws into my flesh. I literally had to pull them off one by one. I looked jealously at Dan and Stu in their "old man on holidays" outfits – hiking boots and long socks pulled up to their knees. I had spent a large part of the morning taking the mickey out of them and was now paying the price. The local kids were laughing and pointing, "Ha, ha, Farangi, they like your white skin." I was agitated and hot and sweaty and at that moment didn't give two damns about seeing churches or anything else.

Eventually we reached the monastery, built in a forest clearing, and out of the reach of the ants. A local monk showed us around his church, which was covered with religious murals of biblical scenes. It was quite clear that these old depictions, originally drawn centuries earlier, had been touched up. My assertions were confirmed when I peeped into an old decorative chest to find tins of paint and brushes.

Nevertheless, it was worth the trip, if only for the musical interlude that was to follow. Fanta appeared with a huge drum and insisted that the monk should play. He literally threw the drum at the monk and ordered him to sing and dance around in a circle while at the same time telling Stu which angle he should shoot from. Fanta was in full Steven Spielberg mode, running between the monk and Stu to make sure his scene was going according to plan. He barked orders at the monk, who was a very quiet and gracious man and could not understand why he had to dance in circles doing the same thing over and over again. It took about an hour to get what was needed because in every shot the monk had a look of utter bewilderment on his face or Fanta would walk into shot and look to the camera: "Is that okay, Stu, does he need to be louder or do we need to move him into the light?" If we had not left when we did, I have no doubt that our pious monk would have become a convicted murderer, Fanta being his first victim, followed by myself and Dan, who spent the hour sniggering behind our hands.

Back in Bahir Dar, we had just an hour to get some pick-up shots of the town. We drove up Mount Bizawit to get an aerial view of the town and lake. This is also the site of the palace of Ethiopia's famous former emperor, Haile Selassie. While the guys took their shots, Fanta and Tony told me the story of their great emperor. Haile Selassie was born Tafari

Makonnen in 1895. He became Ras or prince of the empire in 1916 and took over as emperor in 1930. He was the 111th successor after King Solomon and took the name "Selassie" meaning the "might of the trinity". He is admired and remembered mostly for playing a pivotal role in stabilising the country in times of rebellion and attempting to modernise Ethiopia. His family tree can be traced back to royal lineage, including King Solomon and the Queen of Sheba. This was one of the things that struck a cord with a movement of people in Jamaica in the 1930s who believed (as they still do today) that he was the living god incarnate; thus, the Rastafarian movement was born. The Book of Revelations in the New Testament talks about the return of the messiah and Rastafaris believe Haile Selassie was that messiah, who would lead the displaced peoples of Africa to freedom. In 1966, Haile Selassie visited Jamaica for the first time and could not exit his plane on the runway because of the massive crowds that had gathered. During his trip he never once admitted or denied being the messiah. It was when Bob Marley converted to the Rastafarian movement that it really gained international prominence. In 1948, Haile Selassie donated land 250 kilometres outside of Addis for the use of people from the West Indies; it is still populated and used today.

Later that evening, as promised, Fanta took us to a restaurant for dinner and then down a warren of alleyways to the best Azmari club in town. It was slightly bigger and a little brighter than the room we had been in Gondar, but the atmosphere was just as good. Again people sat around the walls. There was a big square bar in the middle of the room and as we were one of the last groups to arrive, there was nowhere else to stand but behind the bar. The azmari tonight was really on fire, slagging everybody off as he went around the room. We were no exception. He came straight up, looked me in the eye, said something and smiled sweetly. The whole room erupted into fits of laughter. I looked to Fanta to translate and he seemed embarrassed and uncomfortable. "He said you are very pretty." I was not convinced, "Oh, come on, Fanta, what did he say? I'm not going to be offended. I know he was probably being a bit rude, but I like rude sometimes." Fanta smiled and winced at the same time. "He said you are pretty but you must also be very busy with all the men you brought tonight. Especially Tony, who is old, so you have to be gentle." The laughter in the room almost drowned out the music and on and on this went until nobody had gone unchecked by the azmari. Soon we were all out gyrating on the floor, including Tony. I couldn't help laughing at this guy whom I had thought was stand-offish and serious when I met him first but whom I now knew to be one of the most genuine people in the world.

Just before we left with Fanta to get a taste of "modern" Ethiopia in a nightclub down the road, a tall thin guy in a white tracksuit arrived in. "We must not leave yet. This guy is the best dancer in Bahir Dar, maybe even in the whole of Ethiopia," Fanta instructed. The floor cleared and the trancelike music started. People clapped louder and louder as the music began to get faster and faster and then I witnessed dancing like I had never seen before. This guy danced like he had no bones in his body. The way he bent at the neck, shoulders and waist was impossible to comprehend. The speed at which he moved and controlled his shoulders was incredible, rotating one forward while the other ricocheted in all directions in time to the music. Fanta beamed over at me. "I call him Rubber Man." There couldn't have been a more accurate description. For the finale, he was down on the floor with his knees bent and his shoulders touching the ground and moving like a snake being charmed. People clambered over themselves to stick notes to him; the money had become damp in their sweaty hands. Rubber Man had made their night.

We were still talking about him by the time we got to the local nightclub which was again a small packed room but instead of traditional music, a DJ pumped out dance versions of "Country Road" and "California Dreaming". It was so loud we couldn't even attempt a conversation and so I hit the dance floor. It was the first time I had seen Ethiopian women drunk and it took me a couple of minutes to figure out that, in fact, most of them were prostitutes. I looked over and Dan and Stu were lost in a swarm of short skirts and low-cut lycra tops. Having bought most of them a drink, all of us, including me, explained that we would not be availing of any services as we had to leave early in the morning on a flight to Addis. Fanta, looking completely perturbed that we might think badly of his home town, thought it a good idea for us to go, but some of the local girls had other ideas. Dan and I were the first ones to reach the van and get inside. One of the girls managed to jump in with us and clearly wanted to come along for the ride! A crowd had gathered around the van now at the thought of letting three white and therefore "wealthy" men away. Tony tried reasoning with our travelling companion. When this didn't work, Fanta reached inside and pulled her out. We closed the door of the van, which she kicked in disgust as we drove off.

The following morning we flew back to Addis where Abeje was there to greet us with a smile. It was our last day in

Ethiopia and so we just dumped our bags in a day room in the Ghion and headed for the city's famous market. The Mercado is the largest open-air market in Africa, covering a massive twenty-six square kilometres. It is the main retail, wholesale and distribution point for the whole of the city and the highlands, selling everything and anything you could possibly think of from fruit to foreign currency, window panes to weapons. It is a crowded place even early in the morning and we had been warned that pick-pocketing is rife. We were slightly concerned about carrying around the camera gear. Tony thought it was better if we had security and hired two plain-clothed female bodyguards, who were armed, to accompany us around the market.

The place was crowded when we got there but, even pushing through the crowds who thronged the narrow streets, I felt that the general atmosphere was warm and friendly. Ethiopians, I knew at this stage, like to smile. I think it is an innate part of who they are. The sellers were more than happy to be filmed at their stalls. Out of a genuine curiosity for what we were doing, a crowd would gather to try to look into the camera, blocking up the pathways and therefore holding people up. We walked from the metal quarter to the fabric quarter to the spice quarter, which was my favourite part of the market. Mountains of ground ginger, turmeric, paprika and berberis sat on rickety wooden tables framed by long clusters of garlic hanging from the roof. Peeping from the back of this scene was usually the face of a beautiful woman tending her stall, herself a vision of colour in a vibrant headscarf.

We then passed stalls where men furiously worked, bundling and separating huge bunches of green "chat" (or khat) leaves. I had seen these leaves being sold at the side of the road and in markets up in the highlands. The leaves come from the *catha edulis* tree, which originates in Ethiopia and has spread all over East Africa and the Arabian peninsula. The leaves have been chewed for thousands of years as a stimulant and even predates coffee-drinking. The ancient Egyptians even believed it was a "divine food". It is like a mild amphetamine, making people talkative and excitable; but the come-down leaves you tired, lethargic and depressed. Although the World Health Organisation classified it an addictive drug in 1980, it is still not illegal in Ethiopia today – hardly surprising when it is one of their biggest exports. Unlike, say, the betel nut in Papua New Guinea, which you chew and eat with lime, you don't need any other condiments to go with it. You could see the before- and after-effects from different groups of men sitting on the ground around the stalls. Some were animated and laughing amongst themselves, while others sat vacantly staring at nothing. We decided not to join them but instead had a pick-up of a good strong Ethiopian coffee.

Tony organised our last supper at the Old Milk House, where we had eaten our first meal. It had only been a week since we had been there but walking back into the atmosphere of the cosy restaurant felt like something of a homecoming. Ten of Tony's friends joined us for our farewell dinner and, as you might imagine, they were quite an eclectic bunch. It was the perfect way to say goodbye to Ethiopia – sitting at a table surrounded with great food, music and laughter.

We had travelled through a proud country and met a proud people and had the most fantastic travel experience. I cannot compare it to anywhere else I have been, because Ethiopia is uniquely Ethiopian. Its proud and ancient history remains intact but it is also a nation looking to the future. I thought of my first vivid TV images of Ethiopia in 1985 and was under no illusion that parts of this incredible country are still suffering terribly, but Ethiopia needs to progress and tourism can help do that. One of their biggest obstacles, in my mind, is our misconception of their country.

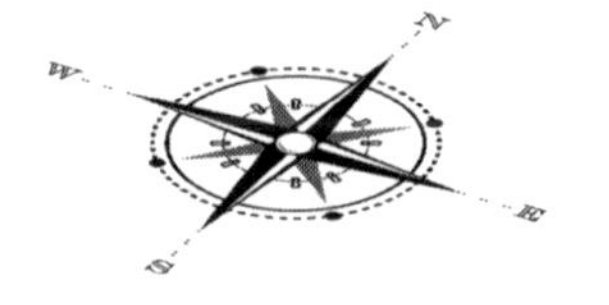

Ethiopia

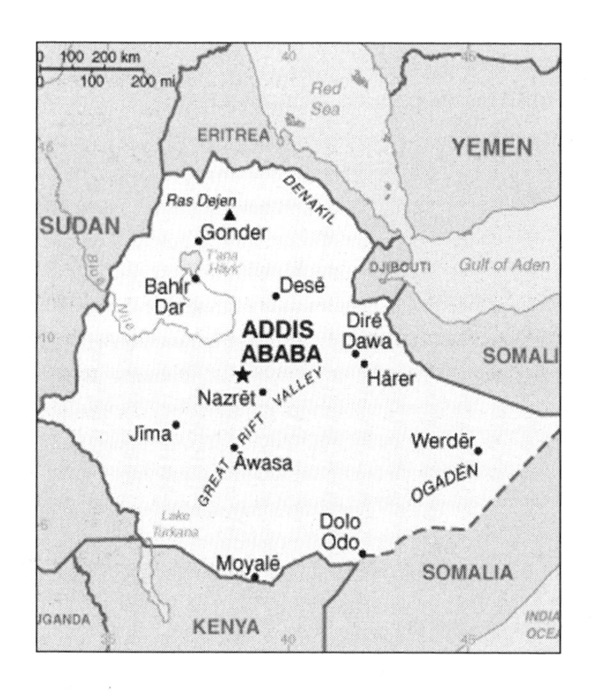

Population: 80 million approx.

Official Name: Federal Democratic Republic of Ethiopia.

Capital City: Addis Ababa.

Languages: Amharic is the official language. English is the medium of instruction at secondary schools, universities and colleges and is widely used in business. Oromiffa, Tigrigna, Somali, Guragigna, Sidama, Afar are among the most widely spoken besides Amharic. Arabic, French and Italian are also spoken.

Size: 1.14 million square kilometres. Ethiopia is bordered by Eritrea to the north, Sudan to the west, Kenya to the south, Somalia to the east and Djibouti to the north-east, and is Africa's second-most populous nation.

Economy: About 90 per cent of the population earns their living from the land, and the principal exports from the sector are coffee, oil seeds, pulses, flowers, vegetables, sugar and foodstuffs for animals.

Climate: Ethiopia is an ecologically diverse country, ranging from the deserts along the eastern border to the tropical forests in the south to extensive plant and animal lands in the north and south-west. Ethiopia has two main seasons, the dry season from mid-September to the end of May and the rainy season from June to August.

Best time to go: The best time to visit Ethiopia is usually from September to May during the dry season but depending on your particular itinerary this may vary to include certain activities and/or events in the wet season.

Who to go with: As you can imagine, tourism in Ethiopia is still developing, I travelled to Ethiopia with Ethiopian Quadrants, www.ethiopianquadrants.com. The company is run by an Irish ex-pat called Tony Hickey.

Time Difference: +3 hours from Ireland.

Currency: The local currency is the Ethiopian birr, made up of 100 cents. It is advised to carry US dollars as these are widely accepted. The use of credit cards is growing in Ethiopia but only two banks (Dashen Bank and NIB Bank) can issue money from foreign cards and this is only in Addis Abba and a few main cities.

Visa Requirements: Irish citizens holding valid passports will be issued a visa upon arrival into Bole International Airport. For more up-to-date information, contact the Ethiopian Embassy in London, www.ethioembassy.org.uk.

Tipping: Tourist hotels and restaurants usually add a ten per cent service charge to the bill. Otherwise tipping is fairly common, but only small amounts are customary. One of the negative impacts of tourism has been to foster a culture of begging. It is better to provide support to local schools and clinics, for example.

Vaccinations Needed: It is no longer necessary for travellers to carry a valid yellow fever vaccination card. It is strongly recommended that you consult your local Tropical Medical Bureau or GP before travelling to Ethiopia for all relevant vaccines. The WHO report malaria transmission in certain parts of the country also. Medical facilities are poorer outside the capital Addis Ababa, although there are private clinics in most towns. All regular medications should be taken with you when travelling and a medical kit is recommended. It is also recommended that you arrange comprehensive medical insurance before travel.

Traveller Safety: For the most part travel in Ethiopia is perfectly safe but certain precautions should be taken when travelling in any poor country. Visitors to Ethiopia should avoid all public demonstrations and large crowds and gatherings. Travel near the border regions (military zones) should be avoided due to unrest and an unstable security situation. Prior to departure, check for any travel advisories issued by the Department of Foreign Affairs. www.dfa.ie

Other Highlights:

- Take a trip on the Historic Route – includes some of the best known historic sites, Axum, Lalibela, Gondar and Bahir Dar. The Historic Route can be done by road, or by a combination of road and air travel.

- Trek in the Bale Mountains National Park – this can be done on foot or by horseback – see Ethiopia's diverse landscape, flora and fauna and wildlife.

- Take a Bird Watching Tour – More than 800 bird species are found in Ethiopia.

- Tailor your own holiday – Contact Ethiopian Quadrants directly.

Fun Facts

- **Ethiopia is about the size of France and Spain combined.**
- **Ethiopia still uses the Julian calendar which has thirteen months and is almost eight years behind our Gregorian calendar.**
- **Ethiopia is the source of the Blue Nile River.**
- **The Jamaican Rastafarian movement originated in Ethiopia.**
- **Ethiopia is one of the world's oldest nations and the second most populated country in Africa.**
- **The oldest human skeleton was found in Ethiopia. "Selam" is a skeleton of a three-year-old girl that carbon dates back 3.3 million years.**

Useful Contacts:

- Ethiopian Embassy, London: www.ethioembassy.org.uk
- Ethiopian Tourist Commission: www.tourismethiopia.org
- General Information on Ethiopia: www.africaguide.com/country/ethiopia
- Ethiopian Quadrants: www.ethiopianquadrants.com

Books to Read: All the relevant travel books – Lonely Planet and The Rough Guide. There are numerous books on Ethiopia available on the Eason's website, www.eason.ie

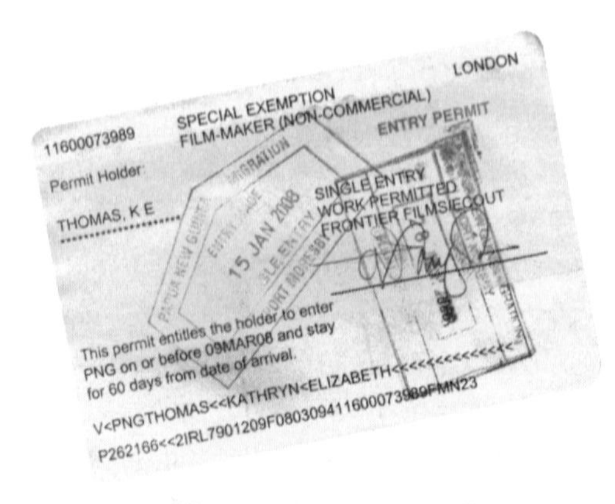

LONDON

11600073989 SPECIAL EXEMPTION
FILM-MAKER (NON-COMMERCIAL)
ENTRY PERMIT

Permit Holder:

THOMAS, K E

SINGLE ENTRY
WORK PERMITTED
FRONTIER FILMS/SCOUT

15 JAN 2008

This permit entitles the holder to enter PNG on or before 09MAR08 and stay for 60 days from date of arrival.

V<PNGTHOMAS<<KATHRYN<ELIZABETH<<<<<<<<<<<<<<
P262166<<2IRL7901209F080309411600073989FMN23

Papua New Guinea

I had wanted to visit Papua New Guinea ever since I saw the shaky black-and-white images of a documentary called *First Contact*, shot by the Leahy brothers from Australia. Their journey into the highlands in 1933 was to search for gold in what they thought was uninhabited territory. Instead, they found a community of over 100,000 people living in the jungle who had no idea that an outside world existed. Can you imagine what this "discovery" was like for both parties, the seekers and the found – those first moments of confusion, fear, excitement and trepidation?

It fascinated me that, on the island of Papua New Guinea, in an age of colonisation, telecommunications and airplanes, the highlands of the country took so long to explore. So I read a lot about this "land that time forgot", its remote mountains and jungles. I read stories about explorers searching for gold and missionaries searching for souls; about tribal warfare and cannibalism that some say is still practised today; about tribes in the highlands that nowadays welcome tourism as opposed to logging and mining industries, which have ravaged and undermined their environment in the past. If ever there was a place that promised adventure, this was it.

For two years I pitched the idea of an off-the-beaten-track adventure trip to the *No Frontiers* team but, because of a lack of tourist board support, the expense of getting there, the cost of internal flights and security concerns, it always seemed to prove too much of a logistical nightmare. Most tourists who visit Papua New Guinea do so to take in the two main highland festivals, the Mount Hagen and Goroka shows, which take place in August and September every year. These festivals originally started in the 1960s as a means for the tribes to interact peacefully. The only previous connection between them had been tribal warfare and these colourful sing-sings were seen as an opportunity to show the amazing diversity of the island people. The other thing that brings the bulk of tourists to Papua New Guinea is the birdlife. There are over 700 species of bird in the country, the native bird of paradise and the huge cassowary being the star attractions. But neither of these was my reason for going. I wanted to travel to different parts of the country, meet the tribal people and try to get a sense of where Papua New Guinea is today.

The island of New Guinea, off the coast of Australia, is divided into two parts: Western Papua, which is part of Indonesia, and Papua New Guinea to the east. Because of heightened tensions along the border and the huge crime rate in the capital, Port Moresby (making it one of the world's least desirable cities to live in), the international press has never been favourable. But after months of research and hard work by the team, our trip to Papua New Guinea was planned and confirmed. We would be a group of three: Mark on camera, Ruth directing and myself presenting. We were to travel with an adventure company that was going to take us off the tourist trails to meet a tribe in a remote village in the highlands and to explore the jungles of the least-travelled area, the lower Gulf Province.

Our itinerary sounded incredibly exciting but also very tough. We would be days without electricity so we had to pack extra camera batteries, we needed protective gear, waterproof gear, a huge medical kit to cater for any emergency, 100 per cent DEET for the mosquitoes and also to prepare ourselves for the leeches that infested the jungles during rainy season – which is, cleverly, when we decided to go! We spent a week checking and rechecking our bags for the seventeen-day trip until there was nothing left to check. Then we flew from Dublin Airport, essentially into the unknown.

Twenty-eight hours later we arrived into Port Moresby airport via Amsterdam airport and Singapore. Standing at the baggage carousel, I noticed two big Digicel posters, and standing underneath was Denis O'Brien himself. I couldn't believe it. We had come to what is referred to as the last frontier on earth, the last true wilderness, and our first introduction to Papua New Guinea was courtesy of one of Ireland's richest citizens. I had met him before through the Special Olympics, but the last place I thought I would see him would be a dusty airport in Papua New Guinea.

"Denis, how are you?"

"Kathryn, what in the name of Jesus are you doing here? Don't tell me you're here promoting holidays! Do you know how dangerous it is?"

He offered us help from his security staff and two mobile phones, which were later delivered to our hotel. We said our goodbyes and parted; him in his private jet on his way to Vanuatu to continue building his empire and us to our hotel in the back of a battered Hiace. The three of us checked into a room in the Gateway Hotel, which is literally outside the gates of the airport.

Two hours later, after a shower and change, we were back in the airport again to meet Aaran, the manager of Eco Tourism Melanesia, and our guides. We were debriefed about our itinerary, talked through what we could expect, what the weather had been like and the difficulty of our first challenge: climbing Mount Wilhelm, the highest mountain in Papua New Guinea.

On board the one-hour flight to Goroka, it felt like the adventure had already begun. From the window as we flew from Moresby, flat grassland turned into huge mountain ranges, covered with forest that stretched as far as the eye could see. Aaran told me that there is no major road linking the capital to the highlands, which is the most densely populated part of the country with a population of about two million, and so all travel has to be by plane. There are over 492 airstrips in Papua New Guinea. There is one key road, the Highlands Highway, which runs from the northern city of Lae to the two main towns of Goroka and Mount Hagen and is considered a lifeline for the region.

Goroka is not a particularly attractive town. We checked into the Bird of Paradise Hotel at that evening and went straight to dinner, where we met Hugo, who was to be our guide for the rest of the trip. Having not slept for two days, I really wasn't looking forward to our 6.30 departure the following morning, especially when it meant the beginnings of a 4,509-metre mountain climb. It was only after I returned to Ireland weeks later that I realised this is the same height as Mont Blanc, the highest mountain in Europe!

I didn't have a clue where I was when the alarm went off at 6.30. Eventually I gathered myself and jumped on board our jeep for the three-hour transfer to Betty's Lodge in Kegesugl. Driving through the highland villages past Kundiawa, I noticed the country's obsession with gardening. The climate up here is spring-like all year round and little colourful manicured patches clung at almost vertical angles to the hillsides. The people of the highlands take two things very seriously – their pigs and their gardens – but not as a source of food or growing crops. These pastimes give social status; the more ornate your garden and the more pigs you have, the better your standing in society.

The higher we got, the more remote the villages we passed through. It was clear that 4x4s were not a common sight up here and people would stare in the window with a look of disbelief and curiosity. As our jeep trundled past, this would change to energetic shouts of welcome, screams of laughter and enthusiastic waving as the children ran after our tracks in the dust. I was struck by how handsome the men looked. They have very strong facial features yet there is a softness to them in their eyes, in their manner, in the way they walked and how they smiled and greeted us. They were far from the fierce warriors of my imagination.

We arrived at Betty's Lodge an hour behind schedule and were welcomed with a traditional "sing-sing". Betty is a local woman who married an Australian and runs a tight ship, organising villagers in the roles of guides and porters for tourists who come to climb the mountain.

After lunch, we set off with high hopes and high hearts for base camp. Our group swelled to twelve, with the local women carrying the heavy rucksacks and camping equipment while the men had the easier task acting as guides. It was quite mild and overcast, perfect weather for walking in fairly steep jungle terrain. This was meant to be the easy part of the climb but after just a short time we were already in a sweat. With all the stopping and starting to shoot, it took us four hours to get to base camp, two hours longer than scheduled.

We arrived at the camp just as it was getting dark. The men went about lighting cooking fires while we rolled our mats out on the floor. We were now at an altitude of 4,000 metres. Feeling slightly light-headed, Ruth went rummaging for her altitude sickness tablets and realised she had left them down at Betty's Lodge! We attributed the headache to one of many things – jet lag, sleep deprivation, physical exhaustion, hunger. Altitude sickness would mean she wouldn't be able to climb. She agreed to wait until the morning to see how she felt.

Unfortunately, after a dinner of rice and vegetable soup by torchlight and collapsing on the floor, morning time came three hours later when we all had to rise at 1.00 a.m. to prepare for the climb. Mark and I had managed three hours' sleep but Ruth hadn't slept a wink. But her headache had subsided and it was clear she wanted to climb. We left our rucksacks behind and stocked up with water before heading off in the pitch dark, with strict instructions for each of us to stay close to our guides with our eyes fixed on their feet in front of us. David was my guide and I saw nothing but the back of his heels for what felt like hours.

It was a hard rocky uphill climb, made even more difficult by the fact that we had to stop and film. It was cold and the wind pierced right through us. David and I, who were leading the group, were told to slow down to try and keep everyone together but that just meant I was getting colder and crankier. I looked up into the darkness. It was the first time I had looked up and not down at the ground and the stars twinkling in the clear sky were incredible. But I didn't care; breathing at almost double time, I had hit a wall, the first of many. After the four-hour climb the day before and lack of sleep, I was physically and mentally exhausted. I was close to breaking point, as was Ruth.

We climbed for another five hours before the sun started to come up. We were scheduled to be at the summit for sunrise, but were still nowhere near the top. We stopped to film the mountain peaks jutting out above the clouds. At this point, Mark, our cameraman, realised he couldn't go any farther. We had to make a decision as to whether we would all go back or whether myself and Ruth would continue to the top with the camera. We had come this far, and I was damned if I was going to let the mountain get the better of me. We continued climbing with Hugo, David and his brother Marcus, while Mark began the long descent back to camp with two of the guides.

At this point in daylight we could see where we were going but we could also see what we had just spent the last five hours' climbing. I believe I was in some sort of altered state of mind. With the sun beating down on top of us, my head had given up, yet from somewhere my body had the ability to keep going, to keep putting one foot in front of the other. David and Marcus told us of the climbers who had died on the mountain, including an Australian army officer and an Israeli backpacker, who both slipped and fell into deep ravines, the Israeli's body only found a year later. I don't think the lads told us these stories to scare us but rather to keep us focused on the challenge. When both of us felt like giving up and that we couldn't go any farther, the guys would take us by the hand and pull us up over the rocks.

It seemed that every peak we climbed would be the last only to get to the top to find another one looming above us. Finally, clinging onto rocky outcrops and looking for footholds, we scrambled to the top. The view across the Finisterre mountain range that engulfed us was incredible. I felt proud and a real sense of achievement standing there, high above the clouds, at the top of the world.

We filmed on the summit for an hour. Then, with one last look at the panorama, and a thank you to somebody somewhere for my health, we began our descent. Although walking back meant very little uphill climbing, it was the longest walk home and our pride and sense of success was soon replaced with sheer exhaustion.

I genuinely don't remember very much about getting down and collapsing in Betty's, but fourteen hours after we had first set out from base camp, I crawled into bed at 4.00 p.m. and died. In what still seems likes a dream, I was woken for dinner about 9.00 p.m., walked out of my room in a trance-like state and into the sitting room to be greeted by about thirty of the villagers in traditional dress of grass skirts and feathers, singing and telling stories to Mark. I don't know what I ate and I collapsed back into bed and slept until 7.00 the following morning.

I was surprised on waking that I wasn't stiff or sore. I felt like a new woman after the first decent night's sleep since we had left Ireland four days ago. Ruth was in the next bed feeling thankful just to be alive. We emerged blinking into the morning light as if we had spent months in hibernation, where Betty, with a knowing smile, served up the best pancakes I'd ever tasted.

Our transfer jeep was two hours late because of a landslide, which unfortunately meant we missed our flight to Simbai and had to instead continue back to Goroka, to the Bird of Paradise Hotel and get a re-scheduled flight the following morning. The next part of our journey would take us farther up into the highlands where we would get to stay for two days in a remote village called Waim. The only access into the village was to fly to Simbai airstrip and walk five hours through the jungle on a narrow goat track carved into the cliff edge. More walking!

The following morning we were waiting outside the hotel at 6.45 for our pick-up to transfer us to the airfield for our re-scheduled 7.00 a.m. flight to Simbai. The new itinerary meant that we would touch down, take an hour to get something to eat and then begin our five-hour trek to Waim. Our driver never turned up and by the time we hitched a lift in the back of an old pick-up truck to the airfield, the fog had come in and we couldn't take off. Half an hour later we were in the air. We flew out over some of the lushest jungle I'd ever seen. The most bizarre part of the journey for me was that at one stage I was looking out the window of the airplane, up at Mount Wilhelm. The plane didn't even fly as high as we had climbed!

Thirty minutes later, we touched down in Simbai and as we taxied along the grass, people seemed to appear out of the trees, running from all directions and gathering at the top of the "runway" to greet us. Ronald was the first person to introduce himself to us. He was the proud owner of the Kalam guest house and he wanted to give us lunch and coffee before we took off on the trek to Waim. On the fifteen-minute walk to the guesthouse we were accompanied by local singers and dancers eager to perform for our arrival and it was quite clear that visitors were not an everyday occurrence in these parts. Music and expression are a huge part of life here and an integral part of a good welcome. Hugo told us that, although a lot of the villagers wear western-style dress, traditional dress is still common among many tribes, not just in times of celebration, which our arrival seemed to be.

Ronald's guest house was very basic with no electricity but again it was set in the most beautifully manicured gardens. I wanted to sit among the flowers in the sun on the big wooden handmade chairs, to relax and stop moving and sleep and take everything in. But an hour later, after three cups of coffee, a bowl of noodles and a banana, we were on our feet again. Before we left, Ronald introduced us to his guard dogs, two tame parrots who never left each other's side, and soon they were taking turns sitting on Ruth's and Mark's heads.

We were a group of about fifteen people: the three of us, Hugo and locals from Simbai, including Ronald and the chief, who acted as porters and guides. The people from both villages, Simbai and Waim, were originally from the same tribe and visit each other often. The sun was up and it was about thirty degrees. We walked across grassland for about half an hour, wading through three rivers at knee height. At the first, I carefully took off my boots and socks, thinking how horrendous it would be squelching around in wet shoes for hours. Soon I realised it was too much of a drama and too much effort to keep re-dressing in the heat, so I just waded in, boots and all.

At first, the landscape was rolling hills and valleys but then we entered the dense jungle and began to climb. It was steep inclines from the start, everyone having to use their hands to hoist themselves up. Every hour we stopped to sit down, get some water and try to work out how much farther there was to go. Finally, Hugo told us that we had made it to the last uphill part of the walk, where we would have lunch before the downhill trek into Waim. A mist had begun to roll in and made the jungle all the more eerie.

The chief of Waim had walked halfway to meet us. He was standing at the top of the hill on a wide fallen log. His colourful feathered headpiece and grass skirt seemed to jump out from the shroud of mist that surrounded him. He was smiling, with his arms slightly outstretched, his spear in hand. It was one of the most mysterious and beautiful images I have ever seen. He shook hands warmly with the chief of Simbai and then with us.

After a quick lunch of crackers and apples (I had begun to think I would never taste real food again), we began our descent into the jungle on the other side of the valley. The walk began to get quite treacherous. The steep jungle paths that we had been climbing essentially disappeared. We were now on what I could only describe as muddy ledges clinging to the edges of the cliffs. It had been raining and many parts of the track had been washed away. For stability, we had to hold onto roots of trees and grab handfuls of long grass to ensure we didn't slip down into the deep ravines below.

Two hours later, we could see the jungle clearing ahead and we were told we were only a few minutes' walk from the village. From this distance I could hear the beating of drums and loud singing and chanting. When we emerged from under the canopy of trees, we could see on the brow of the next hill, hidden amidst plumes of smoke, hundreds of people dancing, performing, welcoming us. My heart beat faster in my chest as we moved toward them and they toward us – men, women and children, covered in paint, wearing grass skirts, kina shell breast plates and beautiful ornate headdresses made of green beetles and birds of paradise feathers, beating drums and singing in our arrival. Some of the men carried bows and arrows and spears and wore a piece of bone pierced through both nostrils.

As the two groups met, led by the chiefs, I could see in the eyes of some of the villagers an element of fear and anxiety. Simbai, although quite a big station, rarely receives foreigners and here in the neighbouring village of Waim, they had only ever received two Dutch tourists, who had trekked here three years earlier. They were suspicious of Mark's camera, even though Hugo himself had come to Waim a couple of weeks ago and explained to the village that we were a television crew from Ireland. Nobody had heard of Ireland or Europe, but "beside the land of the Queen" seemed to suffice as an explanation. Hugo also had to sit with the elders and explain what television was. Some had heard of it, but nobody had ever seen it or indeed seen what makes it. So we were a rather unusual spectacle ourselves. The tribe formed into two lines facing each other and it was customary that we would walk down the middle of them to the entrance of the village. The noise as we passed through was deafening. I was so overcome with emotion that I had to fight back the tears – tears of disbelief, joy, privilege and thanks for the most incredible sensory overload of a welcome!

As I got to the village entrance, four tiny old ladies sat huddled together in the dirt in front of a small fire, wearing only woven fibre skirts. They had been watching the rousing welcome from a safe distance. They seemed quite shy, smiling behind their hands as I approached and crouched down to say hello. We looked at each other for a long time and I felt a real connection had been made as we stood up without saying a word, me towering above them. They took me by the hand and led me into their village. The drums were still beating loudly as people ran in all directions, smiling and laughing.

On arrival into the village, everything quietened down as the chief began his welcome speech in his native language. This was translated into Tok Pisin, which in turn was translated for us into English by Ronald. Tok Pisin, which literally means "talk pidgin" is one of three national languages in Papua New Guinea. It began as a plantation language and so most words are of English origin, peppered with local expressions. In a country that has over 800 indigenous languages, Tok Pisin is the most commonly used, spoken by over four million people. It does take time to get your head around it and the villagers went into fits of convulsions as I stuttered out the few phrases I had learned off. "Nem bilong mi Kathryn. Husat nem bilong yu?" ("My name is Kathryn. What is your name?") "Yu tok isi isi plis" ("Can you talk more slowly please?") "Haus pekpek i stap we?" ("Where is the toilet?") Finishing on that note I was pointed in the direction of the toilet, a hole in the ground that had been especially dug for us, with a bamboo wall for privacy. When I had finished squatting, I emerged to find a small group outside the hut, clearly keen to see my reaction to the toilet facilities they had proudly prepared. "Mi laikim dispela rum!" ("I like this room!") Again, more laughter and an obvious feeling of satisfaction, for both parties!

The village consisted of little groups of huts, built apart from each other with beautiful gardens all around them. Each hut was divided into two parts, partitioned by a bamboo wall. Family members slept on the floors around an open fire.

The huts were extremely smoky and it was much easier to breathe in if you stayed low to the floor. There was a communal hut with no walls, just a thatched roof and a huge fire in the middle.

I wandered up to the top of a hillside, which overlooked the valleys below. With the village at my back, I sat and took in the surroundings – nothing but trees and mountain tops jutting from the clouds. The sense of beauty, isolation and self-sufficiency of the people was astounding and I was slowly beginning to understand how they had remained unknown to the western world for so long.

By 8.00 p.m., it was pitch dark and, with no electricity, Mark, Ruth and I were in our sleeping bags by 8.30, full after a dinner of rice and tuna. Hugo came into our hut as we were preparing to go to sleep to tell us that he had some bad news. The village piped their water from a nearby sacred waterfall, where the spirits of their ancestors resided. A series of bamboo pipes brought water to the village and, since our arrival earlier in the day, the water had stopped flowing. The only other time this had happened was when the Dutch couple had arrived into their village a few years before. One of the elders had already checked to see if there was any blockage, but none could be found, so the conclusion was that our presence had angered the spirits.

As Hugo told us this, in the darkness of our hut, I felt unnerved and uneasy. I dreaded the thought of anyone feeling upset, scared or threatened by us. We had filmed the waterfall earlier in the day because nobody had told us it was a sacred site. We told Hugo that we would delete the images if that would help in any way. He said that two of the elders were going up to the waterfall at midnight to talk to the spirits and to see what offering needed to be made.

We lay down to sleep, our day ending in such an anticlimax in comparison to everything we had experienced earlier. Again, I thought about how our being here would or could affect these people, who have lived without everything that the twenty-first century has to offer. They have survived without money, without clothes, without tourists and without western mentalities. Now that they have a knowledge of an outside world, a much bigger world, they know they could benefit from change, but they don't know the negative consequences of our world and who could blame them for thinking that what we have is better than what they know? Lying in the dark, thinking about their spirit world, I felt that what the west represents on the outside is not necessarily change for the better.

After a restless night, Hugo woke us at around 6.00. To our relief, he told us, "The water is flowing again. The spirits are happy now. They know you come with good intentions. The village did not even have to sacrifice a pig" (which was how the last water shortage had been reconciled). The elders believed the fact that we had arrived a day earlier than expected could have upset the harmony of the village.

I sat up in my sleeping bag, feeling damp and grubby after my night on the floor of the smoky hut. I tried to clean myself as best I could with baby wipes and stepped outside to brush my teeth, using the remains of a bottle of water from the day before. Two of the village children sat crouched on a hill about twenty feet from our hut, hiding behind a small bush, watching me. I waved and they giggled and waved back.

An hour later Ruth and I sat down with the chief and some of the village elders and showed them our footage of the waterfall. They were mesmerised by the pictures from the camera, but they were adamant we should not delete them. We were told there would be a huge feast later in the afternoon, which gave us time to wander around the village. We walked to different homes to say hello and were greeted warmly. There were about thirty families living in the village, with each cluster of family homes built far away from the others, allowing for privacy and cultivation of their own family plots and gardens. There was a church that had been set up by a converted local. It was a beautiful, very simple wooden structure with a wooden ledge for an altar. On one of the pews I noticed a battered bible written in Pidgin English. Next door to the church was an abandoned medical centre. This had been funded and run by the government until funds ran out. The nearest medical attention and hospital was in Mount Hagen, three days' walk away. There were old discoloured posters on the walls with curled edges and old medical jotters lying scattered on the floor. There had not been a doctor out here for eight years and Ronald told me that child mortality in the village was very high.

By the time we got back to the centre of the village, preparations for the "mo-mo" were in full swing. The feast was to be held in our honour and while the women were busy heating stones, digging holes in the ground and sorting out piles of vegetables on huge banana leaves, the men dressed in elaborate costumes began the "sing-sing".

The sense of community was incredible. In traditional Papua New Guinea society, they have what is called the wantok system, which in a way can be described as a social security system. Your wantok is your friend or tribesman and you are obliged to look after them, whether that means giving them food or shelter or to avenge them if necessary. This is one of the reasons they say Papua New Guinea business and government is so corrupt, because *our* supposed standards of transparency and accountability are deemed completely useless. It's all about your friends and neighbours, whom you have an obligation to.

Each family sat in their own circle around a hole in the ground, which was lined with huge banana leaves and filled with hot stones. Sweet potato, ka-kao and tapioca were thrown in and covered with more hot stones. Layer upon layer, the meal was put into the ground and on top, greens such as beans, cabbage and spinach were steamed in the rising smoke. We sat on the brown earth, eating the cooked vegetables straight out of the ground. It was the best meal I'd had since we arrived. The men sang and danced for hours. The whole atmosphere was charged and with the beating of the drums and the music, I felt like I was lost in a magical trance.

We spent two days in the village, and the morning we left, the rain was bucketing down as we said goodbye to the chief. Now that we were friends, he told us, we would be welcome back in his village anytime. Everyone walked with us to the brow of the hill but I wanted to say goodbye to the four old women. I ran up the hill and found them sitting hunched on the ground, weaving in the sun against the most incredible backdrop of blue sky, clouds and flowers. We sat there in comfortable silence, smiling at each other. Then I noticed that one of the women was crying and Ronald translated as she spoke. "Although you have come from a land that we don't know, you are now one of us. We drop tears because we are sad to see you go because we will never see you again. We are old and will not be here the next time you come back. Go on your journey safely." I couldn't help crying when she held my hand in her tiny hand and rested her head on my shoulder. I was sad because, to me, these women represented an untouched, pure way of life that will never be the same again.

Then I noticed the huge tumour on the back of her neck. She was carrying a bilum or woven bag in the traditional way, the strap across her forehead, the bag hanging down her back. The bag covered the deformity, which looked enormous on her tiny frame. It was as big as her head and she had to endure the sickness and pain with no medical treatment. I was in no doubt that she would die of her illness rather than old age and I thought to myself again, who can blame these people for wanting change? Basic health care for themselves and their families would no doubt mean a better way of life.

It was a long walk back to Ronald's guest house, where we rested until our flight the following morning. In bed in my hut, the wind gently blowing through the opening in the thatched wall, I thought of home and of my family and friends. Though I missed them, I didn't long to be there. I didn't feel lonely; I felt happy, my mind full of faces and images of the last few days – smoke rising from holes in the ground; naked women laughing as they tended to fires; old ladies sitting under trees making "bilums" out of reeds and vines; men with painted faces smoking rolled leaves of tobacco; globs of bright red sauce being squeezed from the marita plant onto mounds of pumpkin, kakao and tapioca; and people smiling, always smiling. I thought about climbing Mount Wilhelm, which already seemed like weeks ago, and I thought about what the next leg of our adventure would bring. We were flying back to Port Moresby to transfer to the lowland Gulf Province, where we would be travelling upriver to try and reach an old abandoned gold mine. It is the least visited part of Papua New Guinea, full of jungles and swamps and the promise of plenty of adventure.

We all gathered at the airstrip the following morning and waited for our plane to land. We flew to Mount Hagen and then on to Port Moresby that afternoon. Under strict instruction from the Eco Tourism team, Ruth and I got our hair braided in the local hairdressers. This was to ensure that no leech would go undetected in tangled hair and feast on our skulls without us noticing.

The next day we piled into a van and took off on a long, bumpy four-hour journey up the Hiritano Highway to Tarapo Bridge where two boats awaited us. This is where we met Andrew, John and Jack, who had family in Fishcreek, the outpost we were trying to reach upriver. It was decided that, because we had built a trusting relationship with Hugo, he was to stay with us too, although he had never been to the area before. We motored up the Lakekamu river until we reached Uruala village, which was essentially a couple of huts on an embankment. We were to overnight here before heading deeper inland.

The mosquitoes were out in force by the time we arrived and we all scrambled to get our tents up before dusk. We covered ourselves from head to toe in DEET and hid under the cover of our tents for an hour until it got dark and they eased off. But it wasn't the mosquitoes that bothered me. As the night drew in, the river symphony of croaking frogs and toads started up. Snakes and spiders I can handle; frogs and toads are my worst nightmare, and they were everywhere. I had guessed that, because we were beside a river and it was wet and warm, I would have to contend with them; I just didn't realise how many there were going to be! Ruth had to accompany me to the toilet, which was a hole in the ground about twenty metres from the hut. By the light of our torches, I could see them, hundreds of them hopping all over the ground. I was on the verge of a panic attack. When we eventually reached the toilet, I saw one frog, then another, jump right into the hole in the ground. I dry-retched and decided there was nothing else to do but pee standing up where I was. I dreaded having to go again in the middle of the night and told Ruth in advance that I would have to use a plastic bag in our tent rather than have to face the frogs. She knew I was deadly serious and didn't seem to mind, which in hindsight goes to show how much we had been through together. In an environment like that, behaviour which you wouldn't even contemplate at home all of a sudden becomes the most normal thing in the world.

It was so hot and sticky that night in our tent. I felt dehydrated but refused to drink any water. We had a portable fan which we safely pinned to the roof to try to keep ourselves cool. We both had a restless night. I kept waking up to make sure nothing had got into our tent, while Ruth's wisdom tooth started acting up.

The next day we packed up and set off early. Forty-five minutes later we jumped out of our boats again, this time to begin our trek to Fishcreek. A small group of about twenty people quickly gathered at our jumping-off point where we unloaded the boats. The atmosphere was tense and rather unfriendly. Andrew, who was in charge of this part of the trip, had been assured that he would get some of these local guys to act as porters for a small sum of money. Five of them stepped forward, but it seemed the rest of them were stoned and uninterested in walking anywhere in the heat of the sun. We had to leave two boxes of water behind as there weren't enough people to carry them.

Feeling slightly concerned and with an air of tension amongst the group, we walked for about an hour until we came to a wide, fast-flowing river that we had to cross. We sat down and had lunch so there would be one less box to carry. The guys brought most of the stuff across on their heads. The level of the water was chest-high at its deepest point and the current was strong. It was a struggle, but Mark and Ruth got to the other side and set up the camera to film me wading across.

All of a sudden there was mayhem. A man wearing just a pair of ragged shorts emerged from the bush, running towards us, shrieking in his native tongue, wielding a huge machete. His mouth and chin were stained red from chewing betel nut, which he spat out in between shouting obscenities at our guides on the other side of the river. I have never witnessed anybody so enraged. Standing ten metres away from him, I was rigid with fear when he pointed his machete at me and the two men who were with me. He kicked stones at the edge of the river and slammed his machete off the ground. He demanded that the others re-cross the river and pay a ransom to be on his land.

Because we had changed our route slightly, due to time constraints and flooding, this route had not been checked and okayed with the local landowners. I had a fair idea at this point how important land is in Papua New Guinea and it scared the hell out of me that, in this part of the country where tribal warfare is still a problem, we were entering very dodgy territory. Hugo, Andrew, John and Jack were the first of the guides to come back across the river. They approached the man slowly and after five minutes managed to get him to stop shouting. Hugo felt at this stage that we should turn back, that it was too dangerous to keep going. He took us aside and told us he did not trust that this part of the journey had been organised properly and he felt nobody had recced this route adequately for our trip. He did not trust that the guides knew where we were going.

The three of us deliberated and felt we would not have a programme if we did not continue, so we decided to keep going. Having paid fifty kina to cross, we piled up our bags again and waded into the water. The current was strong and it really was a struggle to get to the other side. Mark was so nervous that €40,000 worth of equipment could end up floating downstream. As everybody clambered out the far side, the heavens opened and, saturated from head to toe, we took off into the dark jungle.

It was overgrown, hot and sweaty. Swamps and streams that blocked our path had to be crossed at certain points by fallen tree. This wasn't easy as the logs were slippery. One wrong footstep meant we would end up ten feet below in leech-infested water. The leeches here were not big, black and fat as I imagined. They were much smaller, with two suckers on either end of their bodies, but they were everywhere and once they attached themselves they were a curse. They seemed to attack everyone together. Our guides explained that they waited on the leaves of trees high above the paths and when they could feel the vibrations of people or animals walking, they fell from a height in the hope of landing on something or someone from which they could suck blood. The first hour of trying to get used to them was terrifying. I was convinced they were in my socks, up my nose, in my cap, and I worked myself into a near-frenzy, frantically swatting all around me.

We were crossing another wet mossy log, Ruth carefully walking across, using a stick for balance. All of a sudden there was a massive crack. The rotten log gave way and she disappeared into the murky water below. Panic stations! "Get me out, they're crawling on me." John and Jack tried to pull her out, but she was thrashing around in the water so much, on the verge of a nervous breakdown, that she kept falling back in. It was like a scene from *Predator* or some other horror movie. Eventually the guys pulled Ruth up onto the bank. She was yanking at her clothes, convinced she was covered in leeches. When she was sure she had none on her, she burst into tears and I knew something inside her had broken. With the pain in her tooth getting worse, the earlier machete threat at the river and a general feeling of uncertainty amongst the group, things were certainly not going according to plan.

We were still walking four hours later and nobody could tell us how far we were from Fishcreek. Nobody knew where we were. The sun was going down and the mosquitoes were coming out. We sat down on the riverbank while John went into the jungle to try to find us shelter. He had seen smoke coming from the trees and knew that a family must be living there. We were all angry – the guides at us because they thought we should have been walking more quickly, though that would mean we would not have had time to shoot anything; and we at them because nobody seemed to know where the hell we were.

The local family very kindly allowed us to put up our tents in their huts built on stilts. When we had finished dinner, Andrew took out a map and explained to us that this area was Fishcreek but that the abandoned gold mine was another two-hour walk in the morning. We were shocked – a walk that should have taken us three hours would altogether take us eight hours if we were to complete the two hours in the morning. Even if we took off at 6.00 a.m., got there at 8.00 a.m., shot for four hours, which is the minimum amount of time to get what we needed, and walked back, we would not be able to make it back before dark. Ruth was not prepared to risk it, especially because the timings since we started our trek had been so far off the mark. In Papua New Guinea, hours and minutes are not held in the same way as they are to us. The people just walk until they get to where they are going. We tried to explain that accurate timings were crucial for us because we had to factor in our filming time, or else there was no point in being there.

Andrew told us that there was a village across the river, twenty minutes away, where they panned for gold. It was decided that he would go there in the morning and ask them if we could film in their village instead of at the gold mine. I was so disappointed as I had been looking forward to venturing farther into the jungle to where the huge rusted dredging machines and carts had been left untouched since the Second World War. There was only one family still living in the village. All the locals had moved out because of the relentless year-round mosquitoes. We tried to contact Aaran on the satellite phone to tell him where we were and that there had been a change of plan, but it wasn't working. So there we were, lost in the jungle, with no satellite phone; we had run out of bottled water and were now boiling and sterilising river water; and the diet of crackers and rice was beginning to wear us down. That night we all reached a low ebb and went to bed tired and tetchy.

The following morning Ruth's toothache had worsened and she could hardly stand up with the pain. She had taken anti-inflammatories but to little avail. We were all physically shattered. Our satellite phone still wasn't working and we had no way to contact anyone to let them know where we were. We set off across the river to the village on the other side. Finally we came across a couple of huts in a clearing where a small group had gathered, awaiting our arrival. The people, who were living in such an isolated place, looked at us warily for a long time. Our guides communicated with them in Tok Pisin and after about fifteen minutes everybody had relaxed except a small child, who was terrified by us. She screamed her lungs off, while the others smiled apologetically, explaining that she had never seen white people before and she thought we were ghosts.

We spent the morning in the village wandering around, learning about day-to-day life, what the locals farmed, how they cooked, how they panned for gold in the river. It was extraordinary to see the men panning for gold and hear how, for one week three times a year, they would get into their boats and head for Mount Hagen, where they would sell the gold and buy washing powder, cloth, clothes, fishing materials and panning equipment before heading back home to live in the solitude of their surroundings.

Ruth only stayed with us for an hour before making her way back to our camp because she was in so much pain. By the time Mark and I returned two hours later, having shot everything we needed, we found her in an awful state. She was so upset and slightly delirious at the reality of the situation. We were lost in the jungle, with no way of contacting anybody, and the only way back was a six-hour trek through the jungle the way we had come.

We decided that it was best for everyone that we pack up camp and start walking to get at least a few hours out of the way before dusk. We would set up camp along the riverbank and continue walking the following morning. It would split the journey and have us back earlier to meet our boat. We coaxed Ruth into the idea and, with the pain that she was in and the sheer exhaustion, I felt a huge surge of pride for her. By the time we took off, the sun was high in the sky and it was hot. My legs and feet felt heavy battling against the current as we crossed the rivers. Again we walked in single file, keeping a close eye on the person in front of us for any leeches.

Eventually we reached a wide riverbank where we set up our tents. The place was swarming with mosquitoes, which were kept at bay by fires we lit along the shore. The porters, who had grown increasingly uneasy with us over the last few days, kept their distance. That night they demanded more money from Hugo to carry our equipment back. We settled down uncertainly, not knowing what to do, while Hugo, Andrew and John kept watch all night. It was horrible to be in that situation – especially when one of them produced a rifle out of his bag the following morning. Whether this was to make a point or whether it was bravado, I don't know. Looking back, I don't know why I did not feel scared or threatened. Maybe I was naive, but I thought the porters were just hustlers and nothing more. My concern was that they might try to steal from our rucksacks, which they were carrying. We made sure that any film equipment, passports and wallets were carried by one of our team.

Finally we made it back to the village where we disembarked. Our man with the machete was there to greet us, this time sober, alert and with a look of apology. He shook our hands and led us to the two boxes of water, which we had had to leave behind. After drinking boiled river water for the past two days, to taste clean water was like drinking nectar!

In a dream-like state, we headed downriver, overnighting again at Urualu. It was extraordinary to think that this village, built on a finger of land in the middle of the river, which had seemed so remote when we had stayed a few days previously, now gave me the distinct feeling of arriving back into town. We had a great meal of barbecued fish, bread and butter. Food never tasted so good. We slept soundly and left early in the morning, finally arriving back at Tarapo Bridge at 2.00 p.m. Eileen from Eco Tourism was there with sandwiches and Coke, which we all wolfed into before climbing into a big open-backed truck. There were two wooden benches running down both sides to sit on. She had brought a mattress and we put Ruth on the floor to try to get some sleep before going straight to a doctor on our arrival into Port Moresby.

Later that night, Ruth was in bed having taken an antibiotic and Mark and I decided we definitely deserved a night out. We called Chris, head of Digicel security and within twenty minutes, two armed vehicles pulled up outside the hotel to take us to the club. We were both dying for a beer and were standing at the bar in the Hilton waiting to order, when I heard, "Kathryn bloody Thomas, I don't believe it, how are things?" I looked around, thinking I must have been hearing things. It was a friend of mine from Carlow who had transferred to Papua New Guinea to work for Digicel. I hadn't seen him for years and stood there for what seemed like ten minutes, mouth agape, utterly shocked at the coincidence of just bumping into him. We had a great night, telling and listening to each other's travel stories. It felt good to let my hair down – quite literally, as the braids had been plaited so tightly to my head.

I woke up the next day feeling absolutely horrendous and put it down to too much beer, but as the day progressed I felt worse and that evening I couldn't get out of bed. I was nauseous and sweating, I had pains in my joints and I thought it was either food poisoning or a bug I had picked up from drinking the infected river water. I tried to sleep but woke up at five in the morning, knowing something was seriously wrong. I rang Mark in his room, who came in and gave me paracetemol, vitamin C and anything else in our medical kit we thought might help until we could ring for a doctor. Ruth, who after two nights' sleep and antibiotics for her tooth was feeling much better, sprang into Florence Nightingale mode. She got a doctor out to the hotel who took one look at me and told me I had falciparum malaria, which was confirmed by blood tests. We were flying out that evening and he told me it was better if I waited a few days. I told him that, as long as I was not contagious or going to die, I was getting out and I was going home.

The flight home was a daze of nausea and exhaustion. I couldn't eat a thing, and it was a struggle even to sip water. Once we touched down in Dublin, I went straight to the Tropical Medical Bureau. I then spent a week in bed recovering, and have been lucky not to have suffered any long-term effects.

Papua New Guinea was definitely the most difficult trip in all the years I had worked on *No Frontiers*, both physically and mentally. But I would also say it was one of the most enjoyable. We had set out to find an adventure holiday and the seventeen days certainly delivered on that front! When you are pushed to your limit, when you are stripped of everything you know to be normal, when you are told to keep going against any obstacle you come up against, you find out a lot about the person you are and what you are capable of.

Papua New Guinea is a fantastic country and, like so many places in the world, it's a land that's changing and that wants change. We cannot stall this process; we can just hope that it is monitored in the right way and that the people of Papua New Guinea are allowed to modernise at their own pace.

Papua New Guinea Fast Facts

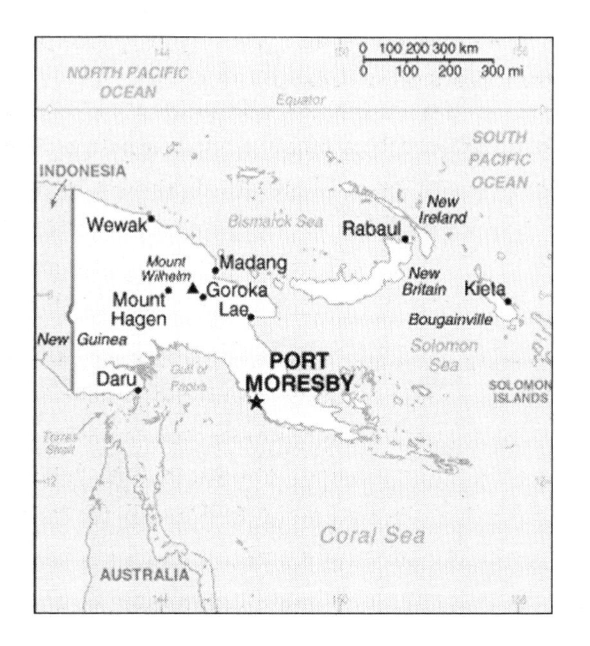

Population: 5.6 million approx.

Capital City: Port Moresby

Languages: There are more than 800 distinct languages. Melanesian Pidgin and Hiri Motu are the two most widely used, but English is the official language in education, businesses and government circles.

Size: 462,000 square kilometres approximately. Papua New Guinea comprises the eastern half of the world's second-largest island, New Guinea; two Indonesian provinces comprise the western part of the island.

Climate: In most places in Papua New Guinea, the wet season is from December to March, the dry season from May to October, though this varies from region to region. Its climate can be described as monsoonal. In the highlands the temperature is cool with occasional snow on the high peaks; it is hot and humid in the low and costal lands.

Best time to go: The best time to visit Papua New Guinea may depend on your personal itinerary. If you are scheduling your trip around one of the cultural shows, they are held between July and October. If you plan on trekking, diving or looking for that elusive bird, you may want to go during the dry season.

Who to go with: There are many tour operators outside Papua New Guinea that can offer guided tours of the country. You should take real care in choosing a company that can provide an itinerary that suits your needs. The Papua New Guinea Tourist Authority provides a list of approved tour operators within Papua New Guinea. www.pngtourism.org.pg

Where I went: Port Morsbey, Goroka, Mount Wilhelm, Simbu Province and the Southern Lowlands.

Time difference: +10 hours from Ireland.

Currency: The local currency for PNG is the kina. ATMs are widely available, with banks in all major cities open Monday to Friday until 4.00 p.m. Credit cards are accepted in most hotels, restaurants and guesthouses in the cities only. Travellers should bring required cash into remote areas as ATMs and credit card services will not be available.

Visa Requirements: Irish passport holders need a visa to travel to Papua New Guinea as a tourist. It should be applied for through the Papua New Guinea High Commission in London – www.pnghighcomm.org.uk

Electricity: Electric current is 220 volts AC (60 cycles). Australian prong plugs are used.

Tipping: Tipping is not customary in Papua New Guinea; you may or may not wish to do so depending on the service provided. Tips for your drivers or guides will be appreciated but bear in mind that their wages are not high so you should avoid tipping too much, as this will set a precedent for others. If you are trekking in the remote regions you may consider leaving money with a local chief or community leader to provide support for the local community.

Vaccinations Needed: It is *highly recommended* that you consult your local Tropical Medical Bureau or GP before travelling to Papua New Guinea for all relevant vaccines. The WHO reports a high malaria transmission throughout this country.

Traveller Safety: Medical facilities are very poor outside of the main cities. All regular medications should be taken with you when travelling and a well-packed medical kit is recommended. It is also recommended that you arrange comprehensive medical insurance before travel. Travellers to Papua New Guinea should exercise a high degree of caution when visiting the country due to the high level of crime in Port Moresby, Lae and Mount Hagen. Private security is available when travelling in the main cities. Check for any travel advisories prior to departure issued by the Department of Foreign Affairs, www.dfa.ie

Emergency numbers: Police Service in Port Moresby is 000. Travellers should ask their tour operator to provide a full list of emergency services available. When trekking in remote regions make sure that your tour operator provides a satellite phone and emergency contact details. Leave your personal contact details and family details with your tour operator prior to heading into remote regions.

Other Highlights:

- **Trek the Kokoda Trail:** The ninety-six-kilometre Kokoda Track passes through rugged mountainous country of rainforest, jungles and valleys. It was here that an inexperienced, ill-equipped, outnumbered Australian force faced the might of the Japanese army during the Second World War.

- **Fishing:** Papua New Guinea's fishing grounds are unique for their natural and pristine state. You can choose from the dense jungle rivers and estuaries, to the ocean's underwater predators of Papua New Guinea's Bismarck and Archipelago Seas, both set to challenge any angler.

- **Visit the Mount Hagen Cultural Show:** Over fifty tribal groups dressed in distinctly different traditional attire come together to perform their respective songs and dances in front of a roaring audience numbering over 50,000 over two consecutive days.

- **Tailor-make your own Adventure Tour:** Get a tour operator to help you decide on your own adventure. Papua New Guinea is the true land of adventure, with breathtaking landscapes, lost cultures, tropical jungles, exotic waters and areas of the country that are still vastly unexplored.

Fun Facts

- **The only known poisonous bird in the world is the hooded pitohui of Papua New Guinea. The poison is found in its skin and feathers.**

- **Over five and a half million people speak around 700 languages in Papua New Guinea.**

- **The Head of State of Papua New Guinea is the monarch of the United Kingdom.**

- **In the Asmat area of southwestern Papua, it is said cannibalism occurred up until the early 1970s.**

Useful Contacts:

- Papua New Guinea High Commission London: www.pnghighcomm.org.uk
- Papua New Guinea Tourism Authority: www.pngtourism.org.pg
- *No Frontiers*, where you can watch my journey to Papua New Guinea: www.rte.ie/nofrontiers (Archive Section)
- Tropical Medical Bureau: www.tmb.ie

Books to Read:

The Lonely Planet – Papua New Guinea & Solomon Islands

Lost Tribe: Search through the Jungles of Papua New Guinea by Edward Marriott

Travels in Papua New Guinea by Christina Dodwell